THE
SERPENT'S
LAIR

Gripping action adventure fiction

The Max Donovan Adventures #3

RIALL NOLAN

THE
BOOK
FOLKS

Published by The Book Folks

London, 2023

© Riall Nolan

ISBN 978-1-80462-140-0

www.thebookfolks.com

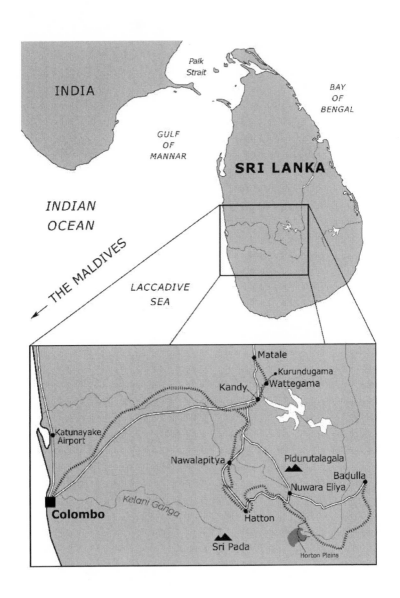

This is for Marina.

PROLOGUE

I woke up to the screech of brakes and tumbled forward as the train slowed. Crawling to the door, I peered outside. The jungle was going by slowly as the train ground to a halt. Then it shuddered to a complete stop and stood still, hot metal pinging in the sudden silence. Two loud explosions came from the locomotive area, sounding like grenades.

Movement at the rear of the train caught my eye. Soldiers were jumping off the top of the fortified caboose as fast as they could, leaving their guns behind and heading for the bush. On the other side of the tracks, men were walking out of the jungle, carrying rifles. From somewhere near the front of the train there was the muted stutter of automatic weapons fire.

Osbert cocked his head. "What's that noise I hear?"

I picked up my shoulder bag and threw open the boxcar door. "That's chickens, Osbert, coming home to roost. Let's get moving."

CHAPTER ONE

At precisely twenty minutes past three in the afternoon the bomb went off, blowing me off the balcony of my room at the Galle Face Hotel, and down into the swimming pool two stories below.

I knew the time because I'd just checked my watch. I had been wondering where my client was, and what the hell was in the brown-wrapped parcel that I held in my hand. Time is a flexible thing in the developing world, here in Sri Lanka maybe more than in most places, but I'd passed up a swim and a run up the beach for whoever was supposed to meet me, and if he didn't show up soon, I'd have wasted most of the afternoon.

Captain Cutlass had brought the note asking for the meeting. He'd materialized the previous night as I sat finishing dinner on the terrace of the Galle Face's seafood restaurant. There'd been a rain squall earlier, a touch of the monsoon licking the island clean, and now breakers were crashing across the low seawall, throwing an occasional shower of spray up onto the terrace.

The party of English tourists had been driven inside long ago, and a group of four Australian air hostesses had just gotten their hairdos drenched and run squawking for the cover of the bar. I sat alone, just out of range – so far, at least – of the breaking surf, sipping an after-dinner *arrack* and looking down the beach at the lights of Colombo Fort. Then someone coughed discreetly, and I turned to see the Captain.

Built in 1864, the Galle Face is one of the grand old Asian hotels, on a par with Raffles in Singapore or the Strand in Rangoon, and its staff upholds tradition. Captain

Cutlass has been the Galle Face's maître d'hôtel for decades, a tradition in his own right. He has a round, pleasant walnut-colored face, a fringe of white hair, and an inexhaustible stock of stories from his years in the Royal Navy back in the days when Ceylon was the jewel of the British Empire. Some of the stories are probably true. The walls of Captain Cutlass's tiny office are decorated with framed photographs of the world's leaders being greeted and led with military dignity to their dining tables.

"Evening, sah." The Captain was all smiles as he snapped off a crisp salute. He wore his usual uniform: a formal white military jacket with broad gold epaulets worn over a spotless white sarong, crowned with a solar topee adorned with cockatoo plumes. A wide gold sash held everything together, supporting the ancient sword of unknown origin which gives him his name.

He extended a white-gloved hand, on which lay a plain envelope. "This has come, Mr. Donovan."

"For me?" I took it and turned it over. There was nothing written on the outside.

"Yes, sah. The porter just brought it." He glanced down at the wreckage of my prawns and curry. "Would sah like another arrack?"

I contemplated my empty glass. I was on vacation, after all. "Why not?" I said after a moment.

Captain Cutlass nodded approvingly and strode away. I ripped open the envelope, and took out the note. It had been written in a clear, firm, somewhat old-fashioned hand, by someone who almost certainly hadn't learned penmanship in the US.

> *Dear Mr. Donovan,*
> *I am writing to ask your help in what is literally a matter of life or death. I need desperately to talk to you, and there is no time to lose. I will come to the Hotel tomorrow, and will meet you there at three o'clock. Please be in your room at that time. Between now and*

then, go to the General Post Office near the Clock Tower and give your name to the clerk at the parcels desk. Do not open the parcel he hands to you. Guard it with your life until our meeting, and say nothing to anyone of this.
S. Wickramanayake.

That was it. No sincerely-yours, return address. I folded the note and replaced it in its envelope as Captain Cutlass approached my table, a fresh glass of arrack in his hand.

"You didn't see who brought this?" I asked him as he set the glass down.

"The envelope? No, sah. You could ask the porter; perhaps he remembers. Ice?"

I nodded, listening approvingly to the ice as it hit the arrack with a friendly cracking sound. I sipped, watching the lights of Colombo Fort winking in the tropic evening. Tomorrow morning, I thought, I'll make a few enquiries. And then I'll go into town and do a little shopping for my retirement. Gems were what I had come here for, a spur-of-the-moment stopover on my way back from Nepal, and if I was lucky, I could probably pick up some sapphires fairly cheaply.

I picked up the envelope and tapped it thoughtfully against my teeth. The post office wasn't far from where I'd planned to be tomorrow morning, and I could at least stop in and see what this mysterious package looked like. After all, what harm could that do?

* * *

The next morning, I questioned the porter, an ancient Sinhalese gentleman whose memory was easily jump-started with a hundred-rupee note.

"Came just at dinnertime," he rasped, hawking red betel juice into the large metal cuspidor beside the reception desk. "Brought by one of the taxi-wallahs. Cheeky bugger came straight up to the desk, dressed in a filthy sarong and bare feet, asking for Donovan

4

Mahattaya." He paused to spit again. "Naturally we couldn't let him wander about among the guests, so I took the letter myself."

"Did he have anyone with him? Anyone in his taxi?"

The old man shook his silver head. "I cannot say, sah. I saw only the driver."

I nodded and wandered out onto the Galle Face Green heading for Colombo Fort. It was early morning, but already the humidity was high and the temperature climbing. On the large open green, couples strolled and children played, their colorful paper kites bobbing in the gentle breeze coming in off the ocean.

I took a deep breath, tasting the air, rolling its tang and texture around on my tongue. South of Gibraltar and east of Rome, out on the world's outposts, the air is a heady stew of sea salt, dust, decay, and a hundred exotic spices and perfumes, under which lingers the scent of open sewers. Just the thing, I'd found, for clearing the brain and sharpening the senses.

I need my senses as sharp as I can get them. I make my living out in places like this, and it's a jungle in more ways than one. I'm a supplier, a sort of Third-World repo man. I spend a lot of my time looking for things – almost anything, really – that might be worth money. Missing people, cash, information – you name it, I'll get it for you. I do a lot of poking around in the dark corners of the world's back alleys, to see what might jump out. Sometimes I get results; sometimes just consequences. Either way, I need to be quick on my feet.

Beside the road, two brown Sinhalese boys shouted to attract my attention, pointing to a large wicker basket which sat on the pavement between them. One of them popped the lid off with a flourish, and an instant later, a large cobra snapped to attention, its head hovering a good three feet above the edge of the basket. The other boy produced a simple bamboo panpipe and began to play, swaying from side to side with the motion of the snake. I gave them five rupees, grinned, and looked around for a taxi.

I hiked up my shoulder bag, thinking of the note inside, as I stepped into the road and flagged down an ancient Morris. It clattered to a halt beside me.

Who wrote the note, and what do they want? Time would tell, I thought, as I opened the taxi door. The bearded desperado behind the wheel bobbed his head in greeting. "*Ayubovan.*"

"And a long life to you, too," I replied, wedging myself into the front seat. I picked up a flat pint bottle of some darkish liquid from the floor and glanced over at the driver. "Whiskey?"

He gave me a dazzling smile. "No, sah. Brake fluid." And with that we were off, sputtering down Galle Road to the center of town.

* * *

I spent the next two hours moving in and out of the gem merchants' shops along Chatham and York Streets in the Fort, pushing my way past elegant sari-clad ladies carrying pastel parasols to ward off the hot sun. I wasn't seriously interested in buying any stones yet; that would come tomorrow, after I'd checked prices and quality. Sri Lanka is one of the gem capitals of the world, and I make it a point to buy a few every time I'm here. Today, however, I was just putting in the time, peering through jewelers' loupes, chatting and drinking countless cups of milky oversweet tea in offices the size of telephone booths with pudgy men who had sharp eyes and smooth tongues.

So I looked and talked, drank my tea and haggled a little as the morning slipped away. I moved from one shop to the next down the narrow streets, past the betel-nut sellers in their dark stalls, smoldering ropes of punk hanging from their shelves for the bidi-smokers. At eleven, I went to the General Post Office on Janadipathi Mawatha near the old British-built clock tower. There I queued for twenty minutes before being handed a brown-wrapped parcel which looked and felt exactly like a ream of typing paper.

Around the corner in the Pagoda Restaurant, I ate a quick lunch of *appa* – thin pancakes made from rice flour and coconut milk. Over them I spooned hot beef curry and *sambol* made from coconut, chilies, onions, lime, salt and dried fish. The resulting mess was delicious, hot and pungent, and I washed it all down with a large bottle of Nuwara Eliya lager. As I ate and drank, I glanced at the brown-wrapped parcel in front of me, my curiosity growing by the minute.

But my meeting with the mysterious S. Wickramanayake wasn't for over two hours. So, after lunch, I took a taxi back down Galle Road to Kollupitiya, and spent the next hour walking through the market stalls, admiring the fruit and vegetables. The fruitsellers smiled at me as I moved through the crowds, offering me durian, jackfruit, jambu and spiky rambutans, and pointing to colorful piles of limes, oranges, tangerines and passion fruits. Smells of vanilla, cloves and cinnamon followed me through the market. I bought a king coconut and waited while a small boy hacked its top off and handed it over for me to drink. When I had finished, I pushed back out into the street.

A crowd of large black crows hopped along the sidewalk, pursuing a fish-vendor staggering under the weight of his catch. I dodged a lunch-packet wallah, his knees angled wide in his sarong as he steered his rickety bicycle through the crowd, a wooden pallet of tiffin boxes strapped precariously behind. I bought the daily edition of *The Island* and walked slowly back up Galle Road, glancing briefly at the new American Embassy, a massive concrete structure looking a little like a cubist phallus, squatting in the sun behind heavy walls and barbed wire.

At a quarter to three I opened the door to my second-floor room, stripped off my soaking clothes, and headed for the shower. Colombo's climate is one of the most miserable in Asia, with nearly one hundred percent humidity, still air, and virtually no diurnal variation. There are only days when it rains, and days when it doesn't.

Ten minutes later I was toweling myself dry, and by the time three o'clock came, I was dressed in a fresh pair of slacks and a sport shirt, ready to meet my mystery client. I took a cold tonic water from the room's tiny refrigerator, and picked up my canvas shoulder bag containing the note and the parcel. Then I put on my sunglasses, and went out on the balcony to see what I could see.

Directly in front of me lay the ocean, gently curved from end to end, stretching away westward toward the Arabian Sea. Sri Lanka – the Resplendent Isle – is a teardrop falling off the end of India, a bright green jewel in a deep blue sea. The Greeks called it Taprobane; the Portuguese, Ceilão; the Arabs, Serendib; the British called it Ceylon. Marco Polo thought it was the finest island in the world, and so did I.

In the old days, they'd shipped camphor, cinnamon, and elephants out of here; today, it was mainly coconuts and tea. It was a fairy-tale country where the magic had turned to terror as wave after wave of political violence had washed across the land, leaving chaos in its bloody wake. The Sinhalese were fighting a desperate sporadic war in the north with Tamil separatists, a war neither side could win and neither could afford to lose. It had been going on for years, and there was no end in sight.

But today on the beach, there was no sign of war or worry. Unlike the night before, the sea today was calm, its waves breaking gently along the beach. Children ran along the sand, trying to loft their kites into the air on the languid breezes, shouting at each other in Sinhala.

Directly below me was the large saltwater swimming pool, its clear blue-green water winking and sparkling in the sun. At strategic locations around the pool stood ancient waiters in long white sarongs, ready to take drink orders. The sun crosses the yardarm early in the tropics, and already guests sat in twos and threes, sipping gin and tonics and talking in relaxed tones about the day.

I finished my tonic and checked my watch. Whoever S. Wickramanayake was, he was now twenty minutes late. I set my empty glass down on the veranda railing and was just getting ready to go back inside in search of a second tonic when the bomb went off.

As I started to turn, I heard a roaring noise behind me. A giant hand slammed into my back, pushing me straight off the end of the balcony and into space. I opened my mouth to shout, but my words were drowned out by an enormous thunderclap which seemed to consume all the available air.

The world fell suddenly silent. And then I was spinning down through the sunlight. I fell endlessly, turning over and over, my eyes watching the patterns made by millions of tiny shards of glass as they flew past me.

Then, nothing.

CHAPTER TWO

"Finally awake, are we?"

I turned my stiff neck to see a nurse entering the room, carrying a tray with a tall pitcher and several glasses. I sat up, feeling a headache start to pound behind my eyes. "Where the hell am I?" I said slowly, testing each word carefully.

The nurse pursed her lips. "Lie back down," she said crisply. "You're in the Joseph Fraser Nursing Home."

"Nursing Home?"

She nodded. "It's a private hospital, actually. Just behind the Police Grounds."

I stared at her. "How did I get here?" I glanced down, and realized that I was wearing nothing but a thin shift. "And where are my clothes?"

Her almond eyes widened. "You don't remember? You were nearly blown to bits this afternoon." She smiled. "Your clothes certainly were." She put a cool hand on my forehead. "How do you feel?"

I lay back down on the cool white sheets. "Happy to be alive, I guess," I said after a moment. I looked around me. "I had a shoulder bag. Did it get blown up, too?"

"Your bag? Oh, yes; it's in the drawer here." She indicated the wooden stand on which she had set the tray. She brought out the bag and held it up. "Do you need something from it?"

I shook my head. "Just as long as it's safe," I said. "My passport and traveler's checks are there."

"Yes, and some sort of a parcel," the nurse said.

I nodded, laying back in the bed and looking around me. The room was clean and airy, and wide windows opened up onto a beautiful garden, bordered by trees and shrubs. The frangipani and bougainvillea pulsed with the soft colors of twilight. In the rain trees, sleepy birds called to one another, announcing nightfall.

"Not a bad place you've got here," I said finally. "Doesn't look much like a hospital, though."

She nodded, pouring orange juice from the pitcher. "No, it doesn't, does it? This was headquarters for the British during the war. The fliers, I think. Mountbatten had an office here. Shall we drink our orange juice now?"

"We shall, most definitely." I was suddenly very thirsty. I lay back and sipped orange juice as she cranked up my bed, gazing out at the garden, imagining what it had looked like during the war. I could almost see the RAF fliers in starched whites, playing croquet on the lawn, their officers' caps tucked under their arms as they applauded a particularly clever wicket by one of the ladies, all the time keeping an anxious eye on the sky for Japanese warplanes.

I finished my orange juice and turned to the nurse. "That feels a little better," I said. "What time is it?"

She checked her watch. "Nearly seven," she said. "It will be dark in a few minutes."

I shifted on the bed, testing my controls. Nothing seemed broken or damaged. "How do I check out of here?"

"Check out?"

"You know, leave. I have to—"

"Sorry, sir," a new voice said. "You're staying here tonight, I'm afraid."

I looked up. A policeman stood in the doorway, ramrod-straight, his swagger stick under his arm. He wore dark olive khakis with razor creases, and his boots shone like obsidian. His dark eyes swept the room, probing the corners, and I felt myself tense slightly. Cops make me nervous, especially when I'm flat on my back in a strange place.

"You're Mr. Donovan?"

I nodded. "I am. And who are you?"

His eyes took my measure before he answered. "Inspector Roshan Abeyratne, CID," he said at last. "Anti-terrorist division. We need to talk, you and I." He shifted his glance to the nurse. "But before we do, Sister, I'll thank you to take your leave."

She looked from him to me and back again, lowered her eyes, and left the room. Abeyratne moved aside a fraction of an inch to let her pass.

He took off his cap and strode to the bed, smoothing down his hair with long, thin fingers. "Congratulations, Mr. Donovan," he said, extending his hand. I shook it, feeling muscled coolness. "You're lucky to be alive."

I looked him over. Abeyratne was in his forties, a handsome man with prematurely grey hair the color of pewter and a neatly clipped military moustache.

"So I've been told," I said. "One minute, I'm standing on the balcony outside my room. Next thing I know, I'm in a hospital bed." I paused. "What the hell happened?"

Abeyratne gave a small, tight smile. "A bomb happened, Mr. Donovan. Rather a good one, in fact. There were thirty pounds of high explosive in a suitcase which had been set against the wall of the room next to yours."

"Thirty pounds? Jesus, that's—"

He nodded. "Quite. There was enough force in that suitcase to lift a locomotive into the air. Fortunately," he continued, "most of the explosion's force was absorbed by the wall. It blew inward, into your room. If you had been inside, of course, you would certainly have been killed." He paused. "Indeed, had the doors to your balcony been closed, you would probably have been sliced in two by exploding glass. As it was, the blast produced a tremendous shock wave which traveled outward, through the open doors. According to witnesses, it blew you straight off the balcony, out perhaps twenty feet." He smiled. "And then, of course, you fell down into the pool. Do you remember any of this?"

I shook my head. "Something hit me," I said. "In the back. Next thing I knew, I was falling through space. Everything was very quiet, absolutely silent, and the air around me sparkled."

"The blast deafened you," said Abeyratne. "The sparkles were shards of glass, of course. You fell into the deep end of the pool, fortunately. You were unconscious when they pulled you out, and so they brought you straight here." He looked me up and down. "Yes, you're an extremely lucky man."

"How did the bomb go off?"

"A simple electrical timer, battery-powered, attached to a detonator," he said. "Set in advance."

"By whom?"

"Ah," said Abeyratne. "Just the question we're trying to answer ourselves right now. An Indian couple – a man and a woman – registered under the name of Mahalingam at noon. They asked specifically for a room with a sea view, and chose the one next to yours. The bellman remembers carrying their bag upstairs, and leaving it on the bed. It could easily have been moved against the wall later."

"And this couple – Mr. and Mrs. Mahalingam," I said, "where are they now?"

Abeyratne shrugged. "Gone into smoke, of course," he said. "They came downstairs, dropped off their keys at the front desk, and said they were going for a walk." He paused. "Naturally, they were never seen again."

"Naturally," I echoed. "Did anyone else get hurt?"

"Two chambermaids who were talking in the hallway when the explosion occurred are in serious condition, although they are expected to live. Both rooms are completely destroyed, of course. The blast tore out most of the exterior wall of one room and a large part of the roof. Six of the large palms surrounding the swimming pool had their tops taken off. Most of the windows in that wing of the hotel were shattered, in fact. The swimming pool is full of broken glass and debris, of course, and the ballroom on the ground floor is covered with plaster and dust." He gave a tight smile. "In short, I'd have to say it was all a bit of a mess."

I said nothing, my mind shuffling fast through the cards I now held. Thirty pounds of explosive was like trying to kill ants with a steamroller, and the fact that someone had gone to all this trouble on my behalf wasn't very reassuring. You can't buy explosives at the corner store, and people who knew how to rig up timed detonators weren't usually listed in the Yellow Pages.

The whole operation showed determination, skill, and connections, and represented a considerable investment in getting me as dead as possible. There was every chance that whoever had set it up would try again as soon as they could.

My eyes shifted back and forth across the wide-open windows. Confined to a hospital bed, I was an even easier target. It was fully dark already, and the lovely garden which had earlier looked so inviting now seemed like an ideal hiding place for assassins.

Abeyratne caught my glance. "Not to worry, Mr. Donovan. There'll be a guard detail here tonight." He paused. "Right now I'm concerned, as you can imagine, with the question of who tried to kill you, and why. Any ideas?"

I thought about it, keeping my eyes on the garden outside. *Who's after me? Who wants me dead badly enough to blow up half a hotel?* From experience, I knew that although friends come and friends go, enemies accumulate. And in my business, I'd accumulated plenty. People who didn't like me were strewn all over the developing world, and they shared a lot in common. They all had long memories, short fuses, and few inhibitions when it came to revenge. If you made your living out on the edge, people like that were an occupational hazard, a form of business overhead. Making a short list of suspects would be almost impossible.

I shook my head. "Look," I said finally, "I've got no idea who did this. All I know is I got a note yesterday from somebody named Wickramanayake, asking me to be in my room at three o'clock." I stopped then, wondering whether to tell him about the parcel I'd picked up. I decided to keep my mouth shut for the time being. I wanted to open that parcel now, no matter what the note said, but I wanted to do it alone, without a cop looking over my shoulder.

Abeyratne sensed something then, and his glance grew sharper. "Just a note, Mr. Donovan?" He moved a step closer. "Nothing more?"

I shook my head. "Nothing more, Inspector." Involuntarily, my eyes darted to the cabinet containing my shoulder bag.

"Do you still have the letter, Mr. Donovan? I'll need it as evidence."

His gaze held mine, and I saw something in his eyes, some tiny movement, that made me suddenly wary. He'd caught my glance at the cabinet, but there was something else. Something's wrong here, my inner voice warned me. Something's not right with this guy.

I shrugged. "The letter's gone," I said. "Blown to bits in the explosion." I had no idea if this was true, but I wasn't giving this guy anything.

Abeyratne's expression changed. He drew himself up to attention and stepped back. He doesn't believe a word of it, I thought. Never shit a shitter.

"A great pity, Mr. Donovan," he said, putting his cap back on. "Well, you're tired, I expect. I'll come back tomorrow morning to take a full statement. But now, with your permission, I'll take my leave."

He turned at the doorway. "You're quite sure there was nothing other than the letter?"

I opened my baby blues wide. "Scout's honor."

He looked at me for a moment, and then he closed the door softly.

I lay quietly in the bed when he had gone, looking out the window at the garden. Close calls were good in both horseshoes and bomb-throwing, and I'd just come as close to losing the game as I'd ever want to.

But I was alive, that was the main thing. And if I could just figure out who had tried to kill me, I might be able to stay alive a while longer.

My eyelids were heavy, and I lay back on the bed, feeling fatigue and mild shock start to creep over me. Somewhere in all of this, a letter-writer named S. Wickramanayake had a role, although I was damned if I could see what it was. Could the bomb have been intended for him?

Just before I began to doze, I wondered if he had any idea how lucky he'd been.

* * *

15

I couldn't have slept more than an hour. The sound of someone tapping gently on the door to my room brought me fully awake. The nurse entered, tray in hand. She smiled prettily. "I thought you might like some more juice," she said, coming into the room and setting the tray down beside my bed. "I brought you some biscuits, too."

"Thank you." I sipped my juice, feeling the delicious liquid make its way down my dry throat. I pointed to the second glass on the tray. "Aren't you joining me?"

She blushed, lowering her long lashes. "Oh dear me, no, sir," she said. "The second glass is for your wife."

I choked on a mouthful of juice, nearly spewing it across the sheets. "My wife?"

The nurse beamed. "I knew you'd be pleased," she cooed. "She arrived just a few moments ago. Visiting hours are over, actually, but of course we made an exception." She dropped her voice. "We didn't know you were married to a Sri Lankan, Mr. Donovan; it was quite a surprise to Matron."

Not nearly as much as it is to me, I thought. I stared at her with my mouth open. "My wife," I finally managed to say. "Ah, where is she?"

"Just coming. They called up from the desk." She looked up. "Oh, here she is now."

I turned my head to see a beautiful Sri Lankan woman standing in the doorway.

She was tall and slim, dressed in a cool blue pastel sari. Her skin was the color of *café au lait*, and glowed with health. She wore a faint brush of color on her full lips, but no other makeup that I could see. Her big almond eyes were almost luminescent, and her wide, radiant smile revealed small, perfect white teeth.

Her hair was jet black, long and spectacular, falling thickly down over her shoulders almost to her tiny waist. She carried a large cloth handbag and a parasol, and as far as I was concerned just then, she was probably one of the most beautiful women in the world.

Maybe, I thought, I'm dreaming all this. Maybe I'm really dead and this is my first day in paradise.

"Darling!" she cried. She swept into the room toward me, her arms outstretched.

CHAPTER THREE

"All right," I said in a low voice, "just who the hell are you?"

The nurse had left the room, leaving just the two of us. She moved until she was standing just beside my bed.

"My name is Shanti," she said quietly. "I have to explain some things to you, and there's not much time." She spoke in British-accented tones, and smelled faintly of sandalwood and coconut oil.

I sat up in bed, took her hand, and felt her cool brown skin. "You're real, aren't you?"

She looked at me with wide doe eyes. "Real? I should certainly hope so. What a strange question."

"Well, it's been a strange day," I said. "You said you had some things to explain."

"So I did." She looked around. "Don't they have chairs in these rooms?"

I moved over. "Sit here," I said.

She nodded and sat primly on the edge of the bed, clutching her handbag. "Thank you." She brushed her thick hair out of her eyes, and smiled tentatively at me. "You'll think I'm mad, coming in here like this, but I had to see you, and there's very little time."

I nodded. *One of us is crazy, for sure.* "Absolutely," I said. "A wife certainly has a right to see her husband, after all."

She blushed. "Yes, well, I'm sorry about that." She looked apologetically at me. "But Matron wouldn't have let me in otherwise, I'm afraid. And of course, I couldn't give her my real name."

"Of course not," I said.

She picked at her sari. "Look, you must believe what I'm about to say, Mr. Donovan. It's quite literally a matter of life or death, as I told you."

"As you told me? Lady, I've never seen you before in my life."

She stared at me. "You mean you didn't get my note?"

Understanding hit me like a pail of cold water in the face. "You're S. Wickramanayake?"

She nodded, her expression somber. "Shanti Wickramanayake. I'm the one who wrote the note."

"Then... the bomb. The bomb was—"

"—meant for both of us," she murmured. "Yes, I'm afraid so. And I'm sorry that you were nearly killed. I was late for our meeting, you see – held up in traffic." She put her hand on my arm. "But look, there's no time to discuss all that now. We've got to get the manuscript out of here, find my uncle, and get him safely to England."

I stared at her. "*We* do?"

She nodded. "Yes, we do. You and I. They know about the manuscript now, you see, and they'll kill both of us to get their hands on it." Her eyes turned fearful. "You've still got it, haven't you?"

"Got what?"

She grabbed my hands. "Aren't you listening? The manuscript, of course. My uncle's book; the one I sent you." Her eyes widened in alarm. "Don't tell me you've lost it?"

I leaned over, pulled open the cabinet drawer, and took out my shoulder bag. It was scuffed and damp, but in one piece. I opened it and peered inside. The wrapped parcel was inside, along with my money, my passport, and my old Zippo lighter. I took the lighter out, curious to see if it would still work.

She reached over, and before I could stop her, she snatched the bag from my hands, took out the parcel and ripped it open. Typewritten pages fanned out in her hands.

"Thank God for that," she breathed, stuffing the manuscript back into the bag. She raised her eyes to mine. "We must guard this with our lives. This is why they tried to kill us this afternoon. Because of this manuscript."

I raised myself up on my elbows. There's definitely a leak in this woman's think tank, I told myself. "And who are 'they'?"

"Us," a voice said from the open window.

Somehow, I knew without looking that it wasn't the Tooth Fairy.

I turned slowly, feeling my muscles protest. A Sri Lankan wearing a black eyepatch and carrying a huge knife in his hand was climbing over the sill, followed closely by another man, also armed with a knife.

One-Eye was stocky and tough-looking, dressed in a T-shirt and striped sarong. His hair fell in greasy ringlets to his shoulders, and he had a tiny, pointed goatee which gave him the air of an unsavory satyr. All he needs, I thought, is a pair of horns. His companion was tall and clean-shaven, with a pointed fox-like face, a long beak of a nose, and a mouthful of cheap metal dentures. From the looks on their faces, they weren't collecting for the United Way.

Shanti gave a low cry and backed up against the wall, clutching her handbag. My bag, containing the manuscript, lay forgotten on the floor in front of her.

I reacted more or less automatically. The one-eyed man with the knife was about six feet away, coming fast, and although the simplest thing to do would be to blow him into bits with my trusty .45, there was one small problem. I didn't have one.

So I did the next best thing. I picked up the heavy pitcher of orange juice and sidearmed it toward him. The sticky liquid erupted from the pitcher's wide mouth, momentarily blinding him. A split second later the heavy base of the pitcher caught him on the point of the jaw. One-Eye gave a grunt of pain and pitched forward, banging his forehead on the cast-iron bedstead.

I leaped out of bed, feeling my muscles shriek in protest. I grabbed Shanti's parasol and jabbed One-Eye in the ribs with its sharp metal end, driving him back a couple of feet.

I held the parasol as far out in front of me as I could manage and felt behind me for the woman. I was suddenly conscious of the fact that I had only a Zippo lighter for a weapon, and that I was wearing nothing but a paper-thin hospital shift, the kind that has ties down the back and plenty of ventilation for your backside. "Come on, lady," I hissed. "Give me a hand, for God's sake."

The two assassins faced me, edging closer, an inch at a time. The one-eyed man I'd baptized with orange juice scowled, wiped his eyes, and gestured with his knife. "Give it to us," he whispered.

I scooped up my shoulder bag, looked at it, then at Shanti. "The manuscript?"

She nodded, glancing fearfully at the one-eyed man as she fumbled with the catch on her handbag.

"Yes, the book," One-Eye whispered. "We want the book. Give it to us and you live. Otherwise—" He scowled again, letting his words trail off into silence.

"Never," said Shanti.

I looked at her in alarm. "Now, wait a second—" I began.

The knife blade hummed through the air as One-Eye advanced on us. "Give it," he spat. "Now!"

I backed away another few feet. He and his crony stepped forward, hissing like a pair of water moccasins as they closed in. The parasol wasn't going to protect us much longer.

"We've got to get out of here," whispered Shanti. We were almost to the window.

"That's obvious," I replied. "But what do you plan on doing about these two?"

"Watch." She opened her handbag and drew out an enormous, very unladylike revolver. One-Eye drew in his breath and stepped back a pace.

Having had some passing acquaintance with various weapons over the years, I recognized what she was holding. It was a rare but deadly Webley & Scott Mark IV revolver, blue-black steel with a six-inch barrel and old-fashioned lanyard ring on the butt. The Webley fired a fat .455 slug with an extraordinary amount of what is politely referred to as 'stopping power.' It could crumple a charging tribesman in his tracks, which was exactly what the British in the last century had designed it to do.

"Where the hell did you get that?" I breathed.

She gripped the Webley with both hands, waving it around like a hosepipe. I stepped back, trying to get out of the line of fire. "It was my great-grandfather's," she said between clenched teeth. "He fought in the Boer War. Ready?"

"For what?"

She looked at me. "To escape, of course. We'll go out of the window."

I looked at the men, and back at her. "Ready when you are," I said.

"We will find you," rasped One-Eye. "You will never be safe until we have the book. Wherever you go, we will follow."

"Listen, we can talk about this," I said. "Work it out, you know? Suppose we–"

Shanti grabbed my arm. "Stop talking," she said. "Out the window, quickly!"

I jumped up on the wide sill. It was a short drop to the ground. Through the window, the moon had risen, filling the narrow slice of sky visible above the rain trees. The garden lay in darkness, waiting. Beyond, the trees were a black blur. If we can make it to the trees, I thought, we might be able to hide.

Hiking up her sari, Shanti clambered up beside me, flashing me a quick glimpse of thigh. Just then, with a roar, One-Eye charged.

Shanti didn't hesitate. She raised the heavy revolver, took a deep breath, and pulled the trigger. There was a dry click, then another and another. "Bugger," she muttered. "Ammunition's perished."

One-Eye lunged forward, snatching the bag from my hand.

"No!" screamed Shanti, starting forward.

I pulled her back. "Don't be stupid," I muttered. "They'll kill us. Leave it."

From the side, One-Eye's companion was closing in, his knife held high.

I grabbed Shanti's arm and pulled her back off the window. We hit the ground running.

CHAPTER FOUR

I pulled Shanti through the bushes and across what appeared to be someone's back yard. It's astounding how fast you can shift gears if you really put your mind to it. Five minutes ago, I'd been an innocent invalid, highly suspicious of the beautiful woman who'd passed herself off as my wife to enter my hospital room.

And although she still might be the Wicked Witch of the West for all I knew, she'd certainly been right about one thing – there were people out there trying to kill us. Faith doesn't need reasons, and in that sense at least, I was certainly a believer. There'd be time enough later on to try and make sense of things.

Right now, I thought as we charged pell-mell through the underbrush, it was a question of surviving the next few minutes.

"Where are we going?" she asked me, not breaking stride. For a woman in a sari, she could move pretty damn fast.

"As far away from here as we can get," I replied, not slackening my pace. "Save your breath, it only slows us down. If they catch us, they'll kill us. You said that yourself, remember?"

We were through the underbrush by then, and after a few moments we emerged on Jawatta Road, a side street running between the suburb of Cinnamon Gardens and the shops at Thimbirigasyaya. I was conscious of my flapping hospital gown, and of the fact that it had what might be called the ultimate plunging backline, an arrangement convenient for infirm patients, no doubt, but one which left my buttocks exposed to the open night air.

We stopped finally beside a drainage ditch at the side of the road and listened. No sound of our pursuers. "Think they've given up?" I asked, gasping for breath.

"They've got what they wanted," Shanti replied, a bitter tinge to her voice. "We've lost the manuscript."

"Not to mention my passport and money," I added. "All I've got left is this." I showed her the Zippo, still clutched in my hand.

"They aren't important."

"They are to me," I replied.

She looked at me. "They aren't important to them, Mr. Donovan. They're after only two things – the manuscript, and my uncle. Now that they've got the manuscript, they'll go after him. We've got to save him." She grabbed the front of my gown. "That's why I wrote to you in the first place – to hire you to save my uncle. You've got to help me, Mr. Donovan."

"Max."

"I beg your pardon?"

"Call me Max." Gently, I disengaged her hand. "Look," I said, "there's a lot I want to know. But—"

"Then you'll help me?"

"Maybe. I don't know yet." I indicated my hospital gown. "I have to get some clothes first. I can't think straight dressed like this."

She looked me up and down. "I'm not surprised."

"And I have to get my bag back."

"And then you'll help me save my uncle?"

I thought about it for a moment. Then I nodded. "Yes," I said. "Yes, I will."

She put her arms around my neck and gave me a hug. "Well, come on, then. We've got to get you some clothes."

* * *

Fifteen minutes later, we stood inside the cramped public telephone booth at the all-night post office on Dickman's Road. I wore a pair of cheap cotton trousers, a tie-dye T-shirt and a pair of rubber sandals from one of the late-night shops. Our heads were close together, listening on the receiver as I talked with the officer in charge at Slave Island Police Headquarters.

"Abeyratne? Roshan Abeyratne?" The OIC's voice was tinny on the line. "I tell you, there's no one here by that name. Are you sure?"

"I'm sure," I said, glancing at Shanti. "Inspector Roshan Abeyratne, CID. Anti-terrorist section."

"Never heard of him," the officer replied. "We've got plenty of Abeyratnes in the police – island's full of Abeyratnes, in fact – but none in the CID, and none anywhere named Roshan. What's his badge number?"

I glanced up at Shanti and cupped the receiver. "He wasn't wearing a badge," I whispered. Her eyes widened.

"Someone's been telling you stories," the OIC was saying. "But if you insist, give me your name, and the hotel where you're staying, and I'll see if I can sort this out for you."

Shanti tugged on my sleeve, shaking her head emphatically. Then she reached over and cut the connection.

I turned. "What the hell did you do that for?" I said.

"Abeyratne was one of them, don't you see?" She grabbed my arm, pulled me out of the booth, and steered me toward the street. "Come on, let's get away from here. They're probably still looking for us."

She led me out into the smoky, humid darkness. Outside the post office, the road was alive with vehicles and pedestrians, hurrying purposefully through the murk. The traffic never stops in Asia, and the streets in most capital cities are almost as busy at night as at noon. The yellow eye of a Bajaj three-wheeled scooter emerged sputtering from the gloom and wobbled toward us. Shanti swept her arm gracefully down, and it swerved, braking to a halt beside us.

The driver was a rail-thin teenager with a downy moustache, flashing eyes and a Michael Jackson T-shirt. He listened to the warble of Sinhala that Shanti fired at him, shook his head in agreement, and revved his motor. We clambered inside, and with a lurch and a cloud of exhaust, we tottered off down the street.

Her hand rested lightly on my knee for balance as we bumped along in the dark. It felt nice, but I needed some answers. "What now?" I said after a moment.

"We have to talk."

"You're telling me," I said.

"But not now. Wait until we get there."

"Get where?"

"Shh. You'll see."

* * *

The Sea Glimpse Wadiya was a ramshackle collection of huts in Bambalapitiya, down across the railroad tracks, at the very edge of the beach. The moon was high over the water by the time we arrived, illuminating a ghostly wrecked hulk just offshore. It made the whole thing look, I thought, a little like a Dali painting. Graceful coconut palms arced out over the waves, just as they do in the tourist posters, and from inside the bar, a string band played *baila* music.

Shanti and I sat out on the beach under one of the small grass-thatched umbrellas, where we could talk over the background of the music, and where the other patrons of the Wadiya wouldn't overhear us. I ordered arrack neat, no ice, and Shanti asked for beer. The barefoot waiter waggled his head, showed us large white teeth, and shuffled away.

The sand was soft and cool under my feet. The breeze from the ocean kept the mosquitoes at bay, and the baila music masked the sounds of traffic from the city which was so close by but seemed thousands of miles away. It was just the thing for my jangled nerves, but there was one question I simply had to ask. "How'd you find out about me?"

She smiled then. "I'm a political historian, Max; a lecturer at the University of Colombo. Three weeks ago, I was at a conference in Berkeley. The same day that I got Bertie's cable saying that Khan had put a price on his head, I met a friend of yours, a woman named Wendy."

I groaned. Wendy Woodward was in the political science department. I'd promised to have dinner with her on my last trip to San Francisco, but finding a stolen painting in Kathmandu had taken up most of my time, and then there was a hospital stay.

"She's certainly good-looking, I must say," Shanti continued. "She was most helpful, Max – she told me all about you, and said you'd help me. Then she gave me your address at the Galle Face." She smiled. "She also said you owe her dinner at Spenger's."

"Good old Wendy," I murmured, making a mental note to devise some particularly horrible form of revenge once I'd gotten myself out of this. I tried my arrack, letting its coconut fire slide down my throat and settle in the pit of my stomach. It's good to be alive, I thought. No thanks, however, to the person sitting next to me. "Let's hear it, then," I said.

She folded her hands, sighed, and bowed her head a fraction. "It's hard to know where to start."

"Begin at the beginning. And when you come to the end, stop."

She smiled. "*Alice in Wonderland.* The King of Hearts said that to the White Rabbit. Uncle Bertie used to read it to me at tea-time." She poured more beer. "Very well, it begins with Uncle Bertie."

"Bertie?"

"Osbert, actually; my mother's brother. His full name's Sunil Osbert Wickramanayake, but no one calls him Sunil. Most of his friends call him Wikkie, actually, but I call him Uncle Bertie." She paused. "Have you ever heard of Kingsley McTavish?"

I thought for a moment. "I've heard the name somewhere," I said at last. "Isn't he a writer of some kind?"

She nodded. "Men's adventure novels. Thunder over the Reefs; High Road to Danger; The Khyber Rogues."

"Of course," I said. "I read *The Khyber Rogues* once, in fact. Pretty blood-and-guts, as I remember."

She grinned. "Awful, isn't it?"

I looked at her. "It wasn't all that bad, to tell you the truth. I was sort of in the mood for it at the time." I tactfully didn't mention that it had been the only thing available to read in the prison camp where I'd spent some time during the Vietnam War. As lurid as *The Khyber Rogues* might have been, its rip-snorting style of freebooting adventure, which pitted brave colonial lads against the scheming barbarians, was just what the doctor ordered.

Eventually, of course, our captors had found the book. They confiscated it and cut everyone's rations for a week, but by that time, we'd all read it at least twice, and like the people in Ray Bradbury's *Fahrenheit 451*, some of us could actually quote large chunks of it from memory.

What we couldn't remember, we made up, and thus Kingsley McTavish's tale grew daily more sexy, lurid, violent and hopeful, passed from mouth to mouth by a bunch of forgotten POWs who didn't have much else to hold on to.

I smiled, remembering. "And how is Kingsley McTavish mixed up in this?" I asked.

She leaned forward. "Uncle Bertie," she said, "is Kingsley McTavish. It's his pen name." She took a precise sip of beer and patted her mouth with a paper napkin. "It's his book, you see."

I took another swallow of arrack. "Are you serious? Your uncle writes trashy paperbacks?"

"He's written dozens of them," she said. "Uncle Bertie's always had an overactive imagination. The strange thing is that he's not really adventurous at all. He's never been off the island; never done any of the things he writes about."

I smiled, thinking about the slam-bang adventurer who was the hero of *Khyber Rogues*. "He could have fooled me," I said.

She nodded. "Oh, yes; he's really quite successful. I mean – and you mustn't tell Uncle Bertie this – they're awful rubbish, really, but sort of fun in a *Boy's Own* sort of way. All my brothers absolutely loved them; they used to come around his house begging for more stories all the time."

"Your uncle must be a rich man, then."

"Not at all," she said. "They're just pulp paperbacks, after all. No, he uses what little money he makes from them on his model train collection – that's his real passion. He has two whole rooms out in the old servants' quarters set up as a sort of tiny railway operation. Everyone thinks he's a bit dotty. I suppose he is, but in a harmless sort of way."

I took a hit of arrack. "Let me get this straight," I said. "You're telling me that the manuscript you gave me – the one the thieves took – is actually one of your uncle's novels? For this I was almost carved into giblets?"

"Oh, no, Max. It's Uncle Bertie's book all right, but it's not one of those. This is a real book, not fiction. A very important book. It's about a man named Iskander Khan, one of the biggest drug dealers in Asia. Khan found out about it, and now he wants to keep the book from getting published. He's put a price on Uncle Bertie's head."

"Must be a hell of a book." I frowned. "But if he's not adventurous, how come Uncle Osbert knows so much about the drug business?"

"He doesn't know much about drugs, to tell you the truth. But he knows how to write. You see, Uncle Bertie ghostwrote this book for someone else, one of Khan's men." She flipped her long hair back. "About six months ago, one of Khan's people decided to leave the organization. He needed money, and so he had the idea of using Bertie to help him write an exposé of the drug ring, and sell it." She paused. "They... they were going to split the money."

I looked at her. She glared back. "Well," she said, "Uncle Bertie's sweet. That doesn't mean he's particularly smart."

I nodded. "Let me see if I can sum this up," I said. "Your Uncle Osbert and this ex-drug dealer wrote a book together, and when Mr. Khan found out about it, he put out a contract on them. Now Osbert and his collaborator are on the run. Am I right?"

"Not exactly. It's Uncle Bertie who's on the run, as you put it. The collaborator is dead."

I looked at her. "Dead?"

She nodded. "Khan's men killed him two weeks ago. Stabbed him in front of his house; in broad daylight."

"And now Osbert thinks they're after him?"

"They *are* after him, Max. Last month, Bertie sent the first three chapters off to his publisher in London. They made an immediate offer of fifty thousand."

"Dollars or rupees?"

"Pounds."

My head came up. "And how much is Khan offering?"

She grimaced. "Khan's offered ten lakh of rupees for Uncle Bertie – alive or dead – together with the manuscript. There's only the one copy, you see."

"And that's the copy we had?"

She nodded. I did some quick arithmetic. One lakh is a hundred thousand, so ten lakh would be a million rupees. About fifty thousand US dollars. That was less than the publisher was offering, and I pointed this out to her.

She nodded. "But it's still more than enough to send every goonda and petty criminal on the island after him," she said.

We were silent for a moment. Then I said, "No other copies, you said?"

"Bertie sent the original of the first three chapters off to the publisher, and those came back with the offer. There was a carbon copy, but it was stolen. We think that's how Khan found out about it."

"Who stole it?"

"Bertie suspects Nandasena, our gardener. Uncle Bertie never liked Nandasena – he kept him mainly on account of Aunt Iris. When she died, Nandasena stayed on. Then one day, last month, he simply disappeared. And so did the only carbon copy of Uncle Bertie's manuscript."

I thought for a moment, gazing out at the moonlit sea. "I still don't understand," I said finally, "why they tried to blow me up this afternoon."

"They weren't after you at all, Max," she said. "They thought you were meeting Uncle Bertie. They must have intercepted the note and thought that 'S. Wickramanayake' was Bertie."

"That's pretty far-fetched, isn't it?"

"Not at all." She leaned forward, putting her hand on my arm. "Think about it. Nandasena steals the carbon copy. Someone else reads a note that comes to the Galle Face. A policeman shows up in your hospital room, but he isn't really a policeman. Don't you think—"

"That's the part I don't get," I said. "That was a real policeman's uniform, and he acted like a real cop. It doesn't make sense."

"Don't you see?" Her voice was low and urgent. "He probably was a real policeman. He just didn't give you his real name." Her fingers tightened on my arm. "Max, Khan has people everywhere on the island – everywhere. We can't trust anyone."

"Just you and me against the world, is that it?"

"Yes, if you want to put it that way." She dropped her voice. "We've got to get Uncle Bertie out, Max. We've got to get him to England." She paused. "And half the advance is for you if we can do it."

That got my attention. I turned my mind to practicalities. "Where's Uncle Osbert now?" I asked.

"In hiding. Somewhere safe."

"Great." I looked around at the night. "I wish I could say the same for us."

I turned it over in my mind. I was broke and without a passport, and if the events of the past eight hours were any guide, I was being hunted by most of Colombo's underworld. The one-eyed man had taken my bag, and with it, Osbert's manuscript. No matter how you looked at it, the first order of business was to get the bag back. Unless I got the bag back, I couldn't very easily get off the island, and if I couldn't get off the island, I was likely to get killed.

But if I did get the bag back, I reasoned, the manuscript would be in it, and the manuscript was worth a lot of money. And if Uncle Osbert was in a safe place, then all I had to do was look out for myself until he and I were wheels-up for London.

And twenty-five thousand pounds, I reasoned, would buy quite a few suits on Savile Row. I didn't wear suits as a rule, but maybe it was time to start.

I checked my watch. It was just past ten o'clock, and the night was young. I stood up. "Let's get started."

"What are we going to do?"

"Well, first you're going to pay for the drinks."

"And then?"

"And then I'll explain the rest to you when I figure it out myself." I smiled. "How's that sound?"

CHAPTER FIVE

Our three-wheeler coughed and lurched as we threaded our way around the potholes on Maliban Street in the Pettah. In the dark, Shanti clutched my arm for balance and peered out at the rows of dingy shops and warehouses going by.

'Pettah' is a corruption of the Sinhala phrase *pita kotuwa*, meaning 'outside the Fort', and from colonial days this section of the city had been the commercial heart of Colombo. The Pettah is divided into sections. Main Street contains shops selling textiles, while Sea Street, beyond it, is for the goldsmiths. First Cross Street is full of shops selling electrical goods; Second Cross Street is mainly for jewelers. Third Cross Street is dominated by hardware merchants. Fifth Cross Street, where I was headed, specialized in tea, spices and ayurvedic medicines.

I wasn't looking for any of those things, however. What I wanted was very simple: information. And if possible, some fresh ammunition.

During the day, the Pettah was choked with noise and dust. Hawkers squatted on the ground, shouting their wares at passersby. Sweating porters pushed wooden carts piled high with chilies, vegetables, and dried fish through the crowd, while underfoot, cats scurried after mice and cockroaches. The narrow streets were clogged with cars, bullock-carts, huge Ashok Leyland lorries and the ever-present sputtering green and yellow Bajaj three-wheelers.

It was well after ten, and business was starting to taper off. The shops were closing, but some were still lit, and as we passed, we could see men seated around low tables, bargaining with each other in the flickering gloom of oil lamps. In the alleys, a few bare-chested laborers in loincloths still worked, unloading goods lorries piled high with bales of cloth and cotton. The heavy smell of spices filled the air, dominated by raw chilies.

Shanti turned to me. "You've got friends down here?" She sounded very doubtful.

"One or two," I said. "What's the matter, don't you like the neighborhood?"

She shook her head. "I just hope you know where you're going."

I leaned forward and tapped the driver on the shoulder. "Stop here."

The three-wheeler swerved and braked sharply before a shabby warehouse, half-hidden in the darkness. I got out and looked the place over.

Gaffar Abdeen's shop stood where it had, from all appearances, been standing since shortly after the dawn of time. Gaffar was a ship chandler, which meant that he arranged supplies of all kinds for the freighters and copra steamers that used Colombo Harbor. It also meant that he knew a lot about how to buy and sell things illegally. The last time I'd been here was during the riots, and Gaffar had sold me enough black-market aviation gas to get myself and my clients the hell off the island.

Tonight, I was hoping that he might be willing to part with some free information. After all, I reminded myself, I'd paid for the aviation gas at more than twice the going rate.

I held up a hundred-rupee note to our driver. "See this?" As he reached for it, I drew back my hand. "Wait for us here and you can have two of these," I said. It wouldn't do, I thought, to be caught down here at night without a ride out. The driver flashed me a nervous smile and quick shake of his head in assent, that odd sideways bobble so common in this part of the world.

Shanti and I got out and hopped carefully across the puddles of rainwater and sewage that formed a sort of shallow moat across the front of Gaffar's shop. The door was open, and inside, a single lamp burned dimly. We went inside.

The shopfront was empty, dusty shelves ranged silently behind a crude wooden counter. Beside the cash register, its drawer open and empty, a large yellow cat dozed. As we approached, it opened its eyes very wide, blinked twice, and watched us carefully.

I walked up to the counter and addressed the cat. "Where's Gaffar?"

The cat got up stiffly, staring at me the whole time. It walked to the edge of the counter and disappeared behind it, moving like a huge furry slinky. A moment later, a door in the back of the shop opened, and in the pool of yellow light, I recognized one of Gaffar's sons. "Come," he said simply, and we followed him into the back office.

Gaffar's office was where real business was conducted, and where the family spent most of its time. In one corner, a pile of ancient clothbound ledgers gathered dust, and in another, a collection of empty Elephant House soft-drink bottles. I knew that Gaffar's warehouse, sleeping quarters, and private rooms extended back from the street like a rabbit warren, but this was as far as he allowed any of his clients to get.

Tonight, only a few of the family were present. In one corner, two more sons, thin and sharp-faced, played a listless game of backgammon. From somewhere in the back, a cassette player ground out a scratchy Oum

Kalthoum tape, the high wailing noises coming through over the aroma of highly spiced curry.

A picture of the Aga Khan graced one wall, a Bank of Ceylon calendar featuring orchids the other. Overhead, a gaudily-painted Korean ceiling fan wobbled unsteadily, trying vainly to move the humid air.

Gaffar Abdeen, sweat beading his large nose and wide-domed forehead, sat behind an ancient wooden desk, counting piles of dirty banknotes and moving his lips silently. Behind him, an old man in a stained kaftan sat in a striped folding chair, slicing betel nut with a wicked-looking chopper and mumbling to himself.

Gaffar Abdeen looked up, blinked, sucked in his breath, and fumbled in one of his ample pockets, finally producing a pair of round wire-rimmed spectacles. Fitting them carefully over his eagle-beak nose, he peered at me with interest.

"Goodness gracious." He smiled, showing us crooked teeth stained by a lifetime of betel nut. "It is Mr. Donovan, no?"

"It is," I said. "How are you, you old bugger?"

He giggled. "Keeping, Mr. Donovan, keeping. And how is your good self, I hope?"

I smiled. No sense in telling Gaffar about my day, I thought. Or trying to correct his syntax. "My good self is fine," I said. I turned to Shanti. "This is Miss Wickramanayake," I added. "She's showing me Colombo at night."

Gaffar smiled broadly. "Is it? Welcome then, madame." He turned to the boys in the corner. "Ali!"

The youngest boy glanced up. "*Appa?*"

Gaffar turned back to Shanti. "*Teda kopida?*"

"Tea, please," she replied politely.

"Same for me," I said.

"Excellent," murmured Gaffar. To his son he said, "*Te thanni konduvar.*"

"*Shari!*" The boy sprinted out of the room.

"Tea and a chat will be ever so nice, I think." Gaffar rose, gathering his khaftan around him. "But first, allow me to wash my hands." He held out grimy palms to us with an apologetic smile, and indicated the piles of money on the counter. "Filthy lucre, as I believe your Bible puts it." He winked at us and disappeared into the back room.

Ali came back a moment later with a tray laden with steaming cups of strong orange pekoe tea and an interesting collection of digestive biscuits. The cat reappeared, climbed on top of the pile of money, and fixed me with a careful eye. I put a digestive biscuit in my mouth and sipped some tea. The cat's eyes never left mine.

Gaffar reentered the room and sat down beside us, taking a cup of tea and blowing on it.

"That's the first watch-cat I've ever seen," I said, making conversation.

Gaffar sniffed. "I don't know why he bothers, frankly. These hopeless rupee notes are practically worthless." He sipped his tea quietly for a moment, and then leaned back and scratched his earlobe. "So, Mr. Donovan. Is it that you are in trouble again?"

I shrugged. "That depends on how you define trouble, Mr. Abdeen. Let's put it this way: I'm in a lot less trouble than the last time you saw me."

Gaffar Abdeen smiled. "That is indeed very good to know. But you have not come here tonight to say good evening, I assume."

"Right as usual," I said. I put my teacup down, glanced at Shanti, and began to tell the story. Part of it, at any rate. I left out everything that had happened before I woke up in the hospital, and I didn't mention either Uncle Osbert or the missing manuscript. The way I told it, I'd been peacefully minding my business, strolling on the beach, when two thugs appeared and took my bag at knifepoint.

Gaffar listened to me, the frown on his face deepening as I talked. He sighed when I finished. "A man with an eyepatch, you say. Are you sure?"

"I won't forget that face in a hundred years."

"That's what I was afraid of." He took a deep breath. "Look, Mr. Donovan, if it is money you require, I can arrange a loan. Passport? I will supply a marvelous forgery in a mere day or two. Let me—"

"Mr. Abdeen" — I held up my hand — "I appreciate your willingness to help." I leaned forward. "But all I want is some idea of how to find the one-eyed man. Do you know him?"

Gaffar Abdeen's nose shone with sweat. "Oh, yes, Mr. Donovan. Most unfortunately so. Everyone in the Pettah knows this man."

"A local businessman?"

Gaffar Abdeen smiled thinly. "In a manner of speaking. His name is Vimal; Vimal Amarasuriya." He paused. "But most people in Colombo know him as Mahasona."

"Mahasona?"

"A kind of devil creature," murmured Shanti. "Something we use to scare the children with."

Gaffar Abdeen nodded. "Yes, precisely. Vimal — Mahasona — is a *mudalali*, one of the most powerful in Colombo."

"A *mudalali*? You mean a gangster of some sort?"

Abdeen shook his head. "More than that, Mr. Donovan. Much more than that. Mahasona isn't an ordinary goonda — he's a kind of underworld king. There was a film, I believe, with that chap Brando—"

"The Godfather?"

"Yes, that one. Mahasona is a kind of godfather — a very powerful and ruthless one. He kills people, you know. And one of his specialties is explosives." He paused. "It is said that he is the one who masterminded the bombing of the Central Post Office a few years ago. Also the Fort Railway Station."

He peered at me over his teacup. "I understand that there was an explosion at the Galle Face earlier today," he said, a thoughtful look on his face. "Your name was mentioned. Can I assume that this is somehow connected?"

I looked at him. "Just tell me how to find this Mahasona," I said, "and I'll make it a point to ask him."

Gaffar frowned. "There is one thing I do not understand, Mr. Donovan," he said. "It surprises me that Mahasona would steal from you himself. He has dozens of underlings who could easily do that." His face searched mine. "Did you have a great deal of money? Or something especially valuable?"

I shook my head. "Not really. Just a passport and some traveler's checks." I dared not glance at Shanti.

Abdeen grimaced. "Then I truly cannot understand it. There would be no reason for Mahasona to concern himself with such a theft. Most curious."

I finished my tea. "That may be so, Mr. Abdeen. But I still want my bag back. How do I find him?"

Abdeen implored me with his eyes. He reached over and put his large sweaty hand on mine. Fear radiated from his moist spaniel eyes as he spoke with quiet intensity. "Don't do this, my friend. Much better you go away now, back to America, and forget this poor island. Mahasona is dangerous, and violent; more so than you can imagine. He has many men with him. You are but one man" – his eyes flicked to Shanti – "and a woman. You cannot hope to contend with him."

I said nothing. After a moment Gaffar Abdeen rolled his eyes and sighed. "Very well. And may Allah forgive me." He dropped his voice to a whisper. "Second Cross Street, near the mosque. There is a wine shop on the corner; Premasiri's. Mahasona and his companions drink there at night."

I stood up. "Mr. Abdeen, you've been very helpful."

Gaffar rose and put his hand on my arm. "Think carefully, Mr. Donovan. You are, as they say, grossly outmatched."

"That reminds me." I opened Shanti's handbag, took out the Webley, and laid it on his desk. "Got any shells for this?"

Abdeen's eyes lit up as he gazed at the heavy revolver. "My word, I haven't seen one of those in years," he breathed.

I hefted it experimentally. "It might even the odds a little, don't you think?"

He smiled then, the merest curling of the lips. "Possibly, Mr. Donovan. Just possibly, for a man with your initiative. And yes, I believe I may have a box of shells somewhere. Won't be a moment." He bustled off into the back of his shop.

Across the desk, the cat sat and stared unblinking at us, its eyes as huge as saucers.

CHAPTER SIX

We rattled through the dark alleys toward Second Cross Street, our driver keeping toward the middle of the road, flitting from one dim cone of light to the next. Most of the shops were shut but from one or two of them, late-night card-players or sweating clerks stared curiously at us as we drifted by. The night was hot and humid, and the smells of cooking oil and charcoal seemed to blanket the Pettah. From the upstairs rooms, baila music drifted down to the street level, the notes descending like party balloons.

We passed the candy-striped Jami-ul-Alfar mosque, its interior dimly lit by several kerosene lamps. From somewhere within its depths came the quiet sounds of prayers being repeated, their cadence rising and falling gently on the night air. And up ahead, on the corner, I could make out a lighted doorway, its single light bulb illuminating a sign in green and red lettering: 'Premasiri's Wine Shop.'

We got down and stood outside the door. "Suppose he's not there? The one-eyed man, I mean." Shanti's voice was a whisper beside me.

I shrugged. "It should be our biggest problem," I whispered back. "I'm trying to think of what to do if he is there. Keep your purse ready."

Premasiri's wasn't what you'd call jumping that evening. There were exactly four customers inside the small smoky room, all dressed in striped sarongs and sweat-stained T-shirts. Mahasona was there, along with his skinny friend, the one with the metal teeth. One of the other two was 'Inspector Abeyratne.'

They were all busy packing away the rice and vegetables, eating *lamprais* with their fingers off wide banana leaves. Water glasses of arrack lay on the table beside them, and I could smell the raw alcohol as I approached their table.

"Enjoying dinner?" I asked.

Their heads swiveled around in near-perfect unison, as if on strings. Mahasona smiled broadly as he recognized me. "Ay-ya!" He levered himself up from the table, staggering a little, sweeping one of the empty arrack bottles aside. It hit the floor and bounced, coming to rest against my bag, which I spotted under the table.

Mahasona said something to his companions. They laughed, showing me white teeth and shining eyes. Mahasona raised his hands as if to bless the congregation. "Stupid," he breathed, smiling at me. "Very, very stupid." He reached into his sarong and pulled out his knife.

I moved closer, pointing to my canvas bag. "No sense in both of us being stupid, is there? All I want is the bag. Give it to me, and we're even."

Mahasona's smile widened. "Even? Very funny." His gaze shifted to his companions, who were starting to circle around us, their faces bright with anticipation. "I think you will die soon," he said with a laugh.

"Think so?" I reached out across the table and picked up a full glass of arrack. It was raw and pungent, well over a hundred proof. With a flick of my wrist, I threw it over Mahasona, soaking his T-shirt, his chest, and his hair. He cursed and drew back.

I took my ancient Zippo out of my pocket. I don't smoke, but I find the old lighter handy in other ways. The last time I'd used it, I remembered, had been to set an embassy on fire. I figured it would work just as well on a person. I flipped open the cap and held it up, my thumb poised on the tiny wheel. "Rare or well done?"

Mahasona let his breath out like a punctured tire, and I saw apprehension cloud his good eye. He drew back some more, and I advanced, coming up even with the table. I had a momentary advantage, but it wasn't going to last long. In a few more seconds the alcohol would evaporate. Time to move things along.

I turned to Shanti. "Your purse, please."

She held it open and I reached inside and drew out the Webley.

Mahasona's lips drew back over his teeth as he saw the Webley. "Gun is no good," he said. "Did you forget already?" He raised his knife and started forward.

I raised one hand, index finger pointing up, like a magician about to demonstrate a trick. "Watch," I said. I levered back the hammer on the Webley, drew down on one of the arrack bottles, and squeezed the trigger. There was a sound like a thunderclap, and the bottle exploded into a million shards, spewing arrack in a fine mist everywhere.

Mahasona and the other goondas gasped and drew back. I beamed at him.

"Works all right now, wouldn't you say?" I raised the pistol until it was level with his chest. "What do you bet I can make it fire a second time?"

Slowly, he put down his knife and raised his hands. "Take what you want," he spat. "Enjoy it while you still live."

Keeping my eyes on him, I bent down and picked up my bag from under the table. I felt through the cloth. The manuscript was still there, together with the leather case I kept my passport and travelers' checks in.

I stepped back. "See? We're even now. That was easy, wasn't it?" I hitched my bag up on my shoulder, keeping the pistol on him. "Oh, one more thing. I'd like that nice piece of cloth you're wearing."

"Hah?"

"Your sarong. Get it off. Now!" I gestured with the Webley.

He fumbled with the knot at his waist. A moment later, I had his sarong in my hand, and Mahasona was trying, not very successfully, to cover himself with his hands. He'd apparently never picked up the habit of wearing underwear.

"What on earth are you doing?" whispered Shanti.

"Escaping, of course," I replied. "What does it look like? Tell the rest of them to hand over their sarongs, too. Make it quick."

A moment later, I had a pile of striped sarongs on the floor in front of me. I picked up a full bottle of arrack and poured it over them. Then I fired up the Zippo.

I waited until the cloth was blazing away merrily, and then I took Shanti's hand and backed slowly out of Premasiri's, all the while watching the naked men carefully. Just before I went out the door, I raised the Webley, sighted carefully, and shot out the single light bulb over the bar.

"Thing's got a hell of a kick," I murmured to Shanti as we ran outside.

Our three-wheeler driver was nowhere in sight, spooked no doubt by the shots, but his vehicle stood at the curbside. "Hop in, quick," I said to Shanti as I stepped on the kickstarter.

Two-stroke engine roaring, we shot away down the cobbled street, just ahead of the band of naked goondas who burst from the wine shop, brandishing their knives and screaming curses to the night sky.

Shanti clung to the side of the tiny cab as I careered through town. "Where are we going?" she said.

"Somewhere far away," I replied, shooting one more glance behind us. "We've got the manuscript back, and I've got my passport and money. The next thing is to hook up with your uncle. Where is he?"

She shook her head. "A long way from here, I'm afraid. Up in the hill country, in a monastery north of Kandy. It'll take us quite a while to drive there." She looked down at the tiny Bajaj three-wheeler. "And not in this, either."

"Then we'll need somewhere safe to hole up for the night."

She thought for a moment. "Drive down by the harbor, along Leyden Bastian Road," she said. "The Taprobane Hotel. They won't look for us there."

I nodded, and we disappeared into the night.

CHAPTER SEVEN

At nine o'clock the next morning, we were on the road to Kandy. The day was hot and bright, and the tires of our rented VW convertible hummed as Shanti drove us out of Colombo across the Kelani Ganga on the old Victoria Bridge and north along the main highway. She was dressed in white trousers and a khaki shirt, and her black hair streamed out behind her as she drove.

Kandy was seventy miles ahead and a thousand feet higher, and it would be cool, I thought as I pulled my damp shirt away from my chest. I looked again at the airline schedule I'd picked up at Quickshaw's, the travel agency where we'd rented the car.

"Says here," I began, "that there's a British Airways flight leaving tomorrow at midnight from Katunayake. Stops once in Bombay, and then straight on to London. How does that sound?"

Shanti nodded. "The sooner the better, I'd say. I won't feel safe until Uncle Bertie's off the island altogether."

"Think we can make it? This isn't exactly a freeway, you know. How far away is this monastery?"

"We won't get there today, Max. The monastery is a couple of hours out of Kandy to the north. Besides, we'll be at the Perahera tonight."

I nodded. The Kandy Perahera, one of Asia's most elaborate spectacles, was winding up tonight. This was the climax of a week-long celebration; the grand torchlit procession through the ancient capital. As we were renting our car earlier this morning at Quickshaw's, the travel agent informed us that a room at the Queen's Hotel in Kandy had unexpectedly come free, for no more than triple the normal rate.

I smiled, passed my American Express card across the counter, and made a mental note to get it all back from Osbert when we arrived in London. It was either that, I reasoned, or sleeping on the floor in the monastery, since there was no chance of getting Uncle Osbert back to Colombo today. I was looking forward to the Perahera, in fact. I'd never seen it, and it would make a change from running through the back streets in my nightgown, or facing down hired killers.

I stretched, feeling relaxed and rested. Shanti and I had spent an uneventful night at the Hotel Taprobane downtown, where we'd taken adjoining rooms. Although we'd arrived just before midnight, a waiter had miraculously produced a tray containing a pot of tea and an assortment of sandwiches, and brought them to our rooms. We ate in silence, looking out at the lights of Colombo Harbor, and then turned in.

We slept with the connecting door open. Shanti had decided that I was probably the better shot, so she passed me the Webley. I slept with the manuscript tucked under my pillow and my hand wrapped around the revolver.

In the middle of the night, I awoke. The darkness was still and quiet, and I could hear Shanti's quiet breathing from the next room. I lay for a while pondering my own heavy heartbeat, loud in the darkness. The night is the time for second thoughts, and I was having plenty. Twelve hours earlier, I had been enjoying life, my face turned to the sun, feeling the warm sea breeze on my cheeks. Now I was a hunted fugitive, trying to figure out my next move in a city where no one could be trusted, and where there was a price on my head.

I rolled over, feeling the reassuring coolness of the Webley's grip. The next move is simple, I thought sleepily; head north, past the ancient capital of Kandy and into the hills beyond, to where Uncle Osbert had taken refuge among the Buddhist monks. Get him, bring him back to Colombo, and spirit him safely out of the country to England.

Do it, I told myself, and you'll make a nice piece of change. Screw it up and it won't matter; you'll be dead. *Plus ça change*, my conscience muttered back; the more things change, the more they stay the same.

And then I had sighed, turned over, and drifted off to sleep, to dreams of fear and falling.

Shanti slowed the car and turned off to the right, away from the main road. I sat up, back again in real time. "Where are we going?"

"There's a temple here," she replied, pointing ahead to where I could see the white spire of a *dagoba* poking up through the palms. "Travelers often stop to make an offering. This won't take long." She parked our convertible in the shade of a rain tree and spent a moment combing her hair back.

Twenty yards away a crowd of children stood naked beside a public water tap, pouring one basin after another of water over themselves. Beside them, their older sisters had their sarongs modestly snugged up under their armpits and were busy soaping themselves underneath the cloth. Sri Lankans waste water the way Americans waste energy, but at least they don't seem to be running out of it. The kids shot shy smiles at us, and one of the girls sent a brown-eyed glance my way that could have melted an icecap.

When Shanti was ready, we walked toward the huge white dome of the dagoba, rising out of the jungle like some sort of extraterrestrial structure.

"It's beautiful," I said, looking at the tall, graceful spire.

"You haven't been here before?"

I shook my head.

"Well, this is the Kelaniya Raja Maha Vihara. It's one of the most important temples on the island. Lord Buddha preached here long ago, which is why this is a special place. I come here often." She took my hand. "Would you like to see inside?"

We left our shoes with an old man at the foot of the temple steps, bought a handful of flowers, and walked slowly up toward the huge hemispherical dagoba. Shanti paused to wash her hands from a stone fountain at the entrance to the temple, and to sprinkle water on the flowers.

In one corner of the courtyard, a group of monks in burnt-orange robes quietly chanted *pirith*. They took no notice of us as we approached. Shanti laid the flowers carefully on one of the small ledges set into the side of the temple, placed her hands together, knelt, and prayed silently for a moment.

When she had finished, I said, "Did you pray to Buddha for something special?"

She shook her head. "Siddhartha Gautama – the one we call the Buddha – isn't a god, Max; just a sort of guide to Truth. We don't really pray to him; we pay tribute to his memory, and we try to follow the Dharma, or doctrine.

"Every temple has things in it to remind us of the Dharma," she continued. "First, there is the dagoba itself." She pointed to the base of the huge spired dome. "See, this one has little carvings of dwarfs all around it, holding it up. You must always walk clockwise around it. Then there is usually a bo tree, and sometimes a *vihara*, or image house."

I noticed other people then, dressed mainly in white, offering flowers and joss. Here and there, monks strolled in twos and threes, their folded parasols giving them a faintly businesslike air. "Do you come often to the temple?"

"Not really. When Aunt Iris was alive, we went several times a week." She lowered her eyes. "Now, I'm afraid to say, I come only on *Poya* – the full moon day." She looked at me. "Anyway, I'm finished now. Shall we go?"

We were almost to the gate when she stopped. "That monk," she whispered, pointing to one of the group we had passed on the way in. "I recognize him. He's from the monastery where Uncle Bertie's hiding."

Just then, the monk saw Shanti as well. He smiled, and beckoned us forward. We approached, Shanti with her eyes downcast, her palms held together in front of her in a gesture of respect. She spoke quietly to him for a moment, keeping her eyes respectfully averted.

The monk looked up at me with alert, intelligent eyes, and nodded. He was as brown as a nut, and shaven bald. I guessed him to be in his early sixties. He wore horn-rimmed glasses and carried a folded black parasol and a paperback book. I glanced at the cover, and was amused to see that it was an adventure story by Kingsley McTavish.

He caught my glance, grinned, and said something to Shanti. She smiled and replied in a torrent of liquid Sinhala syllables. They laughed together briefly.

"What's going on?" I murmured.

She grinned. "He asked me what your name was," she said. "Then he asked if you were one of the sudu mahattayas who come to Lanka to find wisdom in the Tripitaka scriptures. I replied that you would probably be more interested in his Kingsley McTavish book. Then I explained that you're helping me get Uncle Bertie out of danger."

The monk peered at me. "I am pleased to know you, Mr. Donovan," he said in a clear, high voice. "And pleased that we share a similar taste in friends and literature." His English was pure Oxbridge.

"My name is Wimalananda Thero, and I am what you would call the abbot of the monastery at Kurundugama." He dropped his voice to a conspiratorial whisper. "The place where Wikkie is holed up, as Kingsley McTavish might put it." His eyes twinkled. "I was at school with Wikkie – with Osbert, that is – many years ago, before we went our separate ways. I was most distressed when I learned that his life had been threatened. I'm very glad to hear that you are helping young Padmavati get her uncle to safety."

I turned. "Padmavati? I thought your name was Shanti."

She blushed furiously. "Oh, dear," she murmured. "It is – I mean, they both are. My names, that is."

Wimalananda Thero smiled. "Don't be embarrassed, my dear." He turned to me. "I'm the culprit, Mr. Donovan; I gave her that nickname when she was small. 'Padma' is the lotus, of course, and 'Padmavati' means 'lotus-faced girl'."

I looked at Shanti. "It's a beautiful name," I said. "And very apt." Her color deepened.

The monk cleared his throat. "This is a very good thing that you are doing, both of you. We Buddhists believe that there is much karma attached to such actions, however difficult they may be. That is what our philosophers say, at any rate."

I nodded. "So do ours," I said. "'No pain, no gain,' is the way I think they put it."

His eyes twinkled with amusement. "Just so, Mr. Donovan, just so. I can see that you have an enlightened attitude. Are you at all religious, if you don't mind my asking?"

"I, ah, don't go to church very often, to tell you the truth," I said.

"Going to church doesn't make you religious, Mr. Donovan," he said, "any more than going to the garage makes you a car." He smiled. "One of your philosophers said that, I believe." He turned to Shanti. "Are you driving all the way to the monastery tonight?"

"Oh, no," she said. "We'll stay in Kandy and watch the Perahera."

He nodded. "I myself will come to Kandy tonight, stay only for the display of the tooth relic, and continue on to Kurundugama late in the evening. There is a great deal to do, as usual." His glance darted between us. "You have an important task ahead of you both. I wish you luck." He adjusted his robes around his bare shoulder, and drew back.

Shanti placed her palms together and bowed her head. "*Avasaray hamuduruvane,*" she murmured as Wimalananda Thero moved off.

We walked slowly back toward the temple gates. "The abbot used to come to the house often when I was a little girl," she said. "He and Uncle Bertie were at Royal College together, and then he took a degree in Philosophy at Cambridge. When he returned to Sri Lanka, he would spend hours helping Uncle Bertie put his trains together. When I heard about Khan's death threat, he was the first person I thought of."

We reached the car. "We'll stop for lunch somewhere along the way," she said. "I bought a few things in Cargills while you were getting the car." She pointed to a large shopping basket on the back seat.

"What is it?" I asked.

She smiled. "Let it be a surprise," she said, putting the car in gear and moving off.

* * *

Mile by harrowing mile, we fought our way up the Kandy road, Shanti driving like an Indianapolis regular. The road was one long obstacle course, filled with surprises of all kinds, moving at all different speeds. In addition to the usual assortment of ancient Humber and Morris passenger cars, huge red and silver CTB buses roared past us regularly. Crammed with passengers and belching thick black smoke, they crowded everything off the road as they careened recklessly along, horns blaring. Just as numerous – and dangerous – were the wooden-bodied Ashok Leyland goods lorries which charged aggressively straight down the middle of the highway, scattering chickens and pedestrians to the sides. Every wheeled vehicle seemed to have at least two or three grinning men hanging on for dear life to the sides or the back, their sarongs flapping in the backwash.

The buses and the lorries were only one part of the road's rich tapestry, however. Small naked children sat astride enormous water buffaloes, tapping their broad backs with branches as they plodded along implacably on their way to distant rice paddies. Sweating old men hauled or pushed creaking carts piled high with bales and bundles of all kinds. Brightly clad women, their long black hair braided in long plaits, swayed gently as they walked single file beside the road, water-pots and babies on their hips. Crocodiles of schoolgirls dressed in white, their hair done in long braids, giggled and waved as we drove by. Blind beggars and careless drunks wandered across the road near the village marketplaces, accompanied by various four-footed companions. At one point, we stopped for a parade of work elephants, each carrying a large teak log, setting their feet precisely and with massive dignity down as they passed across in front of us.

I was glad Shanti was driving. There seemed to be no rules at all on the road, and too many different kinds of things to watch out for. To calm my nerves, I took out Osbert's manuscript and began to leaf through it. After only a few pages, I looked up. "This stuff is incredible," I said to Shanti. "Is it all true?"

"All true," she replied grimly. "Keep reading – it gets worse."

* * *

An hour later, Shanti slowed the car and pulled over to the side of the road. "Time for lunch," she announced as she opened the door. "There's a nice spot for a picnic in among the trees."

"Let's go," I said, grabbing the basket in one hand and the manuscript in the other.

Shanti spread a cloth beside a bamboo grove a short way into the forest. As she unpacked the groceries, I sat under a shady tree and finished the last ten pages of Osbert's manuscript. Finally, I put it down and turned to her. "Where's the last part?" I said.

"In his head," she replied. "He hasn't done the final chapter yet. He was writing it when Khan made his death threat. I don't know how much he's managed to put on paper in the last few weeks, cooped up in the monastery."

"The less the better, I would have thought," I said. "Given that what he's written so far has gotten him into a pile of trouble. And all of this is true, you say?"

She looked at me soberly. "It's true, Max. All of it. Now you understand why Mahasona wanted the manuscript so badly." She indicated the picnic spread in front of her. "Let's eat."

We sat cross-legged on the cloth, eating sandwiches and the little spicy cakes that Sri Lankans call 'short eats.' The beer was still cold, and delicious. I finished one sandwich, then another. It was cool and quiet in among the trees, and when I had finished my sandwiches, I lay back against a convenient tree trunk, opened a second bottle of beer, and closed my eyes, the better to collect my thoughts.

"Let me see if I can summarize this thing so far," I said at last. "According to his book, your Uncle Osbert thinks there's a plot to take over Sri Lanka and turn it into the South Asian equivalent of Colombia. The man behind the plot is a heroin king called Iskander Khan, who comes from Pakistan but actually lives on an atoll in the Maldive Islands. Khan wants to take over the government and set up processing factories in the jungles here."

I opened my eyes and looked at Shanti. "Now, don't you think," I said quietly, "that all this is just a little too fantastic? That maybe your Uncle Bertie's let his imagination run away with him?"

She shook her head. "Uncle Bertie wouldn't make up a thing like that, Max. His informant – the man who told him all this – was one of Khan's own lieutenants. Uncle Bertie checked as much of it as he could without arousing suspicion, and all of it fit. Even he was skeptical at first, but the more he found out, the more he became convinced that the current political violence on the island has become secondary to what he calls the hidden struggle – which is the title of the book, of course."

"You mean he thinks that drugs, not politics, are what's going to control the island's future from now on?"

"Precisely." She brushed hair out of her eyes. "The trade in opium and heroin is simply enormous in Asia, as everyone knows. The opium comes out of the so-called Golden Triangle, and also out of India, Pakistan, and Afghanistan. That's the part that Khan controls, of course."

"And he ships it through here," I said.

"Yes. The raw opium comes into Sri Lanka via many routes, such as tourists, coastal boats, and freight shipments. We're an island, and the government hasn't a hope of controlling the coastline. Once it arrives, it's split into smaller shipments. Then it goes to the Maldives. Khan's got a network of people working the tour groups – it's easy to find carriers; what they call mules. They also ship it out in merchandise: tea bales, rice bags, that sort of thing. Khan has a processing factory on his atoll. Once he's turned the raw opium into heroin, he uses tourists and tramp freighters to take it out to Europe."

I lay back and sipped my beer. "And according to your uncle, Khan now wants to install his processing factories in Sri Lanka."

She nodded. "If he can set up a secure base of operation here, he can eventually control most of the trade coming out of India and Pakistan, instead of only a fraction of it, as he does now. And if he can get a foothold here, it will be very hard to bring international pressure on him. The volume of business has been increasing every year. There are hundreds of millions of dollars involved."

"I don't doubt that," I said. "But one thing bothers me." I opened Uncle Osbert's manuscript. "He says here – toward the end – that Khan isn't just planning to manufacture heroin here – he's planning to take over the whole island." I looked up. "That's what I find a little far-fetched. I mean, you can't just take over a whole country, can you? How does Khan plan to do that, exactly?"

She frowned. "That's the problem; Uncle Bertie doesn't know. He said that just before his informant was killed, he was starting to describe some secret plan that Khan had. But then Khan's men caught up with him." She paused. "All he knows is that it's got something to do with the Maha Sangha."

I frowned. "The Maha Sangha? You mean the elder monks?"

She nodded. "Yes. The senior Buddhist clergy. The Maha Sangha are a sort of shadow government here, Max.

They operate behind the scenes, but they're incredibly powerful."

"Surely Osbert doesn't think they're mixed up in the drug trade?" I asked.

Her eyes went wide. "Oh, no, Max. The *bhikkus* – the monks, that is – wouldn't have anything to do with drugs, ever. Buddhism prohibits the use of intoxicants, and it would be simply unheard of for a member of the Sangha to be involved with the heroin business."

I looked at her. "Then why does your uncle think the bhikkus are the key to Khan's plan?"

"I don't know," she said in a quiet voice. "And neither does Uncle Bertie. His informant was killed before he could tell him." She picked up the manuscript. "That's why the book is unfinished, you see." She paused. "Whatever the plan, it's something awful. Uncle Bertie's sure of it." She put her hand on my arm. "And that's why we've got to get him out to London, Max. So that people will know. So that they can stop Khan, and stop whatever's about to happen."

We were sitting very close. I could feel the warmth of her body, smell her faint perfume. I looked into her wide brown eyes and felt my breath catch. Her eyes held mine, widened just the tiniest bit, and her fingers tightened on my arm. It was as if a circuit between us had suddenly been completed.

Her skin glowed like dark honey, and her eyelashes seemed to have grown thicker somehow, heavier. I found myself wondering what she'd do if I leaned over and kissed her. Maybe, my inner voice replied, you ought to try it and find out. I was just about to take myself up on it when she tensed and drew back.

Damn, I thought. "What is it?"

She was staring over my shoulder, looking at something behind me. I turned and saw a cobra coiled on the path between us and the car. As we watched, it reared itself erect, its wide hood flaring out. It stayed upright, swaying gently from side to side. Its button-bright eyes gleamed and its tongue probed the air as we watched it, and it watched us.

"Naja," I whispered. "A damned big one, too."

"Yes," she replied. "Isn't it beautiful?"

I'd spent part of my youth growing up in Bangkok, and snakes were no strangers to me. Days when I had nothing better to do, I'd wander down to the Snake Farm at the Pasteur Institute on Rama IV and watch venom being extracted. Although I'd never thought of snakes as beautiful, I'd acquired a healthy respect for them, and for cobras in particular. The Indian cobra, Naja, is one of the most poisonous snakes in Asia, and just about the last thing you'd want standing between you and your car.

I got slowly to my feet, keeping my eyes fixed on the snake. It was about ten feet away, and it didn't seem as if it was planning on going anywhere. Well, I thought, we can easily change that.

"Pass me the Webley," I whispered to Shanti.

She drew back away from me. "Max! You're not going to shoot it, are you?"

"I'm going to shoot at it," I corrected. "That gun of yours isn't all that accurate. I just want to scare it a little, move it off the path." I turned, and caught her disapproving expression. "Why? What's wrong?"

She laid a cool hand on my arm. "Max, don't. You mustn't."

I looked at her. "Don't?" I muttered. "Mustn't? Shanti, that thing's got enough venom to sink the Bismarck. Would you rather get bitten?"

She shook her head. "It won't bite us, Max. The cobra is friendly. In Sri Lanka, we believe that cobras should be protected; never interfered with. Haven't you seen the statues of Lord Buddha with a cobra?"

There'd been one not far from our hotel, I remembered. "You don't mean they're sacred or something?"

"The legends say that Mucalinda, a cobra king, protected Lord Buddha during his enlightenment. The cobra sheltered him from a violent storm, by wrapping its coils around him and spreading its hood. And because the snake protected the Buddha, we protect the snake. They often live in temples; the bhikkus take care of them."

As if on cue, the snake swayed, shifted position, and slowly eased itself back down to earth. Then it glided silently into the underbrush, without a sound.

I watched its tail disappear into the bamboo thicket. "Jesus," I said quietly. "Remind me never to walk around in here without a light."

Shanti smiled. "They won't hurt you if you don't hurt them, Max. It's true. Now, come on — we've still got quite a distance to cover."

CHAPTER EIGHT

It was somewhat cooler as we wound our way up into the hills near Kandy. The deep green of the forest came down to the very edge of the road, making it little more than a narrow ribbon through the jungle. Here and there, a village would suddenly appear from nowhere, neat bungalows arranged around a temple, cloth streamers announcing a celebration or a funeral. In the open fields, I could see men working, naked save for a knotted loincloth, their brown bodies gleaming with sweat as though oiled. And then the jungle would close in again.

We were talking about Iskander Khan, and the plot to take over the island. "He's not the sort of person you'd ordinarily think of as a drug dealer," Shanti was saying. "According to Uncle Bertie's informant, Khan is a Pakistani, from somewhere up near the frontier with Afghanistan. He came to Sri Lanka as a young man and lived here for several years. He was a minor figure in the Colombo underworld, mainly involved in smuggling and extortion. Then he went to the United States. He has an MBA from the Wharton School, in fact. When he finished his degree, he went to Europe for a year, and then he returned to Asia. That's when he began to operate the drug business."

"And now he lives in the Maldives?" I asked.

"He bought an entire atoll," she said. "According to Uncle Bertie's informant, he set up his processing factory there, and stores the heroin in a warehouse. He lives there with a crew of gangsters."

I nodded. "Did your Uncle Osbert ever go out there? To the Maldives, I mean?"

She smiled. "Heavens, no. I don't think Uncle Bertie's ever been off the island in his life." She shot me an amused glance. "You should understand something about my uncle, Max. He's got a very active imagination, but very little experience of the real world. All those Kingsley McTavish stories? As I told you, he made them up, out of whole cloth. He read Kipling as a boy, and Rider Haggard, and that chap who wrote about Tarzan—"

"Edgar Rice Burroughs."

"Yes. And all of it sort of melted in together in his mind. He's a thinker and a writer, Max; not a doer. He's not adventurous; not at all." Her face grew serious. "But Khan's lieutenant needed someone who could write, you see, so he came to Bertie. And at first, Bertie treated it as something of a joke. Until he realized how serious Khan was." She shook her head. "God, this poor island has been through so much. Do you know about the riots we had here a few years ago?"

I nodded, thinking back to those terrible days in July, and the predawn telephone call from a friend which was the prelude to a week-long nightmare of violence. I knew about the riots, all right; I'd been there.

On that first morning the skies were dark with smoke from burning homes and stores as mobs raged through the city, hunting down their enemies. And a few hours later, the first troops appeared on the streets, the air thick with gunfire as they tried in vain to stop the killing and looting.

As usual, I'd been in the wrong place at the wrong time. I'd been squiring a group of Hong Kong businessmen here and there around the island, looking at hotel sites, and the sudden outbreak of violence had stranded us in Colombo. By the afternoon of the third day, with the death toll mounting, they were ready to pay any price to get out.

So I left the hotel and set off on foot into the Pettah in search of my friend Gaffar, hoping to scrounge enough fuel to fly over to the Indian mainland. I passed a burnt-out bus on Galle Road, its charred skeleton still smoking, and walked past endless rows of burned and gutted shops, their merchandise strewn in heaps across the roadway. As I approached the Fort area, the violence mounted. Near the National Secretariat on Lotus Road, I saw a dazed monk sitting in the road, bleeding, surrounded by dozens of rubber sandals left by a panicked, fleeing mob. Overhead, army helicopters tracked the rioters.

It had been a hellish three days, and they were busy converting the hangars at the airfield at Ratmalana into refugee shelters when we finally gassed up at midnight and left, forgetting somehow to have our passports stamped. In the darkness, flying over Colombo and out over the sea toward Trivandrum, I could see the fires below, still burning out of control.

"Oh, yes," I said after a moment. "Yes, I remember the riots."

She nodded. "Things have got worse in many ways since then. There's still fighting, of course, but it's not just Tamils and Sinhalese anymore. There are so many groups now. Some of them are hard-liners like the Janatha Vimukthi Peramuna – the People's Liberation Front. They get arms and support from places like North Korea and Libya. The more radical groups have been assassinating politicians and businessmen. The government's barely in control of things right now."

"A good time for Khan to make his move, in other words," I said.

She nodded. "I'd like to believe that it could never happen, but I'm afraid that it could. There's so much money involved, you see. And Khan's not just one man – he's got dozens, perhaps hundreds, of people working for him."

I nodded, thinking about 'Inspector' Abeyratne, Mahasona, and the others. Paranoia, as someone once said, is just knowing the facts, and it certainly seemed as though the bad guys were everywhere. And if you couldn't trust anyone, that made it damned difficult to get anything done.

I was gazing idly into the side mirror as I thought about this, and I could see a vehicle coming up fast behind us, going like a bat out of hell.

"Better get over to the side," I said to Shanti, "and let this idiot go by us. He's about to climb up our backside."

I turned in the seat to look at the approaching vehicle, and the hairs on the back of my neck snapped to attention. "Uh-oh," I said, digging into my shoulder bag for the Webley.

"What's wrong?" Shanti was staring at me.

"The guy driving that car behind us," I said. "He was one of the crew at Premasiri's last night. He must still be holding a grudge over losing his sarong."

She shot an anxious glance toward the rear-view mirror. "Damn. Are they chasing us?" Her voice had gone tight with tension.

I glanced over, and saw her knuckles white on the steering wheel. "Well, they're coming fast. And I don't think they're hurrying to get to grandmother's house, if that's what you mean."

There were two men behind us in a Toyota Land Cruiser, and they could run rings around our little VW if they wanted to. I doubted somehow that running rings was what they had in mind.

I looked back and saw the man beside the driver unlimber what looked like a shotgun and poke it out the window. The Toyota put on a burst of speed and drew up close behind. "Can you, ah, get some more speed out of this thing?"

Even as I spoke, I knew it was no use.

A few seconds later, the Toyota rammed into us, hard. Shanti screamed and fought the wheel as our tiny car slewed across the road and onto the shoulder. I fired the Webley, but my shot went wide.

"But how on earth did they know we were going to be here?" Shanti said, forcing us back onto the road and shifting down.

Behind us, the shotgun boomed, and I felt something hit the trunk.

"Someone in town must have seen us," I said grimly, blasting another round back at the Toyota. It went wide, but they pulled back a little. "At Quickshaw's, perhaps, or at the hotel. Anywhere. It doesn't matter. What matters now is getting away from them."

"And how exactly do you propose to do that?"

I twisted around, looking at the road in front of us. The forest was thick on either side of the narrow strip of tarmac, giving us virtually no room to maneuver. We were easy targets if we stayed like this. I pointed up ahead to where a narrow side road intersected the main highway. "Turn down there, quick," I said. "Otherwise, they'll blow us away with their next shot."

She nodded and spun the wheel around, hard. The little car's tires screamed in protest as we slewed sideways in the road. She downshifted expertly, sending us shooting down a bumpy dirt track leading off into the jungle. Behind us, I saw the Toyota flash by, and heard the screech of its brakes. We'd gained a few precious seconds, but not much more than that.

"Do you really think they're going to kill us?" Shanti asked. She had her foot to the floor, and we were careening over the bumps and potholes, flashing past groves of palm trees on either side.

"I'm not that interested in finding out," I said. "But if you want a thoughtful answer, no, I don't think they'll kill us right away. I think they want to capture us. If you're right about all that stuff you were telling me earlier, then they're mainly interested in finding out where your Uncle Osbert is hiding." I had my eyes on the road behind us, and I saw the white Toyota coming back into view, gaining fast. I snapped off another shot with the Webley. "So I don't think they'll try to kill us right away. I think they want to catch us and make us tell them where Osbert is. *Then* they'll kill us."

The Toyota was close behind. The shotgun roared again, and I felt a lurch as one of our tires took a hit. Our VW began to slide sideways across the road, and I could see pieces of our shredded tire flying out the side. This is going to be really sweet, I told myself; blown to bits on a remote jungle road by a gang of goondas I haven't even been properly introduced to yet.

I looked around fast; there was a deep drainage ditch to the right, thick jungle to the left, nothing but coconuts up above. All of it went by in slow motion as the VW slewed fully around, facing our pursuers, and started to slide into the ditch. I had time to fire one more shot from the Webley, and then we were falling.

The VW cartwheeled up and over the low earthen bank, and as we dropped I heard the booming of the shotgun again, three quick ones in rapid succession. The bastards must have a pump, I thought. Then we hit the water upside down and started to sink in the warm swampy muck of the drainage canal.

I reached out and found Shanti's arm. Grabbing it, I pulled hard, dragging her along after me as I wormed my way out from under the sinking convertible. It wasn't exactly water that I was struggling through, more like liquid compost, and I held my breath and squeezed my eyes shut as I pushed upwards.

Our heads broke water simultaneously, and I could hear shouting and thudding feet from the road above us, coming up on us fast. "*Hari!*"

"We need to get out of here," I whispered. "Fast."

She looked at me, water streaming down her face. "What are you waiting for, then?" she said, scrambling up the bank like a jackrabbit.

She was scared and she was fast, even faster than last night. I could hardly keep up with her as we crashed through the dense bush, heading away from the road, straight into the jungle. I wasn't worried about what lay in front of us, only about what was behind us.

Our pursuers were coming up fast. Twice more the shotgun roared out, and falling leaves and tiny branches pattered on our heads as we stayed just ahead, just out of sight.

We couldn't sustain this pace much longer, I realized. Running through the jungle at this kind of speed was bound to result in some kind of accident, sooner or later, and we couldn't afford to slow down for even a second. More important was the fact that we had absolutely no idea where we were going, and although there was a path of sorts under our feet right now, it might end at any time, and then we'd be reduced to clambering through the dense underbrush.

The guys chasing us had a pump shotgun and God knows what else, and all we had was the Webley. We had to do something, and fast.

Rounding a corner, the trail suddenly entered a small coconut plantation. The underbrush had been cleared away, removing any cover. I stopped dead and looked up, down, and all around. Nothing but palms as far as the eye could see.

"What the hell do we do now?" I muttered.

Shanti grabbed my arm. "Can you climb trees?"

I looked at her. "I can do anything I need to do right now. What have you got in mind?"

She pointed upward. "If we can get up there," she said, "we might be safe."

I looked up and saw a network of ropes, like a huge spiderweb, linking the tops of the palms together. "You mean–"

"Exactly. Those rope walkways are used by the toddy-tappers. You can get to any tree in the plantation on them. It's our only chance."

I could hear the two men crashing through the bush behind us, getting very near. I stuck the Webley in my belt and spat on my hands. "What have we got to lose?"

The toddy-tappers had cut tiny footholds into the trunk of the palms, and it was possible to climb fairly fast using them. Their feet were smaller than mine, but all I needed was a toehold. It was easier than I thought, but then again, that might have just been the adrenaline. Halfway up, the Webley slipped from under my belt and fell to the ground. I cursed and kept on going.

It took me no more than thirty seconds to reach the top of the tree and the start of the walkway. In the tree across from me, Shanti was already in place.

Below us, the two goondas burst into the clearing. One had the shotgun, the second a long cutlass-like knife. I looked over at Shanti, a question in my eyes. She shook her head and put a finger to her lips.

Just as we had hoped, neither of the goondas looked up. They were searching for people on the ground, and as we watched from fifty feet above them, they ran here and there, searching the coconut grove for signs of us. Neither of them had yet spotted the Webley, lying concealed in the grass at the base of my tree. I kept one eye on them while I looked around me, searching desperately for some sort of weapon.

All I could see were coconuts. The tree I'd climbed had been recently harvested, and all that remained were a few dried and withered husks. The next tree over, however, sported a crop of large, heavy nuts the size of overinflated footballs. One or two of those would come in handy, I thought, as I tested the rope underneath my feet.

The toddy-tappers had linked all the trees together with a complex and clever network of rope walkways, strung far above the ground. For the guys who shinnied up the palms every morning to collect toddy, walking out on these things must have been second nature, but it was too much like being in the circus for me. And unlike circus performers, who at least have a net underneath them, I had a couple of killers below me.

I took a deep breath and edged out onto the triple-stranded rope, gripping the thin guide rope for dear life as I set a course toward the next tree and its fat coconuts. One slip, boyo, and you'll be dog food, I told myself. I moved carefully along the rope, praying that neither of the men below would look up. Shanti watched me, her eyes wide.

In high school, we'd all learned that a falling object accelerates at a rate of thirty-two feet per second squared. I kept this useful piece of information in mind as I inched toward the tree at the other end of the rope. Reaching my goal, I grasped a large green coconut and twisted it loose. I held it balanced in my hand, waiting.

Almost directly below me, the goonda with the knife had stopped moving. Suddenly, he stood still, turning slowly in place, as he swept the area with his eyes, searching for us. The one with the shotgun was somewhere in the bush off to the side, searching the undergrowth.

It was over fifty feet to ground level, I estimated; if I managed to hit him with the coconut, it would probably squash his brains flat. I bounced the heavy nut in the palm of my hand and thought about it. What the hell, I decided – it wouldn't do him any more damage than his shotgun would do to us. I took a deep breath and sighted carefully, feeling like a World War II bomber pilot. Then I let the nut go.

It fell swiftly and silently, catching the goonda on the shoulder. Even from my lofty perch I could hear the sharp sickening crack of broken bone. The man collapsed on the ground, screaming and clutching his shoulder, while his knife went skittering off to the side.

I came down out of the tree like a rat down a drainpipe. I hit the ground with a hard bounce just in time to see the second goonda burst from the bushes. He stopped short when he saw me, his glance darting between me and his fallen companion. I searched the ground frantically, trying to locate the Webley.

Too late. He roared with anger and brought the pump shotgun up, and I heard the snick of a shell being jacked into the chamber. Just then, there was a shout from above us. Both of us looked up to see Shanti balanced on one of the rope walkways, holding a coconut above her head with both hands. She let fly, and the goonda with the shotgun jumped backward. The nut hit the ground three feet in front of him, and his wide grin turned to a grimace of pain as it bounced and caught him squarely in the crotch.

With a shriek of pain he dropped the shotgun and doubled over. I scooped up his weapon, retrieved the Webley, and waved for Shanti to come down. A minute later, she was standing beside me, inspecting the two men.

"Nice shot," I said. "Thanks is a pretty inadequate word, under the circumstances."

She grinned. "Did you know there's no real word in Sinhala for 'thanks'?"

"Really? What do people do, then?"

"Oh, you're just supposed to look grateful."

"That's not hard," I said. I leaned over and gave her a kiss on the cheek.

"Surely you can do better than that?" Her eyes were teasing me.

I nodded, smiling. "I can be a whole lot more grateful than that," I said. "But not in front of strangers." I bent and patted down the two men until I found the keys to the Toyota. "And right now," I said, holding them up, "we need to be on our way."

I ejected the shells from the shotgun, walked over to the nearest palm tree, and swung the weapon at it like a baseball bat, bending the barrel and rendering it useless.

I dropped the gun on the ground and turned to the goondas. "You two boys take care now."

I took Shanti's hand, and together, we melted back into the forest.

CHAPTER NINE

First came the drummers. There were over one hundred of them, and they walked proudly, advancing step by step down the street, feet splayed wide. As they walked, they tossed their heads back with a regal gesture, sending the tassels on their headdresses whipping in all directions. Their long drums lay sideways across their gleaming bare torsos, and as the drummers marched, they beat a steady and compelling tattoo with both hands.

Shanti and I stood at the very edge of the roadway, hemmed in by the huge crowd, watching spellbound as the magnificence of the Esala Perahera advanced toward us. Behind us, thousands of onlookers jammed the sidewalks of Kandy, craning their necks and stretching on tiptoes to get a glimpse of the incredible spectacle that was just beginning.

We'd come the rest of the way up the A1 from Colombo without incident. When we passed the botanical gardens in Peradeniya on the outskirts of town, I slowed down, and pulled over a moment later in front of a hardware store. Dashing inside, I emerged a few minutes later with half a dozen canisters of spray paint.

"What are you doing?" asked Shanti.

"We need to disguise the Toyota," I said, pulling around the corner into a narrow track. "Want to help me paint?"

Twenty minutes later we had changed the white Toyota into a blue one. It was a lousy job, but it would do, I decided. I rubbed some mud over our number plates, and continued into town, driving up the Dalada Vidiya to the Queen's Hotel on the lakefront, just down the street from the moated, pink Temple of the Tooth. Already we could see preparations beginning for the evening's Perahera. Then we'd checked in, cleaned ourselves up, and relaxed for an hour or so before joining the throng outside, waiting for the start of the procession.

And now it was actually underway. Shanti's eyes gleamed in the light of the torches, and she clapped her hands and bounced in excitement as the drummers passed. "Isn't this marvelous?" she shouted in my ear over the booming drumbeats.

"It's incredible!" I shouted back. "But where's the tooth? I thought they were going to display the Buddha's tooth."

"It's coming," she said. She pointed up the street to the pink-hued temple festooned with lights at the edge of the lake. "That's the Dalada Maligawa – the Temple of the Tooth. The holy tooth relic is normally kept there, guarded by monks. Tonight is very special – the first time in many years that the Maha Sangha has allowed the actual tooth relic to be publicly displayed."

"And it really is the Buddha's tooth?"

She laughed. "It is. Or so we all believe, Max. The Portuguese claim that they destroyed the relic, centuries ago, and that the golden casket containing the tooth is actually empty." She paused. "But no Buddhist believes this. The tooth is there, everyone is sure of it." She grabbed my arm. "Oh, look, Max – here come the jugglers."

Down the street, a broad phalanx of nearly naked men approached. Clad only in loincloths and turbans, each man juggled half a dozen firebrands, keeping them constantly in the air. As they strode along, the jugglers chanted in deep voices. The drums were still loud up ahead, and the flickering lights of the firebrands as they swirled and spun in the air lent an otherworldly aspect to an already unreal scene.

From somewhere behind them came a loud crack, and I looked up to see other men, swinging long thick whips around and around their heads. The thick cords made a deep humming sound as they whirled, and I could see the men's bodies gleaming with sweat, muscles standing out in the firelight, as they strained to get the maximum of speed. At some unseen signal, all of them stopped in the middle of the road, took their whips in both hands, and cracked them simultaneously, with a noise like shotguns being fired.

There were scores of them, marching in unison, their long whips thrumming in the humid night air, building up speed, releasing their pent-up energy in dramatic bursts that ripped the evening air and had an almost palpable quality.

"Now, Max! It's coming now!" Shanti was almost squeaking with excitement. There was a gap in the procession, and then a solitary man appeared, walking regally down the center of the road, carrying a large silver elephant goad. As the crowd caught sight of him, they began to shout. "It's the Gajanayake Nilame," whispered Shanti.

"The what?"

"The Gajanayake Nilame; the royal Keeper of the Elephants. The tooth relic is coming."

I peered up past the heaving crowd to where the road curved away toward the temple. In the torchlight, I could make out a line of dancers, their arms and legs gyrating impossibly as they kept time to the frantic drumbeats. Behind them, rows of men carrying long, S-shaped brass horns blew long, triumphant blasts into the night.

And there, looming up out of the darkness, impossibly huge, were the elephants, scores of elephants, dressed in brilliant colors, lit with torches and lights, spangled with decorations, winking with precious jewels.

They heaved along in majestic splendor, each covered with an ornate cloth mantle decorated with tassels, hanging down almost to the ground, extending down and out over the trunk. Eyeholes allowed the animals to see, and they marched ponderously, wonderfully, in near-perfect unison.

All around us, the crowd was growing frantic. Screams and shouts of "Saadhu! Saadhu!" filled the air as people pushed forward frantically to get a better look. I was catching the frenzy, too, my breath coming in short gasps, the sweat running down my forehead. It was almost overwhelming – the shouting, the smoky fires of the torches, the winking of the jewels, the incessant drumbeats, the booming snap of the whips, and over it all, the high, shrill sound of the trumpets.

"Look, Max! Look! The big elephant! It's the Maligawa Tusker. It carries the Lord Buddha's relic." Shanti was practically vibrating with excitement, pointing up ahead.

One of the largest elephants I had ever seen was approaching, its covering cloth lit up with hundreds of tiny electric lights. Its giant tusks were capped with gold, and in front of it, men laid out a white cloth for it to walk on while others showered the massive elephant with flower petals.

I pointed to the illuminated howdah on its back, and the tiny golden casket that sat inside it. "Is that the tooth relic?" I yelled above the roar of the crowd.

"Yes!" Shanti shouted back. "In the *karanduwa* – the golden casket shaped like a tiny temple. Oh, isn't it super!"

I nodded and watched as the magnificent lighted pagoda-like structure approached us, swaying gently.

The crowd was in a frenzy. They surged and swayed around us, pressing forward, faces bright with sweat, eyes shining with mad excitement, voices hoarse from shouting. And then I found that I was shouting, too, straining forward, leaning toward the massive elephant which moved forward, implacably, ignoring the delirious crowd to either side. Head nodding to the rhythm of its heavy footsteps, the Maligawa Tusker advanced, its holy burden blazing with hundreds of lights, impossibly high up on its massive back.

Shanti gripped my arm, hard. "Max! Max, look over there! Isn't that—"

I followed her pointing finger. Not ten feet from us, his face almost lost in the human sea, stood Mahasona. He gazed up at the massive elephant, his single eye shining in the light of the torches. He hadn't yet seen us. I cursed, pulling Shanti to me, and tried to move back into the safety of the crowd.

It was no use. We were trapped by the wave of worshippers pressing forward. The Maligawala Tusker was almost alongside us. The crowd grew frantic, their hoarse cries of "Saadhu, saadhu," beating back at us in waves from the animal's massive flanks, enveloping us in sound. I searched frantically for Mahasona in the crowd, but he had melted back into the sea of faces.

Just then, in the dim light of the flickering torches, I thought I saw something arc through the air and land in the elephant's path. A prickle of alarm flashed up my neck. A second later, the darkness turned to high noon in a hideous strobing fireball. I had an instantaneous thought: here we go again, and then the explosion hit us. The noise was massive and deafening as the pressure wave hit the crowd like an enormous fist, and then there was torchlit chaos everywhere.

The crowd's chants turned to screams as the massive elephants began to panic, spilling their riders. They plunged into the crowd, trumpeting their fear and frenzy to the night skies. Shanti was wrenched from my grasp and went spinning away, lost in the panic. I shouted after her, but she was out of sight in an instant, swept back into the darkness by the surging human tide that was running, scrambling, crawling on all fours, away from the rearing elephants.

I looked frantically from side to side. In a flash of torchlight, I saw a monk lying motionless, his saffron robes almost blood-red in the light of the puddled torches, directly in the path of a charging elephant.

I sprang forward, scant yards ahead of the approaching beast, scooped the monk up with both hands, and bore him to safety. The crazed elephant, blood streaming from its forehead, thundered past us, its panicked eyes seeing nothing.

All around us was terror and chaos, the screams of the crowd punctuated by the shrill trumpeting of the elephants as they scattered into the darkness. Here and there a police whistle sounded as someone, somewhere, tried vainly to restore order.

Holding the monk under the arms, I dragged him along the sidewalk and into a storefront. I propped him up against the wall and peered into his face, trying to see if he was alive. With a shock, I realized that I was looking at Wimalananda Thero, the bhikku we had talked with at the temple in Kelaniya this morning.

He had a gash on his forehead, and I took out my handkerchief and pressed it against the wound. He moaned and stirred. "*Deiyane, mata sanipe ne,*" he said under his breath, brushing at the handkerchief. "*Oluve kaki yeneva!*"

He blinked, opened his eyes, adjusted his horn-rims and looked up at me. "Oh, my goodness." He blinked again, swallowed, and gathered his robes around him. "It's Mr. Donovan. Did you... are you..."

I put my hand on his shoulder. "Are you all right? That's a nasty cut. Your head must hurt."

He put his hand up and felt the top of his head, wincing slightly. "It does indeed. That's what I was saying a few seconds ago, in fact." He glanced anxiously out at the street and the crowd milling about in the torchlight. "What on earth happened? I remember an explosion, a flash of bright light, and then I fell down."

"You were about to get stepped on by one of the elephants," I said. "As for what actually happened, your guess is as good as mine." I looked back out at the street. "I'd say it was a bomb of some kind."

The monk was sitting up, holding my bloody handkerchief to his head. "A bomb? Good heavens, why would anyone bomb the Perahera? What on earth would be the point of that?"

I had a couple of ideas of my own about that, but this wasn't the time to trot them out for discussion. Shanti was still missing, and there might be more trouble. Just then I heard a shout, and looked up to see her running across the pavement towards us, concern written across her face.

She rushed up and hugged me. "Oh, thank God you're all right!" She glanced at the monk. "What happened?"

"The Maligawa Tusker was about to make a waffle out of our friend here," I said, indicating the bhikku. "I dragged him across the street and was just about to come looking for you."

"You saved my life," the monk said quietly. "I am deeply grateful."

"No doubt," I said. "But right now, I think we ought to get you to a doctor, don't you think?" I took him by the arm. To Shanti I said, "Grab his other arm, will you?"

She shook her head. "We're not allowed to touch bhikkus, Max."

The monk grunted. "Exceptions can always be made, my dear. No matter; I think I can stand by myself." Using his parasol, he levered himself upright. "There. That feels all right, actually." He smiled, adjusting his robe around his thin shoulders. "You know, I believe I'm going to live." He looked up. "Ah, here comes the rest of my group now."

He pointed up the street to where a small knot of monks were threading their way through the crowd, using their umbrellas to open a narrow passage. Wimalananda Thero waved, catching their attention, and a moment later, we were surrounded by a bevy of saffron-clad monks. They listened raptly as he recounted his adventures, and then there was a great deal of bowing and smiling as thanks and appreciation were expressed by everyone.

The bhikku turned to me. "They're very impressed, Mr. Donovan. They say you must be very brave. And that I am very lucky."

"I don't know about being brave," I said. "But I agree that you're lucky. Don't you think you should see a doctor?"

He smiled. "I feel quite well now, my friend. And we have someone at the monastery who can examine me." He adjusted his robe and peered at his wristwatch. "In fact, we should be leaving to go there soon." He looked at Shanti. "Would you and Mr. Donovan like to come with us? Or do you have transportation of your own?"

Shanti smiled. "We'll come tomorrow, *hamaduruvane*. Please tell my uncle to expect us early in the morning."

The bhikku nodded. "I will surely do so." He turned to me, and fixed me with his eyes. "You have saved my life, Mr. Donovan," he said quietly. "And although we Buddhists believe that life is an illusion, I must confess that I would rather be alive than dead. I am in your debt."

* * *

An hour later I sat with Shanti in our rooms at the Queen's Hotel, sipping whiskey and listening to the sounds from the street below as the police and medical workers straightened out the mess. The room came equipped with an old-fashioned cabinet-style radio, and I had it tuned to the Sri Lanka Broadcasting Corporation's evening music program.

In some respects, Sri Lanka exists in a kind of time warp situated somewhere during the years between the late 1940s and the start of the '60s. The SLBC English-language programming is a charming mixture of BBC Overseas Service fillers, music of the Andrews Sisters variety, and plays featuring characters out of P. G. Wodehouse books. Right now, Guy Lombardo and the Royal Canadians were playing something I didn't recognize, but whatever it was, it was doing the job of soothing our jangled nerves. I'd had two glasses of whiskey already, and so far, Shanti was matching me sip for sip.

"God, that was awful," she murmured. "It couldn't have come at a worse moment, with all the elephants there." She looked up at me. "Do you think the bomb was meant for us?"

I took her grandfather's Webley out of my shoulder bag and spun the cylinder, watching the way the brass shell casings caught the light. Then I laid it on the table between us. "People don't throw bombs for no reason, Shanti. I think they were trying to kill someone. Us."

"What about your theory that they just wanted to capture us?"

I shrugged. "Maybe they got tired of that. Maybe this is Plan B. Who knows? The only thing that's clear is that we're not safe anywhere on this island."

I sipped my whiskey, watching the fat sausage flies that were drifting in the open window, spinning slowly toward the light. One was down on the floor, one wing off, going around in awkward circles. I feel a lot like that myself right now, I thought. Too much was happening. Yesterday, somebody'd tried to blow me up, and later, Mahasona had tried to rearrange my intestines. Today, we'd been run off the road and nearly stampeded by elephants.

I could hardly wait for tomorrow.

Shanti's hand on my arm brought me out of my thoughts. "Listen," she said, pointing to the radio.

The music on the SLBC had stopped, and an announcer's voice was speaking in that tone that everybody reserves for bad news.

"The Police Commissioner's office in Kandy has just issued the following announcement: earlier this evening, a bomb attack was made on the Esala Perahera, during which the sacred tooth relic was stolen by a person or persons unknown. The authorities have offered a reward of one lakh of rupees for any information leading to the apprehension of the persons responsible and the recovery of the tooth relic. In a related announcement, the Maha Sangha has convened an emergency meeting for tomorrow morning in Colombo. Stay tuned for further details."

We looked at each other in stunned silence. Finally Shanti said, "The Buddha's tooth? Stolen? What do you make of all that?"

I set my glass down and picked up the Webley. "I don't know what to make of it," I said slowly. "All I know is what I started to say a minute ago. I think we'd better get your Uncle Osbert out of here as fast as we can."

She leaned forward. "Then shouldn't we leave now? It's only three hours' drive to the monastery."

I shook my head. "It's after midnight. We'll need some rest if we're to get him on the flight to London tomorrow night. It's better that we sleep now, and leave a little before dawn."

I stood up and stretched. "But we'll need to leave early, and sleep with one eye open between now and then." I started to unbutton my shirt. "You can have the bed; I'll stretch out here in this armchair."

"Do you really think that's necessary?"

There were a couple of ways I could have taken that, but I was tired, and trying to keep my life uncomplicated. There is a time and a place for hanky-panky, and this wasn't it.

So I smiled politely and handed her the Webley. "I do," I said, stripping my shirt off and heading for the bathroom. "Keep me covered while I have a shower, okay, partner?"

CHAPTER TEN

We were on our way just before dawn, out the back door and down the deserted street. I found the Toyota in the back alley where I'd left it the day before. The blue paint job wasn't great, but from a distance, it would fool most people. I checked the vehicle inside and out for signs of tampering before finally getting in and starting the engine.

And then we were off, up the road into the hills, toward the monastery.

We turned off the Matale road after only a few miles and headed northeast, toward Wattegama. As we drove, the road steadily deteriorated until it consisted of little more than huge potholes connected by thin webs of tarmac. Past Wattegama, the road turned to dirt. I put the Toyota in four-wheel drive to take care of the rougher terrain as we pushed on, further into the mountains, toward the monastery at Kurundugama.

We passed a few small villages, their houses built scant inches away from the road, their doors filled with wide-eyed children who peeped shyly at us and flashed us quick grins as we drove past. But mainly it was jungle, dense and close, growing right down to the edges of the narrow track.

As I drove, Shanti explained the significance of the tooth relic to me. "Siddhartha Gautama, the Buddha, was a prince. He lived during the fifth and sixth centuries BC in what is now northern India and southern Nepal. At about the same time as the Buddha achieved *parinibbana* and passed away, the Sinhalese came to the island."

"Came from where?"

"The legends say we came with Vijaya from northern India. And two centuries later, the Indian king Asoka sent his son Mahinda to convert the island to Buddhism. The Buddha himself had already visited the island several times. He even left his footprint on Sri Pada, the holy mountain that the English call Adam's Peak."

I nodded. "I'm with you so far. But what's this got to do with the tooth?"

"Today, Sri Lanka is one of the world's main centers of Buddhism. The Sinhalese have believed for thousands of years that they are the Lion People, chosen to protect and preserve Buddhism. So it was that in the fourth century BC, when the Indian king Guhasiva was facing defeat, he gave the sacred tooth relic to his daughter, the Princess Hemamala."

"It's really a tooth, then?"

She nodded. "The left eyetooth. It was supposedly snatched from the Buddha's funeral pyre. Now stop interrupting and let me tell you."

"Sorry." I swerved to avoid a huge yellow garandia snake sluggishly crossing the road. It slithered on, unaware of how close it had come to attaining the reptilian version of parinibbana.

"Anyway, Princess Hemamala hid the sacred tooth in her hair and escaped to Lanka, disguised as a pilgrim. We have kept it ever since. In 1590, the sacred tooth was brought to Kandy by King Wimala Dharma Suriya I, and later, King Narendra Sinha built the first temple. The Portuguese tried to steal the tooth, but they were unsuccessful. The relic survived. It sits – sat – in the

Dalada Maligawa, the Temple of the Tooth, in its golden casket, the *karanduwa*, guarded by the elder monks."

"But has anyone ever seen it? Recently, I mean? I've heard people say that the casket's really empty; that there's no tooth inside."

"Of course there's a tooth, Max. And it's been there for centuries. The tooth is more than a national treasure. It is the symbol of our religion, our strength, and our nationhood." She turned to me. "The tooth relic is the Sinhalese nation, in other words. Don't you have something in America like that, Max? Something that's a powerful national symbol of who you are?"

I thought for a moment. "Only Mickey Mouse," I said at last. "But if Mahasona stole the tooth relic, why do you think he did it?"

"I don't know," said Shanti. "I don't understand anything that's happening anymore. All I know is that we have to get Uncle Bertie out of here as soon as possible."

Amen to that, I thought to myself as I wrestled the Toyota up the hilly track. This had started out as a relatively simple job, similar to many I'd done before. Find someone, get them to safety, and collect your fee. But this one was starting to slip out of control; there were too many things going on at one time, and I was getting nervous. I shifted down, pressed my foot to the accelerator, and kept going. The sooner we were through with this, the better.

* * *

Three hours later, we entered the tiny village of Kurundugama. Small children clapped and shouted as the Toyota went by, and from the doorways of the cadjan-roofed houses, curious adults peered out to observe our passing. "The temple's down there," said Shanti, indicating a narrow sandy path leading off from the main village square.

Ten minutes of careful driving brought us to the temple gates. White streamers – the color of mourning and death – were strung along the entrance. A knot of orange-robed monks, including Wimalananda Thero, stood on the path, anxiously watching us approach. I parked the truck and together, Shanti and I walked toward them.

The monastery was laid out in the form of a U, with the temple at the base and low buildings flanking it on either side. In the hollow middle, an exquisite flower garden had been planted. The temple itself was a simple unadorned white dagoba. Behind it, the hills rose up sharply, their tops wreathed in mist. It looked like just the place to get away from it all, and I hoped that Uncle Osbert had enjoyed his stay. Things weren't going to be quite as peaceful from now on, I suspected.

As we approached the crowd, Wimalananda broke from it and came to meet us. "Mr. Donovan, Miss Wickramanayake," he said quietly, his face a mask of anxiety and concern. "This is a terrible time for all of us."

I nodded. "Yes, it is," I said. "I, too, am very sorry about the tooth relic."

The bhikku looked confused for a moment. "I'm not talking about the tooth," he said finally. He turned to Shanti. "It's about your uncle, I'm afraid."

Shanti's hand went to her mouth. "Uncle Bertie? What– what's happened? Is he–"

"Dead? Oh, no." The monk paused. "At least, I don't think so. He's been kidnapped."

"Kidnapped?" I looked around at the crowd of monks, watching us with impassive faces. "Are you sure?"

He nodded. "I didn't see it, I'm afraid, but they did," he said, indicating the monks. "I returned here early this morning. My, ah, colleagues met me at the gate and told me what had happened."

"And what did happen?" Shanti was gripping my arm, hard.

The monk sighed. "At about midnight last night – just as we were on our way back from the Perahera – the bhikkus here were awakened by shouting. Your uncle was quartered in the visitors' rooms, down there, at the end of the building. The shouts seemed to come from there. Several monks ran to his room just in time to see your uncle being carried off by several armed men. They marched him out of the gate and into a car. By the time the others arrived, the car was speeding down the road, into the jungle."

"Christ." I glanced guiltily at the monk. "Sorry," I muttered.

He smiled faintly. "Wrong belief system," he said. "No harm done."

"But who could have taken him?" cried Shanti. "Was it Mahasona? The man with one eye?"

"No. They saw who it was," the monk said quietly. "It was Podi Putha."

"Oh, no," breathed Shanti.

I looked from one to the other. "And who," I said, "is Podi Putha?"

The bhikku sighed. "I think that's what's termed a long story," he said. "I suggest we have some tea while you hear it." Beckoning to us, he moved off in the direction of the temple.

* * *

"Podi Putha is a bandit," he began. We were seated at a low table on the veranda of the monastery's dormitory, sipping strong sweet tea. "An insurgent, actually." The bhikku looked up. "Do you know about the insurrection?"

"The 1971 uprising? Wasn't that when a group of young radicals tried to take over the island?"

"Yes," he said. "Unsuccessfully, as it turned out. Most of them were hard-line Marxist-Leninists. But there were also some opportunists and a few outright criminals." He paused. "Podi Putha is one of those. Oh, he's fairly well educated, but he's never been anything more than a thief, a small-time bandit. Podi Putha's not his real name, of course. Before the insurgency, he preyed on travelers, robbed banks and the homes of the rich."

"Like Robin Hood."

The monk smiled. "If I remember correctly, Robin Hood took from the rich and gave to the poor. Podi Putha keeps what he takes, I'm afraid. More like what you would call a highwayman, I think."

"But the uprising was crushed, wasn't it? And it's been a long time since then. You mean this guy is still around?"

He nodded. "I've heard of similar cases – Japanese soldiers that stayed hidden in the jungles of the Philippines, sometimes for as long as twenty or thirty years. Podi Putha's a bit like that. The insurgency is far in the past, but Podi Putha is still living in the past as far as anyone knows. And because of his crimes, there's still a warrant out for his arrest. From time to time he issues a so-called 'communiqué' calling for an uprising, but everyone knows he's just a criminal."

I nodded. The pattern was familiar. Not so long ago, the jungles in northern Thailand and across the border into Burma and Laos had hidden more than one ageing Kuomintang 'general' with dreams of restoring the status quo on the mainland. I'd run into one or two of them myself, and there were probably a lot more still out there. They lived in the hills, commanding small jungle armies composed mainly of mercenary cutthroats. Like rattlesnakes, they tended to keep to themselves, but were dangerous when provoked.

"Where does this Podi Putha hang out?" I asked.

Wimalananda pointed south. "He's rumored to live in the mountains, up near Pidurutalagala. He has only a small band of followers. Every now and then they will make a raid on some government office or bank, escape with some money or supplies, and disappear back into the jungle."

"Is he involved with the drug trade?" I asked.

The monk shook his head. "I shouldn't think so. Podi Putha's not interested in drugs – he's interested in money and politics. More or less in that order. He still claims to want to take over the country, but these days he probably has enough trouble just getting enough to eat."

Shanti leaned forward. "But what on earth does he want with Uncle Bertie? Bertie's never done him any harm, for heaven's sake."

"That's obvious," I said. "It takes money to play Robin Hood. He needs groceries and ammunition, and those things cost money. Your Uncle Osbert would be worth a lot to him, I'd imagine."

Her eyes widened. "You mean–"

I nodded. "Don't forget, Khan's already offered ten lakh of rupees. That makes a kidnapping worthwhile, wouldn't you think?" I paused. "I'll bet he's going to sell your uncle to Khan, Shanti. Cash on delivery."

"I'm afraid to say that I think Mr. Donovan is probably right." The bhikku spoke quietly. "Your uncle is undoubtedly going to be ransomed to whoever has offered the reward."

Shanti had gone pale. "But it's not a reward," she said. "It's a bounty! Khan will kill him! That's what he wants! He wants Uncle Bertie dead, and the book manuscript destroyed." She turned to me. "Isn't there anything we can do?"

"Sure," I said. "We can find Podi Putha."

Wimalananda Thero looked at me with sad eyes. "Good luck," he murmured quietly.

* * *

The Land Cruiser was well-tuned and powerful, and made easy work of the wretched road that wound up deep into the mountainous spine of the island. As we climbed, it grew noticeably cooler. The hill country in Sri Lanka is in a state of perpetual springtime, and the terraced tea plantations were a brilliant green under the bright upland sun.

On the advice of the monk, we were headed for the hill town of Nuwara Eliya, 'the city of light', over six thousand feet high and capital of the mountain region where Podi Putha was rumored to have his headquarters. It would be as good a place as any to look for him, I thought. We had to start somewhere, and we didn't have much time. If Podi Putha had taken Uncle Osbert for the money, then he'd try and sell him to Khan as soon as possible. As I knew from experience, kidnapped hostages are a fairly perishable commodity. The trick to managing them successfully is to get rid of them fast.

It isn't a very reassuring scenario, I thought as I shifted down to take a hairpin curve. There was a lorry coming fast around the other side, straddling the white line. I swerved, gave the other driver the finger, and received a dazzling smile in return.

I went back to thinking. Our options were getting more and more narrow all the time. Metaphorically, we seemed to be heading at full speed down a long narrow passage, and the glimmer of hope that we thought we saw at the other end was starting to resemble the headlamp of an oncoming freight train. I kept my foot as far to the floor as I dared, pushing the Toyota hard as we roared up into the mountains.

Two hours later, we crested a rise to see the massive bulk of Pidurutalagala looming up on our left, and shortly thereafter Nuwara Eliya spread itself out before us. The town was a near-perfect replica of a village in England's Lake District, with tiny parks, flowers everywhere, and large Tudor-style colonial bungalows set back behind spacious lawns and gardens.

"What exactly are we going to do?" asked Shanti as we drove past the racecourse and turned onto New Bazaar Street which ran alongside Victoria Park. To our right, couples strolled on the golf course.

I pointed up the hill. "First, a place to stay," I said. "The St. Andrew's is decent, I'm told." I smiled. "If we're going to look for your uncle, we might as well be comfortable while we do it."

She frowned. "I wish I shared your optimism," she said quietly. "I'm not so sure we're going to find him."

I pulled up in front of the elegant old hotel. "Of course we're going to find him," I said. "Podi Putha may have your Uncle Osbert, but we've got Osbert's book." I winked. "And one's no good without the other."

She stared at me. "What exactly are you saying?"

I climbed out of the car. "I'm saying that Podi Putha and I can do business – one hand's going to wash the other." I checked my watch. "And there's plenty of time to spread the word around a little before dinner."

I opened my shoulder bag and pulled out Osbert's manuscript. "Take this," I said, "and put it somewhere safe. Get us some rooms, hide the manuscript under your mattress, and try and stay out of sight. I'll be back later."

"Where are you going?" she said.

"To do what I do best." I grinned at her. "I'm going to poke around a little bit; stir up the bushes. If Podi Putha's out there, maybe we can arouse his curiosity."

* * *

Two hours later, I had worked my way through most of the shops and stores in the small town. The drill was roughly the same at each one. I'd enter the bar, restaurant, or shop, ask for the boss, tell him I was looking for Podi Putha, and ask directions. Puzzled smiles, much shaking of heads, protestations of ignorance, and then I'd move on.

Towards the end of the afternoon I picked up a small coterie of street urchins, so I told them my story as well, and they laughed and giggled and began to chant Podi Putha's name and clap their hands. I grinned and clapped with them. What the hell, I thought, the more people who know about me, the better.

I was counting on the sidewalk radio to spread the word that there was a stranger in town who wanted to talk.

Eventually, if the word went out far enough, somebody would want to check it out. It might take a day, or two, or three, but sooner or later, if Podi Putha was in the area, he'd come out to at least sniff the bait.

Half past six now, and nearly dark. Time to call it a day. I paused outside the last store, a run-down newsagent and tobacco shop. All the daily papers had headlines screaming the news of the theft of the Buddha's tooth. I walked inside and picked up a copy of *The Island* from the rack. The entire front page was about the theft of the tooth relic, including the text of a statement from the president.

Behind the counter, the shelves of the tiny store were filled to bursting with cheap Chinese firecrackers, their gaudy colors causing my eyes to blur. The proprietor was a sad-faced Tamil who shook his head when I tendered a hundred-rupee note for the paper.

"Sorry, sah. No change. Trade is very bad today." He pointed to the newspaper headlines. "This is terrible business. I am a Hindu, but just so, this very bad indeed. Who can do such a thing?"

"Let's hope we find out," I said. "You can't change even a hundred rupees?"

"No, sah, sorry." He brightened. "But wait. You can take change in kind, not so?" He scooped up a handful of firecrackers and pressed them into my hand. "There, all even."

I looked down at them. "You seem a little overstocked on these, don't you?"

"Yes, sah. Today was to be our annual Merchant's Day. Big celebration, lowest prices, much noise and merriment." He indicated the fireworks behind him. "The bangers were for that, you see. Many people would come to buy, light them in the street, make big noises. Very nice, no?"

He shrugged his shoulders in a Gallic gesture of defeat. "Now, all of it is spoiled. The tooth relic is gone, everyone is afraid, and no one comes to buy." He implored me with his eyes. "Take them, sah. There is no money here."

When I hesitated, he ducked under the counter, coming up a second later with two large cherry bombs the size of ping pong balls. "Take these as well, sah. Much better quality." His eyes sparkled. "These have a very big bang, most definitely, sah."

I knew when to be a good sport. I smiled and thanked him, stuffing the fireworks into my pocket and picking up the newspaper. This guy had enough problems without arguing with customers, and anyway, I wanted to get back to the hotel for some dinner.

I drove the Toyota up the hill to the St. Andrew's and was locking it up in the parking lot when two men approached me. One of them opened his jacket just far enough to show me the automatic pistol he was holding.

"I'm impressed," I said, stepping back and holding my hands out in plain sight. "That was a lot quicker than I'd expected."

"You've been looking for Podi Putha," the man with the pistol. It wasn't a question. "He wants to see you."

"Now?"

"Now. At the Hill Club."

"The Hill Club?" I looked down at my shirt and trousers. "Don't you need a jacket and tie to get in there? I'm not properly attired."

The pistol jerked. "That's the least of your worries," he said. "Now come on. We're wasting time."

CHAPTER ELEVEN

The Hill Club was set back from the road. It was a grey stone mansion on a low hill overlooking the golf links, on the way out of town toward the racecourse. It lay nestled among old trees, its neat lawns recalling the days of colonial splendor and the glories of the British Raj. It dated from the 1870s, and looked every inch the part. I'd dined here two or three times on previous visits to the island, and found the atmosphere to be almost frighteningly evocative of another time.

We entered the castle-like building through a side door and moved quietly through the halls. It was still a bit too early for diners, and our footsteps echoed down the corridor. The walls were of dark oiled wood, hung with fading sepia photographs of British soldiers and their regimental flags. In the pictures, the men held their plumed helmets proudly, their young faces set in the serious expressions of the day, chins thrust forward to meet the challenges of the future. Silver competition cups stood ranged over the mantlepiece of the huge fireplace in the main reception room, where thick logs blazed, dispelling the early-evening chill that had crept over the town.

Through the open doors I could see into the main dining room. There, elderly waiters drifted to and fro, setting up the tables for the evening. The man with the pistol took me by the elbow. "Not in there," he said, pulling me through a side door. "Up here."

We went up two flights of narrow stairs and into what was obviously a private function room of some kind, dominated by a huge billiards table in the center.

"Wait here," the man with the pistol growled.

He shut the door and I heard a key turning in the lock. I let my breath out and turned slowly, examining my surroundings. The room had polished oak panels along one side, where obscure regimental colors alternated with hunting prints and several large stuffed fish. On the other side, mullioned windows looked out onto the darkness of the woods. Over the windows hung the heads of boars and sambur deer, staring down on me with glassy eyes. At the far end, a wood fire burned brightly, taking the edge off the chill, and at the other, deep-set bookcases contained a varied collection of encyclopedias, *Country Life* magazines from two decades ago, and a pile of old newspapers.

I was about to settle in with the magazines when the door opened, and a tall man in military-style fatigues entered the room carrying what looked like a whiskey bottle. I stood up.

He locked the door from the inside and turned around. "Good evening, Mr. Donovan," he said in a low smooth voice. "I am Podi Putha." He held up the bottle. "Will you take a glass with me? We have several matters to discuss."

In his early fifties, he was thin to the point of emaciation. His thick salt-and-pepper hair was long and curly, and his teeth were large and prominent. His skin was very dark, and his eyes glowed with an inner light from their deep sockets. At his hip, he carried a pistol.

"I, ah, didn't realize they let bandits in here," I said.

He laughed, richly and without hesitation. "No one knows we are here, Mr. Donovan. One of my men is on the staff, and he arranged this informal meeting." He gestured at the room. "This is the board of directors' private meeting room; used very little. It is highly unlikely that we will be disturbed."

"And if I yell for help?"

Podi Putha looked at me, and then down to his pistol. "Then I will shoot you, Mr. Donovan. And escape out of the window if necessary." He smiled. "But I do not think you will call for help." He produced two glasses from the cabinet under the bookcase. As he poured, he asked, "Do you play billiards, Mr. Donovan?"

"I've been known to play," I said after a moment.

He chuckled. "Then take a cue and let's have a game," he said. "Here's your drink." He handed me a glass filled with clear liquid. "Not brandy, I'm afraid. Banana whiskey. We make it ourselves. I think you'll find it acceptable."

I took a sip and choked, feeling the fiery liquid rush down my throat like molten steel, to land in my stomach with a splash and a hiss. "Aaah," I wheezed, blinking back tears, grabbing the edge of the pool table for support.

"Superb body, don't you think? I always like a good, hearty drink. Husky. That's what the English say, I believe." He rummaged in the pocket of his fatigue jacket and handed me a thick brown torpedo. "Here, have a cigar and let's get started. The cues are over there, in the rack. What do you feel the stakes should be?"

I thought about it for a moment. "If I win," I said, "I get to walk out of here with Osbert Wickramanayake."

He laughed. "No, no, Mr. Donovan. If you win, you might get to walk out of here all by yourself. Alive."

* * *

Half an hour later, I was two balls up, on my third glass of banana whiskey and my second cigar, feeling very little in the way of pain. As the saying goes, the prospect of being hanged concentrates the mind wonderfully, and mine was working at top speed, trying to figure out a way to enjoy tomorrow's sunrise.

Like all good Asian businessmen, Podi Putha was taking his time about coming to the point, preferring to let a conducive atmosphere develop. In this particular case, that meant trying to get me drunk on banana whiskey. I politely refused his offer of a refill, set down my cigar, took careful aim, and blasted the 12 ball into the far corner pocket. Podi Putha made a small sound of disgust.

I took a deep drag on the cigar, holding it away from me as it popped and spit a cloud of sparks. Choking, I blew out a rich cloud of foul-smelling blue-green smoke. "Great stogies," I croaked through the haze. "Where do you buy them, at a tire recapping factory?"

Podi Putha beamed. "Local tobacco, Mr. Donovan. We grow it ourselves, in the jungle. Excellent quality, actually. Burns nicely – never go out on you. We are largely self-sufficient, you know." He took two more cigars and stuffed them into my shirt pocket. "Here; take these for later."

I stroked another ball into the side pocket. "Are you self-sufficient in everything?" I asked.

Podi Putha chuckled. "No, of course not. We must beg, borrow, or steal things like medicine and ammunition." He paused. "Which is why I brought you here tonight, Mr. Donovan, for our little talk."

I slammed another ball home. "Too bad we're not betting on this game. Two more and I'll sweep you."

He smiled. "We are betting, Mr. Donovan. In a sense, at least." His eyes narrowed, and suddenly he looked a lot less friendly. "This afternoon you went through town, asking for me. You must have asked a hundred people, knowing that some of them would report to me. I don't know who you are, Mr. Donovan, and I don't particularly care. But I am betting, if you like, that you are an intelligent man who values his life." He set down his pool cue.

"I had you brought out here tonight to give you a very simple message: stay out of what is none of your business." He looked around the room. "I could have you killed, Mr. Donovan, and your body deposited on the steps of the St. Andrew's Hotel in less than half an hour."

"That's impressive," I admitted.

"It's also true," he said. "So I'm betting that you are a smart man, and that you will forget any idea you might have about persuading me to release Osbert Wickramanayake. You see, I know that you're traveling with his niece."

I sighed, plugged the last ball into the side pocket, and straightened up. "There are a couple of things you don't know," I said. "I've been looking for you to make a deal."

His eyes narrowed. "A deal? What are you talking about?"

I leaned back against the pool table and twirled the cue like a majorette's baton. "Simple, old chap." I was feeling the banana whiskey now, but still more or less in control. "The way I hear it, you're all horse and no hat. You talk big, but you don't have much in the way of money, guns, or even ammunition. Have I got it right so far?"

Podi Putha sipped his whiskey and watched me. His eyes had gone flat and narrow now. "Keep talking," he said softly.

I took another drag on my cigar and washed it down with more whiskey. "Okay," I said, when the tumult in my throat had subsided. "So here you are, out in the boonies, still dreaming about making it big." I raised the pool cue as if to emphasize a point. "Then you hear that someone's offered a lot of money for Osbert Wickramanayake. And you think, why not? He's hiding out, but it's a small island, right? Everybody knows everybody else, so it's not that hard to find him."

I paused, holding the cue up like a conductor's baton. "That reminds me; how did you find him? He was supposed to be hiding, after all."

"One of my men spotted him walking in the monastery grounds. Pure chance, in a way. We took immediate action."

"Shows a lot of initiative," I said. "So you go to the monastery, the monks are all upset about the theft of the tooth relic, and you grab the old man." I paused. "Now you've got him hidden somewhere up in the hills, and in a day or so, you're going to turn him over to Khan's people and collect the reward."

"Get to the point," Podi Putha said.

"That is the point," I replied. "Collecting the reward. That's the deal I want to talk to you about. That's what you need me for."

"To collect the reward? Are you mad, Mr. Donovan, or just stupid? I've got Osbert, haven't I? What more do I need?"

I smiled. "You need Osbert's book," I said. "That's what Khan really wants, after all."

"Nonsense. Khan wants Osbert."

"Wrong," I corrected. "Maybe you never heard the whole story. You're a long way out in the jungle, after all. Do you know why Khan wants Osbert? No? Then let me enlighten you a little."

I spent several minutes giving Podi Putha a modified version of the story. "He doesn't want Osbert alone," I concluded. "He really wants Osbert plus the book. Give Osbert to Khan, and the book is still out there. Once it's published, Khan's plans are shot. Give Khan the book, on the other hand, and Osbert's still out there; he can always write another." I paused. "So Khan needs both. And if he gets both, he'll pay more. A lot more."

"How much more?"

I smiled. "A London publisher's offered Osbert fifty thousand pounds for the rights to the book." I paused. "That's more than Khan's offering." I paused. "I think we ought to hold an auction, don't you?"

I had Podi Putha's full attention now. "Where's the book?" he said.

I finished my whiskey. "I've got the book, my friend. And if we go in together, we ought to be able to raise the price quite a bit." I set down my pool cue. "Want to make a deal?"

"What about Osbert's niece?" he said finally.

I shrugged. "She wants her uncle back, but she can't pay. The girl will just have accept the situation."

Podi Putha's eyes and teeth gleamed in the soft light of the billiards room. "What's your plan?" he said.

* * *

Midnight now, and it had turned very cold up on the high plateau. I'd hidden the Toyota miles away, up a narrow logging trail, and now I was moving easily through the tall grass, using the moonlight to help me keep to the path. I kept my mouth open to improve my hearing, and moved my eyes from side to side, alert for movement within the shadows. Podi Putha and his men knew the area a lot better than I did, and I didn't want to walk into an ambush. It reminded me of the times in Vietnam when I'd go on night patrol, working my way through Cong country. Old times, but not particularly happy days.

I was twenty miles from the hotel, up on the Horton Plains, a wide expanse of open grassland and twisted moss-covered trees. The Horton Plains were actually one vast plateau, high above the surrounding countryside and shrouded in mist most of the time. The plateau ends fairly spectacularly, in a sheer cliff appropriately known as 'World's End', dropping down several thousand feet into the jungle below. The cliff's edge was where I had arranged to meet Podi Putha, in about two hours' time. It was real Ray Bradbury country, enough to give someone the creeps in the middle of the night. Apparently, the Sri Lankans thought so, too. The Horton Plains is one of the very few places on the entire island that is uninhabited.

I'd left Shanti back at the hotel after a late meal and a weak story about meeting an old friend for a drink, my feeble attempt to explain the fact that I'd shown up for dinner over an hour and a half late, reeking of alcohol and cigar fumes. She was on edge and clearly exhausted, and I had no trouble persuading her to turn in for the night. I'd even offered to tuck her in. She gave me a small tight smile and a level glance and said that she could manage very well, thank you, and that she'd see me in the morning.

I waited an hour until I was sure she was asleep. Then I loaded the Webley, picked up my shoulder bag, and slipped out through the lobby to where I'd parked the Toyota.

Now I shivered slightly as I moved silently through the grass. It wasn't just that I wanted to be on time. I wanted to be there first. I was betting that Podi Putha would come with reinforcements, but I was also betting that he wouldn't be there yet. And that might give me enough time to set him up.

At least, that's what I hoped.

* * *

Ninety minutes later, I heard them coming. I was lying flat on the ground, staring dreamily out over the edge of the world. Far below me, the jungle was little more than a misty dream-image in the moonlight, floating in space. The wind sang softly in my ears as I became aware of the sound of an approaching motor.

I got to my feet, stretching my muscles. I'd spent the last hour carefully scouting the terrain, trying to figure out what to do when the time came, and so far, inspiration hadn't struck.

I could hear them approaching slowly, a low growling noise as Podi Putha's vehicle made its way slowly up the rutted track leading to the cliff edge. I brushed the leaves from my jacket and faded back into the shadows. Ready or not, I thought; here we go.

CHAPTER TWELVE

There were three of them, and they came single file – one, two, three – clearly illuminated in the moonlight. I recognized two of them. First in line came Podi Putha, carrying his pistol. The last man in line was the one who'd picked me up in the parking lot earlier. He held a Sterling submachine gun, and was using the barrel to push the third man along in front of him.

I watched the third man carefully. He was tall and thin, with white hair and a wide handlebar moustache. He carried a bamboo cane with a brass handle, and he moved with grace and dignity. He was dressed in a Nehru shirt and white trousers. Hello, Uncle Osbert, I thought.

Hidden in the grass, I watched them approach. They were taking their time, looking from side to side, stopping every few minutes to listen. I didn't blame them. Honor among thieves and all that bullshit, but it wasn't going to stop them from being damned careful. As far as they knew, I was alone, but they'd be assuming – rightly – that I was armed, and they'd know that I was dangerous. But nothing bad would happen unless somebody made a mistake.

The internal logic of it all was rock solid. They had Uncle Osbert, and Shanti and I had the manuscript. Either one, without the other, wouldn't be worth squat on the market. No, they would only be worth real money if they were used together. And that's what was happening out here in the misty moonlight.

We were about to enter into a kind of unholy marriage, but I, at least, had no intention of saying 'I do'. And, I was betting, neither had Podi Putha.

I smiled in the darkness. Now it was fast coming down to the basic question, the oldest one of them all: who is going to be the screwer and who the screwee?

I watched them walk by me toward the edge of the cliff while I took stock of my resources. I had the Webley, a small clasp knife, my old Zippo, and a folded newspaper in my shoulder bag. Plus the firecrackers I'd been given in lieu of change earlier in the afternoon. They should be useful for something, I thought.

I wormed my way backwards through the grass, back up the ridge to where they'd parked their jeep. We'll just see, I thought, what sort of mischief I can get up to here. The jeep was parked in plain sight two hundred yards away. Once I got there, I crawled all around it, sniffing the night air and checking things out, thinking hard.

There are a lot of ways to mess up a vehicle, some of them better than others, and over the years, I'd gotten to be somewhat of an expert. The ideal thing would be to get under the hood and take off the distributor cap, but that would make noise, and in the bright moonlight, there was a chance they'd spot me if they were looking back in this direction. I could also let the air out of their tires. A kid's trick, but effective. But bleeding the tires would take time, and it would make noise as well.

I felt in my shoulder bag for my clasp knife. What the hell, I thought; might as well keep myself busy while I think it through. I eased the driver's side door open and wriggled in behind the dashboard. I located the ignition wires, gathered them together in a bundle, and sawed through them. Then once more, making sure there wasn't enough wire left to be able to make a splice.

I crawled out from under the dashboard, stood up and turned slowly around, listening to the night air. That should hold them for a while, I thought. Everything was quiet. Podi Putha, the gunman and Uncle Osbert were at the end of the trail now, close to the cliff edge at World's End.

I sat back on my haunches, thinking. Disabling their vehicle had been easy, but I needed something bigger. I needed an attention-getter. Something grand – a big, spectacular diversion, something that would give me an opportunity to grab Uncle Osbert and make good our escape. Something sharp, short, and shocking.

An explosion.

'Energetic disassembly' was how my buddies in Air America had referred to it all those many years ago, and I smiled in the darkness as I set to work. The last time I'd done this, I remembered, it had been an act of public service, performed on a drug dealer's vintage Chrysler Imperial. The Imperial had been fire-engine red, with tiny rear taillights that stuck up on little thin sticks like cocktail hors d'oeuvres, and a friend and I had blown it all to bits with a coffee can full of C4.

I pulled the firecrackers out of my bag and inspected them carefully. What can you do, I thought, with a couple dozen inch-long poppers and two fairly hefty Chinese cherry bombs?

Just about anything, I decided. I set to work unravelling the fuses from the double strings of poppers, retying them until I had one long fuse.

I held it up in the moonlight, inspecting my work. Damned near perfect, I thought. But just to be sure, I cut the long fuse in half. Now I had redundancy built into the system, something any good demolitions expert would have approved of.

I carefully tied the end of each fuse to a cherry bomb. Then I opened the gas cap on the jeep and slowly lowered the cherry bombs down inside, paying out the two fuse cords like fishing line. When I felt the lines go slack, I let out my breath and stood up.

I led the fuses down to the ground and made a nice dry place for them with part of the folded newspaper. Then I stepped back to admire my handiwork. Excellent, I decided. Time to start the show.

From my pocket, I took one of Podi Putha's homemade cigars. Extracting my Zippo, I fired up the stogie, cupping my hands around the glowing tip to hide the flame, drawing in hard and long, until I had the foul-smelling thing stoking away like a potbellied stove in a blizzard.

I took the cigar out of my mouth, spit once to get rid of the taste, and picked up the loose ends of the fuse cords. Wrapping both fuses around the stogie about halfway down, I propped the contraption up against a flat stone, up off the wet ground. If the stogie didn't burn out, I figured on maybe ten minutes of lead time before one of the fuses caught. And if one fizzled out, there was always the other.

Time to start the countdown, then. I took the Webley out of my shoulder bag and stuck it down the back of my shirt, in the small of my back. I turned and walked down the trail, hands in my pockets, admiring the sheen of the grass in the moonlight and whistling softly under my breath.

* * *

"Hi, guys."

I stepped out from behind a tree, holding the Webley loosely in my hand, a kind of hey-folks-don't-take-any-of-this-too-seriously grip that I'd learned to adopt in my dealings with various midnight ramblers over the years.

The man with the Sterling hissed and brought up his weapon, but a barked command from Podi Putha stopped the rise of the gun barrel. Everybody moved back a pace and looked around, sniffing the air like dogs in a strange neighborhood.

"Put your gun away, Mr. Donovan. We are all friends here, aren't we?" Podi Putha's voice was the sweet sound of reason on the night air.

"We are indeed, Mr. Putha," I said, tucking the gun back under my belt. "Friends and businessmen." I raised my chin in the direction of Uncle Osbert. "I take it this is the subject of our discussion tonight?"

Podi Putha nodded. "This is Osbert Wickramanayake," he said.

I nodded at him. Osbert looked back at me with careful eyes, his face expressionless as he studied me silently. If he had caught my name, he gave no sign. Keep your mouth shut, Bertie, I prayed, and maybe we'll get through this in one piece.

I turned my face slightly and winked at him. I wasn't sure, in the moonlight, whether or not he caught the gesture, but he seemed to relax ever so slightly then. Despite his age, he looked fit and healthy, and I hoped he'd be able to run like hell when the time came. If all went well, in a few minutes he was going to have to be as loose as a goose if we were going to get out of this alive.

"Have you brought the manuscript?" Podi Putha's voice was harsh in the deserted night air.

I patted my shoulder bag. "Right here," I lied.

Podi Putha smiled then, showing me all his teeth. "How do you suggest we do this?"

"Very simple," I said. "Each of us has part of the package. Put them together, and we have a deal." I saw Uncle Osbert's eyebrows go up, but I kept talking.

"Khan's man in Colombo is a one-eyed *mudalali* called Mahasona. Perhaps you've heard of him?"

Podi Putha's smile disappeared. "What you call in English a nasty piece of work."

I nodded. "Very nasty. But he's Khan's agent. Mahasona will pay us when we deliver this man" – I pointed to Uncle Osbert – "and his book to him in Colombo." I paused. "Cash on delivery."

My internal clock was counting the minutes, wondering where the hell the fireworks show had gotten to. Had the cigar burned out? Had the fuse sputtered and died? Jesus, that's all I need, I thought. Caught up here on the edge of the world with two desperadoes and an old man, and me with nothing more than an antique revolver.

"Now we have to talk details," I said, stalling for time. "How do you want to deliver the package to Mahasona? I assume you're not planning to come down into Colombo yourself. As I understand it, a lot of people down there would like to get their hands on you – something about an uprising years ago?"

Podi Putha laughed. "Not to worry, my friend. Of course I won't go myself. I'll send Jaya here." He indicated the man with the Sterling, who grinned from ear to ear.

"Jaya is unknown to the police, you see. You and Jaya, Mr. Donovan – a fine pair of birds, what?" He laughed again. "No, Mr. Donovan, while you two are collecting the money, I will be here in the mountains, thinking of the guns and ammunition that all this money will buy."

His eyes glowed in the dark, like a cat's.

"And I will be thinking of all the fine mess and bother that I can make with them." His voice dropped to a soft whisper. "One day, my friend, we will come out of the jungle for good. And on that day–"

He never had a chance to finish his sentence. There was a flash, and the night disappeared in a hellish orange glow. Podi Putha stopped talking and threw himself to the ground. A split second later the roar of the jeep's exploding fuel tank washed over us with a hot dry wind. A fireball climbed toward the moon, propelled by the roar of blazing gasoline.

Jaya, his Sterling held high, sniffed the air like a wary bear, firing bursts into the darkness, sweeping the muzzle back and forth across the bush, seeking an elusive target.

I waited until he had paused to reload. Then I pulled the Webley out from under my shirt and tapped him hard, just behind the ear, with the butt. Jaya groaned and went down. Shoving the Webley back in my belt, I scooped up the Sterling with one hand, and grabbed Uncle Osbert's arm with the other.

"Hi," I said. "I'm Max Donovan, and it's time to leave now. Follow me, sir, and run like hell."

"Stop!"

I turned to see Podi Putha, his pistol at the ready, crouched in front of us. My finger tightened on the trigger of the Sterling, but all I got for my effort was a dry click. "Shit," I breathed. I'd forgotten it was empty.

I scrabbled for the Webley, caught somewhere in the folds of my shirt. I saw Podi Putha's eyes narrow as he straightened up.

He was just bringing the pistol to bear when Uncle Osbert's cane caught him across the nose with a noise that sounded like Willie Mays hitting one out of Busch Stadium on a fine summer afternoon.

Osbert leaned forward and scooped up Putha's pistol from where it had fallen. He turned to me, his eyes bright with excitement, his moustache tips quivering. "As you said, Mr. Donovan, run like hell, eh?"

And then we were off, scampering off into the darkness like Halloween goblins, the old man moving surprisingly fast, while behind us the Guy Fawkes bonfire of the blazing jeep lit up the night sky.

* * *

It was nearly three o'clock in the morning when we turned the Toyota into the long drive leading up to the St. Andrew's. "Ten minutes, that's all," I was saying to Osbert. "Just time to pack our things. You wake Shanti up while I take care of the bill. He's got people in the Hill Club and God only knows where else."

"Good God," Osbert said. "I had no idea things had reached this stage. What on earth are we going to do?"

"Drive straight down to Colombo. There's a daily flight to London leaving at midnight. I've got a friend in the Pettah who'll hide us until evening. If we stay out of sight, we ought to be okay."

"Whatever you say."

I pulled up in front of the wide doors and hopped down. The bellman was still awake, and came down the steps to meet me. He held an envelope in his hand. "You are Mr. Donovan?"

I stared at the envelope, dread already building in my mind. "Miss Wickramanayake departed an hour ago," the bellman continued. "With her uncle. They left this for you." He handed over the letter.

Osbert and I looked at each other as I ripped the envelope open.

"Her uncle?" Osbert's voice was a croak.

"Yes, sir. The gentleman with the eye-patch. He said he is well known to you, Mr. Donovan. He left the note for you, sir, telling you not to worry."

I ripped open the envelope.

> *We have the girl. If you want her back alive, bring us the manuscript, and Osbert. He knows where to find us.*

"Sir, are you all right? Sir?" The bellman's voice was barely audible over the thudding of my heart.

CHAPTER THIRTEEN

The whine of the engines rose suddenly, the brakes released, and the Air Lanka TriStar began its takeoff, picking up speed rapidly, pressing us back into the seats. I looked over at Osbert. His face was bathed in sweat, his hands clutching the armrests in a white-knuckled deathgrip. I smiled and shut my eyes, thinking back over the past twenty-four hours.

I'd headed for Gaffar Abdeen's the moment we hit town. Bells would be sounding up and down all of Mahasona's network now, and unless we stayed out of sight, Osbert and I had the approximate life expectancy of a turtle on the freeway. So I holed up in the Pettah, drinking tea and watching Gaffar's cat drift in and out of naps, while Gaffar arranged a couple of passports for Osbert and me.

We were going to the Maldives to find Shanti. Osbert and I had discussed it pretty thoroughly on the way down from Nuwara Eliya, as I spun the Toyota down the mountain roads in the darkness.

"We'll have to go after her, of course," said Osbert as we left the St. Andrew's and headed down the road.

"Of course," I replied. But unless we wanted to swim, I thought, we were going to need valid passports to enter the country, and that meant getting help from Gaffar, the supplier's supplier.

I could go on my own passport, of course, but that would be like flashing a neon sign if you took the attitude, as I did, that Khan might have watchers at the airport, and that anybody – anybody at all – could be one of his men. We were going to need new identities if we were to stand any chance of making it out the doors at the other end of the arrivals building.

It had taken Gaffar most of the day to get the two passports ready, but by ten o'clock the next morning, Osbert and I were standing in line behind a German tour group at Katunayake Airport, getting ready to hand our tickets to the Air Lanka hostess in the red sari behind the counter.

I wore a sun hat and dark glasses, and Osbert had improvised a sort of turban from a length of towel he'd taken from the men's room. Gaffar's passports had turned out better than I expected, and I gave us a better than even chance of getting through security.

I handed over our tickets, smiling mechanically at the woman behind the counter. I was thinking about the Webley. I'd packed it inside a cheap cardboard suitcase that I'd bought this morning, and I was hoping that they wouldn't inspect the cases closely. I hadn't put a name tag on it, and there was no way they could trace it to me, but it would be embarrassing if they found the revolver, and bad news for us if we arrived in the Maldives without a weapon of some sort.

I was carrying the manuscript in my shoulder bag, not letting it out of my sight. In Nuwara Eliya, before taking Osbert down to Colombo, I'd searched Shanti's room at the St. Andrew's, finding the manuscript – as expected – hidden under the mattress.

"Mr. Pemberton?"

I came to with a start. "Hah?" Was that my name? I'd looked only at the photograph.

"Smoking or non-smoking?"

"Ah, non-smoking," I said.

"And you, Mr. Mohammed?"

"Ah, yes, the same please, miss," said Osbert in a pure babu accent.

"Any bags to check?" I handed over the suitcase, mentally crossing my fingers.

Ten minutes later we were in the departure lounge, and half an hour after that, we were boarding the red and white Air Lanka TriStar.

Now we were becoming airborne, the coconut trees forming neat needlepoint patterns on the ground below as we climbed, heading straight out for the coast. The TriStar rose sharply, leveled out, and started a slow bank to starboard, sliding smoothly around a column of billowing thunderheads drifting innocently along over the Bay of Bengal, on their way to a landfall rendezvous somewhere to the east.

Osbert wiped his brow with a large, checked handkerchief. "Absolutely fascinating," he murmured, staring out the window. "So quiet. I always thought there'd be more noise."

"Haven't you ever been in a jet before?"

He smiled at me. "My dear Mr. Donovan, I've never been in any sort of aircraft, ever in my life." He paused. "I was in a boat, once, out on Beira Lake, down where the temple is."

I looked at him. "You're a brave man, Mr. Wickramanayake," I said after a moment.

"Oh, dear me, no." He practically blushed under his nut-brown skin. "It's you who are the brave one. I'm—well, I'm really just along for the ride, as you Americans say." His eyes shone with excitement.

I nodded, settling back in my seat and watching out the window as the shadow of the TriStar moved across the bright water, moving us slowly closer to the danger that was waiting somewhere close, just over the horizon.

* * *

We came in so low over the clear green water that I could see the brightly colored fishes playing in the shallow coral below us. There's nowhere in the Maldives that's really big enough for an airstrip, and the runway on Hulhulé Island had been built on crushed seashells, right out into the ocean. If I hadn't seen the coral strip when we banked to make our approach, I'd have thought we were ditching in the open water.

The TriStar shuddered and bucked as the thrust reversed suddenly and then we were rolling easily up the runway. We came to a quiet stop and turned, the engines revving up again to push us toward the low terminal building. The doors opened and we got out, blinking in the fierce sun. The humidity felt like a barber's warm, wet towel around my face.

So far so good, I thought. Khan would assume that sooner or later we were going to show up, and he might have watchers at the airport. The Maldives was small enough so that any newcomers would be noticed almost at once. Unless they were part of a tour group.

We walked across to the low customs shed. It was little more than an open hangar, with a limp flag hanging listlessly over the entrance and the words 'Welcome to Malé, Capital of the Maldives' in English and Dhivehi painted in black on the cinder-block wall.

The plump Germans were just in front of us, all busy clicking away with their expensive cameras, yakking back and forth to each other about food, drink, sun and sex. I hurried to catch up.

I retrieved my single bag and followed Osbert past the customs officers, making very sure to stay as close to the Germans as possible. Group excursions were unlikely to get their bags checked, and I knew that neither Osbert nor I would be able to give convincing answers to even the simplest questions. I smiled, looked dumb and nodded a couple of times, and then we were through.

We stood on the hot tarmac at the wharfside, blinking in the bright sunlight, Osbert turning slowly around, taking it all in. "What do we do now, Max?"

"Get over to the main island," I said, pointing across the water to Malé. "And hope nobody's spotted us."

A cinder-black kid with bright button eyes and a high squeaky voice beckoned at us from an Evinrude-powered dugout. "Heyyyy, Jack! Wanna ride across? Fi' dolla, 'kay?"

"Kay," I said, and threw him my bag. We clambered down into the dugout. As we sped across the water, I contemplated our next move. I'd been to the capital, Malé, years ago, and unless it had changed, it was a classic backwater in the very best Graham Greene-Eric Ambler tradition. It consisted of a dozen or so rutted streets, some dusty shops, and no alcohol whatsoever; all this on an island barely a mile across. The population, related to the Sinhalese, spoke Dhivehi, which is written with an obscure group of squiggly characters that look like little black worms.

There's nothing to do in the Maldives unless you like to swim, fish, or sunbathe. The islands are tiny, perfect tropical jewels ringed with white sand, each containing an acre or so of palms and perhaps a small lagoon. There are several thousand of these, almost all of them uninhabited. Some of the larger ones have been turned into resorts for the tourists.

And one of them was now home to Iskander Khan, drug baron and bad guy extraordinaire. He had Shanti, and maybe he also had the Buddha's tooth for all I knew, but I was mainly interested in Shanti. He'd kidnapped her for one reason only, and that was to get his hands on Osbert and the manuscript, and destroy them both. And we were in the process of obliging him right now, with every pulse of the tiny outboard as we sped toward Malé.

He'd be expecting us, and he'd be ready. And given the geography of the islands, where you could look off your front porch and almost see the curvature of the earth, he'd spot us coming a hell of a long way off. No way, really, to sneak up on him.

And no way to deal, either. Because Khan didn't really want anything other than our heads. He didn't want to talk, he didn't want to bargain. There was nothing that we could do for him except die, so the agenda wasn't going to be very complicated once we arrived at his hideout.

He had Shanti, and Uncle Osbert and I had the manuscript. Osbert and the manuscript were the last two pieces, and Osbert was on his way. Khan was betting on Osbert's sense of decency, compassion, and fair play to draw him to his island lair in search of his endangered niece. And once he showed up, Khan would take the manuscript and kill them both.

But Khan hadn't figured on one thing.

Decency, compassion and fair play might have loomed large in Uncle Osbert's character, but not necessarily in mine.

* * *

Twenty minutes later we stepped out on the crushed-seashell road that ran along Malé's waterfront. I admired the ancient cannon left over from centuries past, and the way the sun lit up the gold dome of the mosque. Out at sea, I could see the sails of local fishing dhonis on the horizon, and here and there, a green smudge indicating a tiny island.

"Tell me about Khan's island," I said after a moment.

"Well," Osbert began, "it's called Madirifushi, and it's north of here, about a hundred miles as the crow flies. It used to belong to the British, I believe. It had a radar station on it, something to do with the old Royal Air Force base at Gan. After the British left, the fishermen used it as a stopping-off place. It has a freshwater spring, apparently."

"Is it on the charts?"

"Oh, yes. I looked it up myself once, in the Colombo Public Library. Five years ago, Khan bought the island, turned the fishermen away, and built himself a virtual fortress."

"Terrific," I said. "A fortress. What else do you know about his setup?"

He shook his head. "Nothing. He's supposed to be heavily guarded, but one would expect that."

"Any idea how we can get inside?" I said.

He turned surprised eyes to me. "None whatsoever, Mr. Donovan," he said. "I rather thought that would be your department."

"That's what I was afraid of." I shaded my eyes and looked out at Malé harbor, where a forest of fishing-boat masts swayed on the tide. "Well," I said finally, "the first thing is to find some facilities."

"Facilities? What kind of facilities?"

"A boat," I said. I pointed out to the limitless ocean. "We need a boat to get up to Madirifushi."

Uncle Osbert looked around at the tiny harbor town. "I'm not sure they have much for rent here, actually."

I smiled at him. "I wasn't thinking of renting, to tell you the truth."

CHAPTER FOURTEEN

"You do realize that theft is highly illegal?" Osbert said to me as we wandered through the crowded fish market, gazing at the harbor.

"So's kidnapping," I said. "Have you got a better idea?"

It was high noon, and the sun was boring into my head like a giant celestial heat lamp. Osbert and I threaded our way around piles of glistening fish and bright vegetables, smiling and nodding at the vendors who waved and called out to us.

As we walked, I kept my eyes on the harbor. There were plenty of boats, but most of them were local fishing dhonis. I needed something better. If Madirifushi Atoll was a hundred miles north of here, that was the maritime equivalent of the remote jungle outback. I needed something that would get me there fast and in one piece, preferably some kind of ocean-going inboard. I also needed something that I knew how to operate. Sailing has never been my strong point, but I can hot-wire the ignition switch on just about anything.

My eyes lit up as I spotted the large launch moored at the end of the next-to-last jetty, over by the repair yards. 'CLUB MED' was painted in bright blue letters on its hull, and *'Delphine'* was neatly lettered on the transom. She bobbed gently in the swell, with nary a sign of anyone on board. I looked over to shoreside and saw three Europeans dressed in tourist togs, shoulder bags at the ready, threading their way through the market crowd. All right, I thought. Practically perfect.

"Come on," I muttered to Osbert. Glancing quickly from side to side, I walked out on the jetty, acting for all the world as if I owned it.

I was almost to the end of the dock before I heard a voice behind me. "Oy!" it said.

I kept walking.

"Hey, you!" The voice was louder this time, tinged with anger. I turned, all wide-eyed innocence. A fat, tanned bon vivant in a sea captain's hat and a sporty pair of Aussie bush shorts emerged from the tiny office. His T-shirt read 'Silly Buggers for Christ.'

"We're not leaving until three," he said in an exasperated voice. "Didn't Monique tell your group that? And besides," he added, jerking his thumb at the boat, "we're not going back in this one." He frowned. "I thought they told you that."

I smiled brightly. "Sure did. Yep, I knew that, all right." I watched him carefully, wondering what I was going to do about him.

"Then why in the bloody hell–" He glanced at my shoulder bag. "Oh, sorry, mate. You're the mechanic they called for, aren't you?" He smiled. "Cripes, nearly mistook you for one of the bloody guests."

He reached into his shorts and tossed me a ring of keys. "Well, take a dekko and see what you think." His beefy arm swept out beyond the breakwater. "I was you, I'd take 'er out there and open it up. You'll see what Cedric was on about." He caught sight of Osbert and his eyes narrowed. "Who's this, then?"

"Him? Oh, he's my helper," I said.

"Helper? Little long in the tooth, isn't he?" He shook his head. "None of my business anyway." He held the line taut for us as we clambered into the boat. "Mind you're back soon," he warned. "Cedric said he wanted you to look at the runabout as well."

I gave him the thumbs-up as I started the engine. "Right you are," I said as I eased away from the dock. And then we were roaring away from the dock, heading for the breakwater and the open sea.

When we'd cleared the harbor, I turned to Osbert. "That was a lot easier than I'd thought it would be," I said. "Having fun so far?"

"I've never stolen a boat before," he said thoughtfully. "In fact, I don't believe I've ever stolen much of anything, really." He smiled. "Except mangoes, when I was a child in Cinnamon Gardens."

"Stick with me, sir," I said as I pushed the throttles all the way up. "I'll show you how to steal all sorts of things."

* * *

I'm not much of a sailor, but then again, neither was Osbert. He spent most of the next two hours hanging over the side, praying to the God of Stability and Stillness, while I fought down my own nausea and struggled with the wheel. The *Delphine*'s engine was in terrible shape, and a thick black cloud of exhaust made us visible miles away. Just peachy, I thought as I fiddled with the choke control, trying to even out the roughness in the diesel. As if Khan needed even more advance warning.

The *Delphine*'s charts showed Madirifushi as a small circular island surrounded by a reef. There was an even smaller island several miles away to the west, and I planned to use it as cover, coming in behind it, counting on the setting sun to make us hard to see.

At this rate, however, we wouldn't be there before nightfall. Osbert had recovered enough by this time to be useful, so I handed him the wheel and showed him how to steer a straight course. He'd found a captain's hat from somewhere and he set it at a jaunty angle. All he needs now, I thought, is a parrot.

While Osbert drove the boat, I poked about in the *Delphine*'s lockers and cabinets, taking inventory, whistling softly between my teeth. I had no idea yet of how we were going to get ashore at Madirifushi Atoll, but I was hoping that something on board would give me an idea. We had the Webley, of course, but that alone wasn't going to persuade Khan to lower the drawbridge. I needed something a little more persuasive.

I wasn't likely to find it here, I realized. The *Delphine* was basically a ferry, used to carry well-heeled tourists from Malé out to the resort islands and back again. It was constructed along the lines of a Parisian *bateau-mouche*, with padded seats in rows and along the sides, and with plenty of room back in the stern for baggage. It was also fitted out for snorkeling and scuba-diving, with a stair-transom that could be lowered to provide easy access to the water, and an impressive collection of modern diving gear. I checked the pressure on a couple of the air tanks — all of them were full. I found a couple of wicked-looking spear guns, half a dozen diver's knives, and a shark billy, but nothing that I'd really call a weapon.

I sighed. Oh, well, I thought, at least we had a boat of sorts, with plenty of fuel and water on board. I got a beer out of the large cooler amidships, pushed my cap down low over my sunglasses, and settled down to enjoy the ride, letting my right brain work on the problem of how to avoid getting killed at the other end.

* * *

Three hours later we were still far away from Madirifushi, somewhere out in the middle of the Laccadive Sea, roughly midway between Fadiffolu and South Miladummadulu Islands, and if that's not an awfully long way from nowhere, then I don't know what is. The water was deep here, the current swift, and our forward progress had slowed to a crawl.

I was fiddling with one of the scuba tanks, listening with one ear to the laboring of the engine and trying to calculate our running time to Madirifushi when I heard the engine cough, miss, and then cut out momentarily.

"Oh, drat," muttered Osbert.

I came up beside him. "What's wrong?"

He shook his head. "Not quite sure, actually." He tapped one of the dials. "Does this mean anything?"

I looked over his shoulder. It was oil pressure, and it was dropping. Beside it, the temperature gauge was edging up toward the redline. "Yeah," I said after a moment. "It means we've got problems."

Just then there was the deep clunk of something breaking. The engine sputtered, burped, and abruptly died.

The sea was absolutely silent as we coasted to a stop and rode the gentle swell, the odor of burning bearings wafting forward from the engine compartment. "Well, shit," I said finally.

I moved aft and pulled off the hatch cover. Thick grey smoke billowed out of the engine compartment. Waving it away, I regarded the ruined engine with disgust. Osbert materialized beside me. "Can you fix it?"

I shook my head. "No chance. Smell that? I think the engine's seized. There must have been a weak gasket – a blown ring, something like that." I looked around at the limitless sea, waiting patiently for us. "They must have brought it into town to repair it – that's why the fat guy said they were taking the other boat back in the afternoon." I gave a mirthless laugh. "There's not even a pair of oars on board."

Osbert looked around. "No, but I saw a radio, up on the bridge. We could call for help, couldn't we?"

I nodded. "Sure. And then we'd get arrested for boat theft. We need to get to Madirifushi, not go back to Malé. Especially not if it means going to jail. Khan's probably got half the cops out here on his payroll. No, we can't trust the authorities, that's for sure."

I picked up the chart and studied it for a moment. "We're smack in the middle of the channel," I said after a moment. Unless somebody comes by, we could be stuck out here for days." I glanced back at Osbert, who was busy scanning the horizon with the binoculars. "Don't waste your time," I said.

"No, wait." He pointed to the eastern horizon. "Look, I believe that's a fishing boat coming now. Perhaps our prayers have been answered."

I grabbed the glasses from him and focused. Sure enough, there was a ship out there, and she was headed our way. The name on the side was the *Bombay Duck*, and it was low and sharp-edged in the water, painted in camouflage striping.

It doesn't look like a fishing boat, I thought. More like a warship. In fact, I decided, it looked a lot like one of the mosquito boats they'd used in Vietnam. Was this the Maldivian Coast Guard, come to arrest us? I focused the glasses more closely and swept the *Bombay Duck* from stem to stern, but found no trace of a flag or other marking.

Just then I saw someone emerge from the wheelhouse holding what looked like a length of thick pipe in his hands. As the boat approached, I could see that it was an M16 assault rifle.

I put the glasses down, took the Webley out from my belt and stashed it under some rags. "Grab your socks, Osbert," I said quietly. "I think these guys are pirates."

CHAPTER FIFTEEN

"Hey, Johnnie, how you doin'?" The big Indian stepped over the gunwale with a smooth, practiced movement, holding his weapon easily in a big hand. It was a 9 mm Czech Skorpion, just the thing for close work. "I'm Vish," he said. "Captain Vish."

He was about thirty, I estimated, big-boned and well-fed, but I was willing to bet that there wasn't much fat on him. I watched him carefully as he came toward me, trying to figure out a way to keep us from getting killed in the next few minutes.

I grew up reading Robert Louis Stevenson and watching Kirk Douglas and Tony Curtis at the movies at the Embassy on Saturday afternoons, cheering with the rest of the kids as the good guys swung down from the ratlines, swords in hand, wading into the pirates as they swarmed aboard the ship.

Like most folks, I kind of assumed that piracy was where we'd been, not where we were going. But a few years in Southeast Asia had knocked that silly notion out of my head once and for all. Piracy was a growth industry out in that part of the world, and a while back I'd had some hands-on experience of my own up in a muddy river estuary on Malaysia's east coast. Since that time, my respect for pirates had increased in inverse proportion to my liking for them.

Modern piracy is a filthy business, practiced mainly by seagoing psychos who wouldn't last ten minutes on dry land, given their overall set of attitudes and operating procedures. They get away with it mainly because the seas are vast and empty, and because the victims are usually helpless and weak.

Anybody with a basic knowledge of the wind and the waves, a propensity to murder innocents, and a total disregard for his own life can be a successful pirate. Especially if you don't care who you rob and kill. Stranded sailors, boat people, and shipwrecked passengers make the easiest pickings, of course. Merchant ships can be good, if they're carrying something valuable that's small enough to be easily handled. Drug-runners used to be excellent targets, although lately they've gotten more willing to slug it out.

Pirates aren't much interested in fighting, though. They're interested in stealing, and anyone who's likely to give them a hard time usually gets a wide berth. Pirates go for the easy, soft pickings.

They go, I thought, for folks like us.

Vish stopped a few feet away from me, his bright black eyes darting this way and that, checking us out. The *Delphine* had no below-decks, and what you saw was what you got, so he was making sure he saw everything before he made his next move.

"Got engine trouble, Johnnie?" He smiled, his wide mouth revealing teeth stained red with betel juice.

"Yeah," I said. "No oil pressure. I think the engine's seized." I glanced sideways as I spoke, noting the position of the two spearguns lying against the forward bulkhead. He caught the eye movement and moved smoothly sideways, placing himself between me and the wall.

Then Vish turned and said something to his crew. Everybody laughed for a moment and glanced slyly at us the way people do when an in-joke's been made at someone else's expense. They were speaking in Tamil, and they were probably from Trivandrum or one of the other coastal towns down below Madras, maybe from the

Laccadives. Counting Vish, there were four of them, all young, all armed, all smiling as they looked us over. They were checking us out, trying to figure out how dangerous we might be, and in a minute or two, they'd have made up their mind about that. And if they decided we were harmless, they'd kill us and take whatever we had. And unless I could come up with something damned good, that's what was going to happen.

"Too bad, Johnnie," said Vish. "If your engine's buggered, that's no bloody good, is it?" He grinned again. "I think maybe you're in trouble now."

I looked up at him, keeping the smile on my face. Just a hometown kid, I thought, that's all I am. My hand tightened on the neck of the scuba tank, my fingers searching for the valve lever. It was a lousy weapon, I knew, but if all you've got are lemons, you make lemonade.

A full scuba tank holds air at a pressure of about 2500 pounds per square inch. If the valve snaps off, a tank can behave like a rocket, shooting off with enough force to punch through a cinder-block wall. In a sense, a scuba tank's a very dangerous piece of equipment, but under normal circumstances, they're perfectly harmless.

These were far from normal circumstances, of course. I watched Vish's eyes and calculated the distances as he looked slowly around the boat, taking everything in. He needs to be closer, I thought. Osbert was standing quietly back by the engine hatch, his eyes moving back and forth between me and the pirate chief.

Vish walked over toward me until he was about two feet away, just inside my private zone. He was trying to intimidate me, and that suited me just fine. "Don't move, Johnnie," he said softly. "We need to talk a little, okay?"

"Talk? Talk about what? You guys are thieves, for Christ's sake." I cranked my voice up into a mid-level register of fear and indignation.

"Not thieves, Johnnie. Pirates." He jammed his face into mine, his eyes gone all hard and snappy now, his breath stinking of fish and hot spices as the muzzle of the Skorpion bit into my belly.

Good, I thought; I had him nice and close now, just where I wanted him. I felt everything slow down to half speed as the part of my brain that had been waiting for this moment decided to throw the switch, press the button, start the action.

Just then, Osbert reached into the piles of rags, drew out the Webley, and fired it into the air. Everyone jumped.

Well, now or never, I thought. With one smooth motion, I brought the scuba tank up, aimed the valve nozzle at Vish's face, and opened it up full.

Air under high pressure coming out of a tiny nozzle can hit you like a fist, breaking teeth or putting out an eye. It hit Vish square in the nose, snapping his head back like a punching bag. Before his scream was past his lips, I let go of the valve, transferring my hand to the bottom of the tank, and then quickly rammed the valve head upward into his chin, with all my might.

As he fell, I yelled to Osbert to hit the deck. I ripped the Skorpion from Vish's hands. Bright red blood was pumping from his nose now, and he made wet choking sounds as he writhed on the deck. I kicked him once in the back of the neck to get his attention, clicked off the safety on the Skorpion, and hauled him to his feet.

I positioned the gun close behind his ear and let off a couple of rounds for effect. On board the pirate ship, the other three men stood stock still, players in some bizarre game of Statues. "Drop your guns!" I shouted across to them. "Drop your guns, or I kill him!"

Vish yelped with fear, twisting in my grip, and I brought the heavy butt down hard on his neck. "Stay still, you bastard," I growled. "Next time I fire this thing, it'll be straight into your ear."

One of the crew yelled something in Tamil to Vish. He opened his mouth to reply, but Donovan's Rules of Order were in force here now, and so I let off a burst a few inches over their heads. "Drop them!" I shouted. "Now!"

Three Armalite rifles hit the deck with a clatter. "Get over here," I said to them. "One at a time." I turned to Osbert. "Nice work. Now search each one for other weapons. Throw anything you find back into their boat."

"*Their* boat?"

I grinned. "Yeah. We're trading up."

Five minutes later, Osbert had herded all the pirates onto the *Delphine*, and a small but impressive collection of knives and small-caliber pistols lay piled on the deck of the *Bombay Duck*. While Osbert kept everyone covered with the Webley, I trussed them up one by one, making the knots nice and tight. When I'd finished doing that, I transferred the diving gear from the *Delphine*, ran a hose from her fuel tank, and started pumping her out.

"Hey!"

I turned to see Vish's stricken eyes. "Got a problem, friend?"

"My God, you are leaving us here to die, no?"

"Not really," I said. "There's some food and water in the lockers. No fuel, but your engine's seized anyway, remember?" I indicated the shortwave in the wheelhouse. "Play your cards right, don't run down the battery, and you ought to be able to raise someone on the radio in a day or so. You'll stay alive till then, I reckon."

I grinned. "What the hell, hoss, you might spend a few days on your own, but that's better than being sharkbait, right?"

Vish nodded. Even a pirate recognized a good deal when he had one. I finished transferring the fuel, and when I was done, I turned and waved goodbye. Nobody waved back.

Then I pushed the twin throttles forward, and Uncle Osbert and I roared off north, on course for Madirifushi Atoll once more.

CHAPTER SIXTEEN

It was a fine day in the islands, and the *Bombay Duck* was powerful and responsive, planing effortlessly over the waves as we moved north. From time to time we would see small islands on the horizon, and Osbert or I would check them on the big chart, marking them off, noting our position, moving by degrees closer to Madirifushi and Khan's stronghold.

I had to hand it to the pirates, they were well equipped. Although the boat was generally filthy, it was in excellent running condition. As I'd suspected, the *Bombay Duck* was a converted WWII mosquito craft, one of the old PT boats with the tubes and deck cannon taken off. Its original gas-guzzling Packards had been replaced by more economical but no less powerful twin Napier Deltic diesels, capable of pushing the boat at speeds of over 50 knots through smooth water. They'd added extra fuel tanks, almost tripling its range.

They had a big Hallicrafters shortwave up in the wheelhouse, a radar transponder, and a depth indicator. The galley was stocked for a week or so of open-ocean running, and there was a fine supply of alcohol. There was also a collection of skin magazines, some tape cassettes of Indian and Western pop music, and what looked like hashish in a plastic bag.

High jinks on the high seas, I thought, as I tossed it all overboard. I wasn't interested in drugs right now. Or in sex or rock 'n' roll, for that matter.

I was looking for firepower.

I found it down below the forward bunks, neatly disassembled and packed away, wrapped in oil-impregnated canvas to protect it from the salty sea air. I breathed deeply as I hauled out the parts one by one and inspected them, my eyes shining with excitement.

I finished assembling it and lugged it up on deck. Osbert turned back from the wheel. "What on earth have you got there?"

I smiled. "Osbert, you're looking at one of the finest implements of murder and destruction ever designed." I clicked the last piece into place and patted the long barrel. "Meet the Browning M2 heavy machine gun; the Cadillac of rapid-fire infantry weapons. Where the hell they got hold of something like this, I'll never know. You don't see many of them outside the US and Central America."

I held up one of the ammunition belts. "But there's plenty of ammunition here, Osbert. Look at that – those shells are half an inch across. Hell, Osbert – we're contenders again. In Vietnam, I saw people blow down whole stands of palm trees with one of these things."

Osbert stared at the heavy gun, a frown on his face. "Don't you think a weapon like this is a little, ah, excessive, Mr. Donovan?"

I smiled up at him. "Never get into a war you don't intend to win, Osbert." I got to my feet. "Now shut the boat off and help me set this thing up on the forward deck. I want to see if it works."

We spent the next half hour setting up the Browning, bolting its tripod to the deck and fitting the heavy gun to it. Finally, we were ready. I showed Osbert how to insert and feed the belt, and then it was time for practice.

I tossed an empty oil drum overboard and let it trail out behind us until it was fifty yards astern. I swung the big gun around and stepped aside. "She's all yours," I said.

Osbert looked at the gun, and then at me. "Are you sure?" he said hesitantly.

"Go for it," I said. "I'm counting on you to back me up once we get there. This is what backup means, my friend."

He gripped the twin handles and raised the gun.

"Sight across the top," I said. "Pull the trigger and kind of walk the gun up toward the target. Hold tight now – she kicks quite a bit."

Osbert nodded. He pulled the trigger, and the machine gun began to cough, shuddering violently. Bullets stitched a deadly arc through the water as he slowly brought the gun up. The bullets made little waterspouts as they crept toward the bobbing drum. Suddenly there was a puff, a cloud of fragments, and the oil drum simply disappeared.

Osbert turned to me, grinning from ear to ear. "I say, Max, that was fun. Can we do it again?"

I nodded, watching the horizon. "Oh, yes," I said after a moment. "I'm sure we'll be doing it again. Very soon, in fact."

CHAPTER SEVENTEEN

We lay in the sandy underbrush of the tiny atoll, staring at Madirifushi across the channel, and waiting for sundown. We were taking turns looking at Khan's hideout through the binoculars, and talking about what to do and how to do it.

Khan's lair lay straight across the water in front of us, about two miles distant. Earlier that afternoon, I'd brought the pirate's ship into the shelter of the smaller island to the west, using the setting sun as cover. We'd made a wide approach, keeping the island between us and Madirifushi, and I was pretty sure that they hadn't seen us coming.

After making sure there was no one waiting for us on shore, I eased us through a break in the lagoon and up into a narrow inlet which nearly split the island in two. The underbrush was thick, and it nearly covered the deck as we nosed into it, but Osbert and I still spent twenty minutes cutting palm fronds and leaves for makeshift camouflage.

It would be dark in a few hours, and if anyone spotted us before then, well, the fight would just start a little earlier, that's all.

I scanned Madirifushi with the glasses, whistling softly through my teeth and wishing the pirates had had the decency to lay in a supply of sirloin steaks in their galley, along with the bags of Bombay onions, chilies, and green lentils that seemed to constitute their staple diet. I could plot and scheme better on a full stomach.

In addition to the Browning machine gun, the hold of the *Bombay Duck* had held several more treasures. I'd found a crate of hand grenades, two boxes of dynamite and a rusty coffee can full of detonators, a roll of fuse cord and a nice collection of weaponry, everything from pistols and switchblades to Armalite rifles. We had enough firepower to arm the Congolese army, I thought as I sorted through the junk.

Well, not quite. It was really the element of surprise that was the wild card in all this, the key to everything. Khan knew we were coming, of course. That's why he'd kidnapped Shanti; to lure Osbert to him. He didn't really care about the woman, all he wanted was the manuscript and its author. And unlike Podi Putha, he wouldn't settle for some half-baked 'deal' cooked up over a billiard table. No, Khan was the real article, and there was only one way to deal with him.

Fast, head-on, and hard.

He'd be expecting us, but he wouldn't know when, or how, we'd be arriving. It was a small edge, but important if we wanted to get out of this thing alive. I scanned the shoreline very carefully, looking for something, anything, that would build up the odds in our favor.

Khan's island was about half a mile wide, roughly round in shape, no more than eight or ten feet above the high tide level, and nearly flat. A ring of dazzling white sand surrounded it, giving way to palms, wild bamboo, and dense undergrowth in the center.

The only sign of habitation was the presence of a small single-engined seaplane with Sri Lankan markings moored just outside the reef. I was very curious about who it belonged to.

Madirifushi was unremarkable when seen from a distance; passing ships wouldn't give it a second glance. But once you took a look through the field glasses, things took on a different aspect. Poking up out of the top of the palms was a radio mast, and there, back under the shadow of a dense grove of palms, I could make out the low roofs of a compound. I could see at least three cinder-block buildings, and back in the bush behind them, an even bigger structure, little more than a shadowy outline.

Down at the water's edge was a low jetty, painted a sandy color which almost exactly matched the beach. I moved the glasses a fraction of an inch, peering into the shadows at the edge of the shore, where the jungle met the sand. In the late afternoon sun, I could see three or four sleek hulls, long and pointed, hiding under the tree cover, and what looked like sets of rails leading down to the water's edge.

I looked at them for a long time. They looked like cigarette boats, super-fast torpedoes, capable of incredible speeds across open water. More than a match for the *Bombay Duck*. With extra fuel tanks they'd be able to cover the distance from here to Malé in a matter of a few hours.

Just then there was movement on shore, and a moment later, one of the cigarette boats slid down its ramp and into the water, bouncing across the lagoon and out over the reef. It made a wide circle and slowed to a halt beside the seaplane's pontoons. Mahasona and another man got out and climbed up into the tiny cockpit. The third man stayed in the boat, and handed them up a large parcel. He handled it carefully, as if it contained glass or pottery. Then he waved, got back in the boat and gunned it toward shore.

A moment later the seaplane's prop jerked and caught, and then they were moving, spanking over the waves until they rose, the fading sun glinting off their wingtips, and headed northeast, toward Colombo. I let my breath out slowly and went back to looking at the island.

I took my time, scanning the lengthening shadows carefully and slowly, familiarizing myself with the contours of the island and the way the shapes shifted as behind me, the sun moved slowly down toward the edge of the world beyond the water. I needed to know as much as possible about the layout of the place, because it would be dark when I made my move, and although there would be a moon later on tonight, I couldn't count on it being much help to me.

I put the glasses down and rubbed my eyes. I was going to have to go in blind, and although I didn't much like it, there was nothing I could do about it. Khan was snugly fitted into his little island hideout, and I'd be willing to bet that he had then place rigged up as one big booby trap. He had built a highly successful business, and he had to be ready for a hostile takeover – other drug lords wanting a piece of the action, or even just up-and-comers who figured that the quickest way to make a name for themselves on the block would be to take on the big guy.

Although it looked like a sleepy little island in the setting sun, it was probably anything but. With that in mind, I walked back through the sand to the *Bombay Duck* and climbed aboard. I spent the rest of the late afternoon sorting through the diving gear I'd brought from the Club Med boat, testing and adjusting the equipment until it was perfect. Then I started on the pirate's junk, picking it over, looking for something I could use.

I finally settled on the dynamite. Dynamite was a nice attention-getter, and although it's a pretty piss-poor explosive, it can do a fair amount of damage when properly used.

I selected eight sticks, and wrapped them in two bundles of four sticks each, using some duct tape. I poked a hole in the end of each bundle with my knife, inserted a detonator, and secured it with more tape. Then I cut a foot of fuse cord for each one and knotted it to the detonator wires. Finally, I wrapped each bundle in a plastic bag and tucked them away inside the roomy pockets of my diving vest. Maybe I could use these, maybe not; but it didn't hurt to plan ahead.

I laid out all the rest of the diving equipment, checked everything one last time, and sat back, waiting for night to fall. Osbert pottered around in the primitive galley, eventually producing an edible meal of rice, lentils, and sweet biscuits. I ate slowly and sparingly, my mind on other things. Neither of us talked much.

As usual, the sun took an abrupt nosedive into the water and, fifteen minutes later, darkness had settled like a cloak over the sea. I finished the last of my rice, washed it down with a mouthful of warm water, and stood up. "It's time," I said.

We pulled off the camouflage foliage, started the *Bombay Duck*'s engines and backed her out of the narrow inlet. Moving slowly, running lights off, we nosed her out of the lagoon and around to the other side of the tiny island, directly across from Madirifushi. Then I started to suit up.

It took a long time to get all the equipment on, and when I was finally dressed, I felt like an overweight astronaut. Fortunately, the human body weighs a lot less in water than on dry land, and the added weight would be useful for keeping me at a safe depth. I'd have to swim at least two miles to cross the channel between our island and Khan's, and I needed to do it unobserved. The safest way to do that was to stay underwater. The prospect of crossing a deep ocean channel at night, underwater, didn't exactly appeal to me, but I couldn't see any other way to do it.

If Madirifushi was like most of the other atolls, there would be a broad coral reef surrounding the island, out anywhere from fifty to several hundred yards from shore. The reef would be very close to the surface of the water, and would prevent all but very shallow-draft boats from entering the lagoon behind it. Normally, there would be numerous small breaks in the reef big enough to run a boat through, but I didn't know where those were, and in any case, I didn't need them if I were going in on my own.

Behind the reef, the lagoon would be shallow, warm, and relatively safe. The deep ocean channel – the part that lay just in front of me – was the part I feared. The chart in the wheelhouse of the pirate's boat showed the channel to be over forty fathoms deep, and that was enough to be scary all on its own.

Sharks were my main worry. Many of the more aggressive species forage at night, and they hunt by tracking vibrations in the water. In the dark, I'd have no warning at all of an approaching predator, and my torch would be of little help. So I picked up the long shark billy, checked to see that it was loaded, and strapped it on.

A shark billy – also called a powerhead – looks very much like a cop's bobby stick, and you use it pretty much the same way. Shark noses are sensitive – they use their nose to check out the edibility of objects in the water – and if you give them a good tap on the snoot, that's usually enough to discourage them. But if that won't do the trick, the shark billy has another little feature: it shoots a 12-gauge slug out the end if you press the firing stud. You only get one shot, and it was definitely a last-ditch remedy for a shark attack. But as they say, life's not fair.

I attached the large diver's knife, added four kilos of lead weight, and buckled on the wide belt. I strapped a compass to my left wrist and a depth gauge to my right. I patted my vest pockets, feeling the reassuring bulk of the dynamite.

Grunting with effort, Osbert helped me into the tank harness. It was a long swim and I was going to be using up plenty of air and energy, so I'd opted for a two-tank rig. It was a lot heavier, but it would give me double the normal 70 cubic feet of air contained in a single tank. I figured I'd need most of it to get across the channel and through the lagoon at the other end.

I looked longingly at the Webley lying on the deck beside me. "Aren't you going to take it?" Osbert said.

I shook my head. "I'll pick up something once I get there," I said.

"What's your plan, then?" asked Osbert.

I picked up the big torch and strapped it to my thigh. "Very simple," I said. "I go over there and get Shanti, bring her back to the boat, and then we get the hell out of here."

"Yes, yes, of course," he said. "But I mean, how are you actually going to set about it?"

I spat into my mask, rinsed it, and put it on. "No idea," I said. I gestured across the water in the darkness to Madirifushi, where two tiny lights gleamed out of the underbrush. "Who knows what he's got on his island, Osbert. And I won't find out until I get there."

I cracked the valve on my tank, blew a few blasts through the regulator, and took several breaths. Everything seemed to be working.

Osbert plucked nervously at his shirt. "Well, what am I supposed to do, then?"

"That's easy," I said. "Wait here until I come back."

"All right," he said doubtfully. "But what if you don't come back?"

I looked at him. "Osbert," I said patiently, "if I don't come back, it'll be because I'm dead. And in that case," I added, "you're on your own."

Then I pulled my mask down, stuck the regulator in my mouth, and jumped off the side of the boat.

CHAPTER EIGHTEEN

It was cold out in the channel, and as I swam along, I could feel the heat slowly draining from my body, a fraction of a degree at a time. Most people think of tropical waters as warm, and for short periods of time they are. But out in the open sea, you can die of exposure just as surely as you can in the North Atlantic. It just takes a little longer, that's all.

I was about fifteen feet under the surface, moving along slowly. The moon was up, its wan filtered light making the thousands of plankton motes in the water glow with an eerie phosphorescence. It distorted perspective and orientation, making it seem as if I were a spaceman cast adrift in the limitless void. There was no noise except for the harsh metallic rasping of my regulator, no feeling save for the ache in my muscles as I pushed on doggedly through the water – nothing to tell me that I was even alive.

This must be what they mean when they talk about floating in limbo, I thought as I swam. Under the surface, there was no longer any up, down, forward or back. There was only the water and the dreamy sensation of floating. It would be easy to just let go, I thought – to stop swimming and just drift, without direction or bearing, sinking slowly into the darkness.

Except for the fear.

My heart was hammering like a Harley with a thrown rod, and only part of it from the exertion of swimming. I was about as wired up as I could get, all systems on full alert, adrenaline flowing through my system like oil through the Ras Jebel pipeline.

Flying, as any pilot will tell you, is largely long periods of boredom punctuated by short intervals of intense terror. Scuba diving was the reverse, at least the way I was doing it. I was stroking through the water in a modified dolphin kick, trying to conserve energy but wanting desperately to keep my speed up as high as possible and still have some air left at the other end. The channel was wide and deep, and God knows what might be swimming along in here in the darkness with me.

If I can get across the channel fast enough, I thought, I might not have to find out.

I sucked air in through my regulator, blew it out through my nose, and tried as much as possible to keep a smooth, strong stroke, one that wouldn't send 'hurt fish' vibrations out into the water like a distress signal, attracting the interest of everything with teeth for miles around.

I checked my watch. I'd been in the water nearly half an hour. Snapping on my torch, I looked at my pressure gauge. Three quarters empty; time to switch over. I took a deep breath from the regulator, popped the valve on the new tank, and felt the air kick in again. A fully charged tank can last a diver up to an hour, but air consumption varies too much to make this any sort of guide. The amount of air used depends on depth, physical condition, and what you're doing. Deep diving, or lots of work underwater, will cut the time drastically.

I've certainly been working hard, I thought, adjusting my buoyancy compensator to take me a little closer to the surface. I was performing the equivalent of two or three miles in pool laps, underwater and in pitch blackness, with my nerves like scraped bone, and it was going to eat up a lot of air, to say nothing of peace of mind.

I snapped on my torch briefly, checked my wrist compass to make sure that I was still on course, and then swept the torch briefly out into the blackness in front of me. All I could see were millions of tiny motes in the blackness, stars like grains of sand in some galaxy out on the edge of the universe, no depth or form, stretching away forever to the end of time. This is what it was like before the beginning of the world, I thought. Out there in the cold void.

Well, maybe not exactly, I thought as I caught the merest glimpse of movement on the periphery of my vision. The big bang theory didn't say anything about sharks.

Was it a shark? I snapped the torch on again and probed the water, seeing nothing. Probably just a big fish, I told myself. A tuna, maybe, or some kind of sea bass. Any one of a hundred kinds of fish, all harmless. Sure, Donovan, my brain replied.

The tropical seas are full of nasty creatures, and a great many of them are active at night. Sea snakes abound in the warm waters of the Indian Ocean. In addition to being the most venomous creatures on the planet, they're also one of the most inquisitive, and if they spotted me, they'd just naturally want to get up close for a better look. Jellyfish floated freely on the tides and currents, trailing a forest of poisonous tentacles in their wake. I had a very healthy respect for the creatures since I had seen what one of them had done to someone off the coast of West Africa, and in the dark, I could swim into the thick of their tentacles without warning.

But sharks are what I fear most, I thought, feeling sweat breaking out under my mask. Sea snakes were venomous, but unaggressive, and although they might swim close to get a look at me, they wouldn't bite unless badly frightened. Sharks, however, needed no excuse to go for a man in the water, and if you were going to try to invite a shark attack, there was hardly a better time than the night.

This is because the shark can 'see' in the dark, using its super-sensitive nose and its lateris system which senses vibration in the water. And I couldn't; without my torch, I was totally blind. Even with the torch, I could only make out objects in an area roughly two feet wide and about ten feet out in front of me. That was almost the same thing as being blind, if you thought about it.

A shark could come up and start his attack run before I'd even spotted him, and there wasn't a damn thing I could do about it except get the hell out of the water. God knows I was trying my damndest to do just that, but I couldn't stop swimming until I'd reached Khan's island.

And then, I reminded myself, my real problems would start.

I bled air into my BC and drifted slowly to the surface, trying not to think about what might be underneath me, ready to bite off one of my legs. I broke water soundlessly and stopped swimming, staring up at the stars with grateful eyes and letting my brain get itself reoriented.

After a moment, I turned slowly and located the outline of Madirifushi Atoll, less than a quarter mile away in the soft darkness, outlined in the moonlight, the dim glow of lights coming from somewhere inside the jungle near shore. I nodded to myself; not long now. The reef would be somewhere between me and the shore, and I hoped it was as far out as possible, because once I was inside the shallow lagoon, I wouldn't have to worry about the sharks anymore.

So let's get going, lad, I told myself. The sooner you put your ass in gear, the sooner you'll be safe inside the reef. I rinsed my mask, stuck the mouthpiece of the regulator back between my numb lips, and slid under the water again.

* * *

Fifteen minutes later, I hit the reef. My feet brushed against something, and I snapped the torch on, seeing pale fronds of fire coral caressing my flippers. Fire coral contains thousands of tiny poison sacs tipped with what amounts to miniature hypodermic needles. If you swim into the stuff, it can put you into anaphylactic shock, but my wetsuit was protecting me from harm.

I shone the torch cautiously around the bottom. The reef reared up abruptly out of the dark depths of the channel, a riot of color and texture, everything from massive brain coral to tiny delicate anemones. Squads of striped fish paraded in and out of the various plants, feeding eagerly on the plankton and other tiny forms of sea life.

The reef came almost up to the water level. I could float across the tops of the waving fronds of fire coral if I lay flat, but there was no way that Osbert was going to be able to bring the *Bombay Duck* in over this mess, not unless I could find a passage through the reef. I started swimming slowly parallel to the reef, looking for the openings that I knew had to be there.

It took me almost forty-five minutes to circumnavigate the island, and in the process I learned one very interesting thing: there was no channel through the reef at all. Khan – or someone – had plugged whatever natural passages there had once been with a jumble of concrete and rough stone. Given the fact that neither material is readily found in the Maldives, he had certainly wanted to ensure his privacy by making sure that no one brought a boat in across the lagoon when he wasn't looking.

It seems a bit excessive, I thought as I drifted on the current, only my mask out of the water, looking like a large frog, peering at the lights on shore. And in any case, plugging the holes in the reef wasn't really going to keep people out. Not if they were as determined as I was.

I smiled in the darkness. Drifting on the surface, careful not to brush against the sharp coral mere inches below me, I pushed myself across the reef and into the calm, safe, peaceful waters of the lagoon beyond.

CHAPTER NINETEEN

The lagoon at this point was about two hundred yards wide, as calm as a mirror, and about ten degrees warmer than the open ocean had been. I floated quietly just under the water, letting my eyes accommodate to the darkness, grateful for the dim light of the rising moon over my right shoulder. The shoreline was distinct now, backlit by the lights of the buildings hidden in amongst the undergrowth. As my pupils dilated, letting in more light, I could see the outlines of the jetty, extending far out into the lagoon, and beside it, the hulls of the sleek cigarette boats I'd seen earlier that afternoon.

There was no movement from the shore, no sound, no sign at all that anyone was there at all. But I knew better.

What's next? My brain was asking the difficult questions, but my guts had no answer. Most of life is like that, I thought, you make it up as you go along. The first thing to do, I decided, would be to get on dry land, get rid of the diving gear, and map out the lay of the land. Once I'd figured out where things were, I could decide what to do.

I looked out at the shoreline. It might be booby-trapped, but I doubted it. Land mines, tripwires and Claymores were fine for the bush where you didn't plan on doing any fighting yourself, but wiring up your own island might not be too smart, especially if it was as small as this one. It would give you restricted mobility, and if you were planning to repel unwelcome guests, that might be the last thing you'd want.

The easiest thing for me to do would probably be to swim right across the lagoon to the jetty, stash the diving gear down under the pilings somewhere, and make myself invisible in the forest for a while. I flashed the torch briefly down into the water, noting with relief the clear, sandy bottom less than twenty feet below me, perfect for a nice, relaxing swim. I checked my air supply, cracked the valve on my BC, and dropped down until my toes brushed the bottom. I started stroking slowly across the lagoon.

I had gotten a little more than halfway across when something brushed against my leg. I twisted awkwardly in the water, looking back. In the dim, filtered moonlight, I saw something big and bulky move off into the darkness, and my blood froze. I snapped on the torch but whatever it was had gone, disappeared into the watery murk. A sea turtle, I told myself, wanting desperately to believe it. They often frequented the shallow lagoons, especially during egg-laying season. Either that or a manta ray which I'd disturbed as it lay half-hidden on the bottom. I snapped off the torch and resumed swimming.

Thirty seconds later it happened again. This time it wasn't a gentle contact, but a hard, jarring jolt as something big rammed into my upper thigh. I turned, scrabbling frantically for my torch, the panic messages from my brain's basement flooding into the switchboard. I knew what I'd see almost before the torch lit up the water around me.

There it was, an enormous hammerhead shark, turning in a tight circle back toward me, its dead eyes showing no emotion as it scythed through the water. At the outer reaches of the light beam I could see other shapes, large and indistinct, but you didn't need an advanced degree to figure out what was going on.

I could feel my breathing ratchet up into high gear as I began to hyperventilate. Sweeping the torch from side to side, I realized that what I had assumed was a peaceful, quiet lagoon was alive with sharks, big ones, and most of them seemed headed in my direction.

It hit me like a flash of lightning then: of course, that's why there'd been no passage through the reef, why Khan had blocked the natural openings with stones and concrete. He'd created a one-hundred percent authentic shark-filled moat around his island stronghold, simply by blocking off the lagoon.

He must have gotten a few big hammerheads from somewhere, fishermen probably, and stocked his little pond after he'd blocked off the entrances. It would be so simple – feed the beasts once in a while, enough to keep them alive but not enough to dispel their ravenous hunger. That way, they'd go for anything that entered the lagoon, unless it was steel-clad.

And now they were getting ready to go for me.

One of the hammerheads nosed out of the pack and bumped me again, hard, on the upper arm. I struck it a glancing blow on the nose as it swept by, but knowing sharks, that probably only whetted its appetite. There were at least a dozen of them out there now, circling me in an intricate choreography of long figure-eights, getting ready to make their move. I dropped to the bottom and crouched there, sweeping my torch in fast arcs through the water.

Sharks are hungry, vicious, and aggressive, but they're not stupid. They like to know what they're about to bite into, and the way they usually go about it is to nose into their intended prey once or twice, sizing up the situation, trying to figure out whether the object is good to eat or not. I've had diving buddies who've had their scuba tanks bitten by sharks, who then decided that anything that hard and metallic would probably be tough to digest, and left them alone. Somebody in a wetsuit, on the other hand, probably feels lovely and squishy, just right for a quick snack.

The usual attack pattern was to circle for a while, making a run or two, nosing in to get an idea of texture and resistance. Then, on one of the next close passes, a slight turn to the left or the right, a powerful thrust from the tail fins, and the mouth would open, exposing multiple rows of backward-sloping teeth.

Sharks are seagoing pit bulls; they bite, fasten hard, and worry their prey, ripping off huge chunks of flesh which usually go down the hatch immediately, as they're coming out of their turn. And they're very good at biting; an average shark can apply over 6,000 pounds of pressure per square inch with its jaws. Blood in the water excites them, and if they're hungry enough, they'll go into a feeding frenzy where they'll snap at almost anything, including each other.

I ran through my options. One way to deal with hungry sharks is to simply change your position in the water, by moving up or down thirty feet or so. Sharks are territorial, and seem to operate on some sort of complex pattern of water temperature and pressure. But the lagoon was only ten feet deep, so that possibility was out.

Another defense is to get against or behind something, something that makes it difficult for them to make one of their veering passes. Coral heads, wrecks, or anything that sticks up from the seabed will do.

Unless, of course, you happen to be in the middle of a lagoon with a smooth, sandy bottom. It might as well have been a sports arena for sharkball, for all the protection it offered me. I kept the torch on and waved it from side to side, trying to figure out where the next one would come from, and thinking hard, because there were a lot of them, they were very hungry, and sooner or later, they'd get me. I knew it and, probably, so did they.

I had the knife, of course, but it would be useless against the tough sharkskin. There was also the dynamite, but that would be like destroying the village in order to save it. I had no wish to either give myself an underwater pressure concussion or to send Khan's men a loud and clear signal that I was on my way to their office.

That left me with one real weapon, the only one I could use. The shark billy.

I unclipped it from my weight belt and slipped the rawhide thong around my wrist. It had a good heft and a nice balance, and I managed to get in a good knock at another one of the hammerheads as it bore in on me. The shark flinched and spun off. Irritating, probably, but not discouraging enough. So my next step had to be carefully timed and perfectly executed.

I had to shoot one of the sharks through the head, and, while the rest of them closed in on their dying comrade, I had to get the hell out of there and up on dry land.

Khan's thugs might be a problem, but they were my next problem.

I turned the ring at the end of the billy and felt it click into place. I curled my fingers around the handle, resting my index finger lightly on the firing stud. I had only one slug in the billy, and I had to get it right. No reloads, no practice shots. And if I hit the shark anywhere other than the brain, it might do very little damage at all. Or it might enrage the shark into attacking suddenly.

I cracked the valve on my buoyancy compensator, bleeding my vest of all its air. I needed both feet solidly on the bottom for this next act, and I needed enough weight to be able to swing and hit without floating off in the opposite direction as the laws of motion took over. I got into a fighter's stance, standing straight up on the bottom, my feet flat against the sand. I held the billy in one hand and the torch in the other. A couple of hammerheads nosed by, but neither came close enough for what I had in mind. I needed a serious shark, one which had already made up its mind to have a bite, because that one would come straight in without stopping, and that was the one I wanted to shoot, right in the brain.

I stood on the sand, moving in a slow circle, feeling like some strange kind of underwater cowboy in a shootout. Three or four other sharks glided in and out tentatively, and then I spotted my target.

I picked him up in the torch beam from about fifteen feet out, moving fast. He was big and he was mean, and he didn't waste any time. He held his jaws half open, threshing the water powerfully as he sped toward me.

I barely had time to react. He bored straight in, turning slightly on the way, the jaws wider now. As his terrible image grew larger, filling my field of vision, I brought the billy up.

I held myself rigid, ignoring the panicked screaming of my nerves, until the very last second. Then I turned sideways, like a bullfighter. As the shark flashed past me I jammed the billy hard into his head just behind one of his terrible dark eyes, and pulled the trigger.

There was a sharp crack, and the shark convulsed, throwing me backward. In an instant, the water was full of confusion, as blood poured from the wound in a dark cloud. The other sharks moved to the attack, excited by the scent. I dropped flat to the sand and began moving off, using a breaststroke, feeling like a tadpole at a kingfishers' convention. I looked back only once. The other hammerheads were tearing their dead brother to pieces, the water thick with blood and gore.

And for a few moments, they'd forgotten about me. Stroking with all my might, I sped across the sandy bottom toward where I thought the jetty would be, flashing my torch every few moments to light my path. If someone on shore could see my light underwater, well, that was just too bad.

A few moments later, I spotted the pilings, looming up through the dark water like ancient Roman columns, together with a rusty ladder along the side of one of them. I glanced at my air supply gauge: three hundred pounds left. Enough for another ten minutes or so if necessary, but I intended to be on dry land in a matter of seconds.

I quickly unbuckled my weight belt, took off my buoyancy compensator, and shucked off the backpack containing the two air tanks. Keeping the regulator in my mouth, and scanning the water for the reappearance of the sharks, I bound up the buoyancy vest and tanks with the weight belt and pulled the buckle tight. Once on shore I'd find some place to stash the gear in case I needed it again, although God knows I wasn't looking forward to entering the waters of the lagoon ever again.

But I also knew that other terrors might await me on dry land, and who could say at this stage whether the lagoon might look like a safe haven in comparison with what else was out there? One way or the other, I'd be finding out very soon now.

I kept my wetsuit and the diving vest with its roomy pockets. I'd sweat underneath the close-fitting rubberized fabric, but it was dark and offered quite a bit of protection. I also kept my knife, torch, and underboots; I didn't feel like running across the island barefoot.

I was ready in record time. Taking one last long hit off the regulator, I picked up my bundled gear in one hand, and climbed the ladder to the surface.

The night air was cool and sweet and a welcome relief after the canned stuff I'd been breathing for the past hour. There was a gentle, warm breeze coming off the ocean, and the accumulated heat of the day felt good against my face. I eased carefully up onto the varnished wooden planks of the jetty, glancing out at the lagoon in the moonlight. I could see ripples a hundred yards offshore, and what looked like a dark stain spreading across the surface of the water. I shuddered, picked up my gear, and turned toward land.

I'd gotten almost to the end of the jetty before I saw the dogs.

There were two of them. They were large Dobermans, and they sat quietly in the sand, watching me with bright eyes. Their ears were back and their mouths open, and in the moonlight I could see their long pointed teeth. They'd been waiting for me.

I stopped and stood very still. "Nice doggies," I whispered, hoping I'd see their little stubby tails start to wag in welcome.

No such luck. Their muzzles came up and their lips drew back. Killers, I thought. Trained killers, taught to attack silently and without warning.

Like right now.

As if responding to a thought signal, both dogs bounded to their feet and came leaping toward me. I reacted instantly and instinctively. I turned and ran for my life, back along the jetty.

No time to draw my knife from its sheath on my lower leg, no time to even begin to think about a strategy for overcoming the two dogs. I was perhaps fifteen feet out in front of them, but that wouldn't last long. There was a metal flagpole marking the end of the jetty, and it was coming up far too quickly. In the water beyond, I could still see ripples where my friends the sharks were finishing their impromptu evening snack. I had perhaps another ten yards of jetty left, and then I'd be joining them.

The dogs' claws rattled and skittered on the slick varnish of the jetty's planks as they closed the distance between us. They were finding it tough going over the slippery surface, but they'd got the stride just about right, and they were literally nipping at my heels. Another few seconds and they'd be on me, and once that happened, my wetsuit would be almost no protection at all. They'd go for my throat first, trying to rip it out, and something as flimsy as a quarter-inch of tough rubber and nylon insulating fabric wouldn't even slow them down.

Almost to the flagpole now. I shot a glance backwards to see the dogs only inches away, and when I looked up, I was out of jetty. I reached out with my right arm, crooked it around the flagpole, and swung myself out and around like a tetherball. With my other hand I let go of my diving gear, sending the bundle straight off the end of the jetty into the water.

The dogs were fast and they were mean, but they weren't particularly bright. They shot straight off the end of the jetty, following the equipment, with hardly a second thought. One of them gave me a mild look of surprise as he sailed by. I whispered "Sayonara" as they hit the water.

They went in and down without a murmur – either they'd actually had their vocal cords cut or else someone had trained them awfully well.

And then the water boiled and grew dark again as the sharks discovered that the second course was being served.

I let out a deep breath and turned away. Easy come, easy go. And although the SPCA might not have approved, I didn't figure that anyone else was going to miss the dogs too much. I just hoped there weren't any more of them on the island. I was running out of energy, and I needed time to scope out the scene and figure out what to do. It would be nice, I thought, if I could do that in relative peace and quiet.

I walked to the end of the jetty and faded into the forest. Now, I thought, for the tricky bit.

CHAPTER TWENTY

I paused at the edge of the beach, listening to the night. The breeze murmured gently through the palms, and from somewhere in the interior of the island I caught the quiet hum of a motor. That would be the generator, I thought – the power supply. Maybe that should be my first stop.

Then I remembered the cigarette boats that I'd seen through the binoculars. Perhaps it would be a better idea to take a look at those first.

A burglar friend of mine once told me that the most important secret of success in his business was to always check out the exits before you did anything else. The last thing a burglar wants is to be trapped inside a house or apartment. Before you go in, he said, make a plan for how to get out again.

My diving equipment was now lying either at the bottom of the lagoon, or inside some hammerhead's belly, so that way was out. And since Osbert wasn't going to be able to get the *Bombay Duck* in through the reef, I needed to know, before I got started here, what my other options were going to be.

There were three boats, all of them on metal rails, ready to go. Khan's men probably used them to ferry raw opium in from Malé, and finished product back again. Across an open ocean, one of these babies could really rip, and although they gulped fuel like a drunk on a weekender, I didn't figure that operating expenses were much of a worry for Khan.

I hunkered down beside one of them, keeping the torch off, letting the moonlight help me. I didn't know if there'd be anyone else wandering around on the island at night, but I sure as hell didn't want them to see my light. I figured that if they were running this show the way I would have done it, they'd let the dogs out at night, and everyone would more or less stay out of their way, because it got too confusing and dangerous for the dogs to have to distinguish between friend and foe. Easier to just train them to attack anything that moved, and let it go at that.

That's the way I'd have done it, at least. And if they'd done it that way, too, then I had nothing more to worry about from that particular quarter. Unless, of course, there were more than two dogs patrolling the island.

I worked fast, my senses on full alert, expecting at any minute to hear the scratching of paws on the sand behind me. I checked the fuel tanks, and found all of them fully gassed up and ready to go. I looked in the onboard lockers, searching for weapons, but found nothing usable.

I opened the bilges on the first two boats and buried the threaded plugs a few yards away in the sand, smoothing it over afterwards. When the time came, I figured everybody was going to be wanting to leave the island in a hurry. But my own agenda was to promote a selective departure policy.

Then I cut the fuel lines from the tanks to the carbs. Taking a roll of black electrical tape I'd found in one of the lockers, I taped the cut ends together to make it look as though they were okay, and then replaced the lines under the decking, as they had been before.

I went to the last boat in line, got out my knife and cut the ignition wires. I scraped the ends free of insulation and positioned them so that I could hot-start it in a hurry. I sat back and inspected my work.

The way I had it rigged now, the third boat was going to be my own private getaway craft. I'd noticed an automatic control to lift the prop, which would take care of the problem of getting it out across the reef and into the open sea. If Khan's men were chasing us, they'd be able to get the other two boats started, using the fuel already in the carburetors, but it wouldn't get them very far. And the open bilge would eventually fill the boat.

If I got there first, I stood a decent chance of getting away. Anyone who tried to follow me would find his engine running out of fuel, and his boat filling up with seawater, before he even cleared the lagoon.

Cruel and unusual punishment? I hadn't given it much thought, to tell the truth. It wasn't me, after all, who'd set up a shark farm in the lagoon and neglected to put up 'No Trespassing' signs. And anyway, I doubted that the cigarette boats would sink completely. Most modern craft have built-in buoyancy chambers, designed to keep them afloat even when full of water. I figured that as long as the folks in the boat stayed where they were, they wouldn't turn themselves into hors d'oeuvres for our finny friends.

I stood up, brushed over my tracks as best I could with a palm frond, and slipped into the underbrush, thinking about my next move.

This was going to call for some careful research. I had no idea what the layout of the island was, but stumbling around in the dark way wasn't an ideal way to find out. The fact that they'd been using dogs meant that there probably weren't any mines or tripwires around, but if they were really intent on security, they might have installed sensors or wires higher up, which would either trigger an alarm or just simply blow the hell out of whatever happened to set them off.

So caution was the watchword. I moved silently, half-crouched, through the bush, as nervous as a pregnant fox in a forest fire. I needed to get my bearings to figure out roughly where everything was, and then to make some sort of a plan. For starters, I needed to know how many men Khan had on the island, and what kinds of toys they had to fight with. Once the curtain went up, there wouldn't be any time to revise the choreography. It all had to happen fast and perfectly, without the benefit of a dress rehearsal.

I spent the next half hour making a quick tour of the periphery of the island, not bothering with the compound hidden back in the forest, just looking at how the outer perimeter was set up. There were no other boats, no other jetties. Here and there paths wound back into the bush, presumably toward the compound, but I passed up the temptation to follow one of them. I needed to wait until I'd seen everything out here before I investigated the interior.

By the time I'd circled the island, I was getting impatient. My watch told me that it was many hours until dawn, but I wanted to get started. Sooner or later, somebody would wonder about where the dogs were, and once they realized that they were gone, all hell would break loose.

I needed to be in position and ready to go before that happened. I swung away from the beach and started into the bushes, down flat on the ground, trying to think like a dog. Or at least not like a human; if there were traps in here, they'd be for humans, not dogs.

The underbrush was thick, but I moved easily through it. I'd had lots of practice years ago in Vietnam when a buddy and I had worked our way down the Indochina Peninsula trying to find our unit after we'd escaped from the prison camp. We'd moved mainly at night, and we'd had to learn in a hurry to be better than Victor Charles at the craft of jungle invisibility.

Like riding a bike, it was a skill you never really forget. Especially if you learned it under life-and-death conditions.

I edged my way forward, toward the glow of the compound lights two hundred yards ahead through the jungle, my ears and eyes open wide, thankful for the fact that there were no hordes of birds and monkeys in the trees ready to start shrieking my presence as I passed by below.

After ten minutes, I saw the outline of a cyclone fence ahead of me, topped with sharp-looking ends of twisted wire. As I came closer, I could also see ceramic insulators every few feet. So much for simply climbing over.

I climbed a convenient tree instead. Stretched out on a wide branch, I inspected the setup. The compound sat back inside the fence, four small buildings and a larger one that looked like a warehouse of some kind. Lights were on in two of the buildings, but the two others and the warehouse were dark.

One of the lighted buildings was up on short stilts and had the look of a prefab bungalow. I figured that for Khan's own place. The other lighted building lay far back along the compound fence. It had a radio mast on the roof, and I could hear a generator grinding away from somewhere behind it. That would be the nerve center;

where the radio would be, and the alarm signals, if there were any.

The other two darkened buildings worried me. They were windowless Quonset huts of corrugated steel. They lay side by side, their twin humps looking like a huge tin can sliced up the middle and opened out on the ground. They might be storehouses for food and equipment, or dormitories for a pack of highly trained killers. I needed some idea of how many people were on the island, and so whatever else I did, I was going to have to check out the Quonsets sooner or later. But most of all, I wanted to take a look in the warehouse. I figured that was where Khan had his heroin lab, but I was also hoping I'd find some more useful things as well.

Weapons, for example. In my experience, drugs go together with weapons, and I needed a lot more than a couple of sticks of dynamite, a knife and a flashlight if I were planning to get myself and Shanti out of this snake's nest alive.

I watched and waited for fifteen minutes, until the tree trunk began to grow hard and uncomfortable. No one came out of any of the buildings during that time, no one moved. I checked my watch. Nearly midnight.

Just then I heard a noise. I shifted position on the tree branch, watching as a stocky Indian emerged from the radio shack and approached the gate. He had a Kalashnikov slung carelessly across his shoulder and a dog's food dish in each hand.

Grunting, he set them down, extracted a ring of keys from his pocket, and opened the gate. He stepped outside, placed the food dishes in front of him, and whistled twice.

I smiled in the darkness, took a deep breath, and got ready.

CHAPTER TWENTY-ONE

I was tying the last knot in the guard's gag when he woke up. He squirmed, his eyes rolling in terror. I picked up his Kalashnikov and patted his cheek affectionately. "Relax, friend," I whispered to him. "You're getting the best deal of the bunch, believe me." Then I pulled him back into the shadows under the trees and slipped through the gate into the compound.

I tried the radio shack first. Moving as quietly as I could, I slipped up to the lighted window and peered cautiously inside. The noise of the generator would cover the sound of my feet, but I didn't want to take a chance on getting discovered at this stage. Time enough for that later on.

The room was empty, so I moved inside. A single wicker chair stood pushed back from the rough wooden table. A tattered paperback lay open beside a cracked saucer ashtray in which a long, foul-smelling cigar burned. Behind the table, on the wall, was the radio equipment. I scanned the array carefully, looking for something connected with an alarm or booby-trap system, but saw nothing but the standard shortwave equipment, including a big Zenith transmitter, a scanner and two multi-band receivers. One of the receivers was tuned to All-India Radio, and skirling Hindu music filled the tiny room.

I was tempted to fool with the radio equipment, but we were a long way from help, and I had other things to do first. I needed to get a look at the warehouse, and also to figure out who or what was in the two Quonset huts. I helped myself to a roll of electrical tape and a small coil of nylon rope, closed the door to the radio shack carefully and faded back into the darkness.

The two Quonsets had obviously been military surplus, designed for storage; they had no windows, and only one door each. Air conditioners had been fitted into each Quonset, which made me suspect that there were people inside. I circled the huts warily, keeping as quiet as possible. If Khan had a squad of heavies to take care of intruders, this is where they'd be sleeping, and I wanted them to rest undisturbed for the time being. I crouched beneath one of the air conditioners, listening hard. I couldn't hear a thing over the thump and rattle of the compressors, but that didn't mean they weren't in there.

I sat back on the balls of my feet and tried to figure things out. Each Quonset hut was about twenty feet long. They'd probably been part of the original RAF station, converted later by Khan into sleeping quarters. If you subtracted some space for a kitchen and a toilet, there'd still be room for four or five men to sleep inside. I figured five here, and five in the other Quonset. Plus Khan and maybe a few others.

I was dealing with a dozen men, maybe more, and the odds weren't encouraging. In an open, fair fight, I'd stand no chance at all. But I'd learned a long time ago that when you can't win the race, you move the finish line. So I cut the nylon rope in half, and working carefully and quietly, used each piece to tie the doors of the Quonset huts shut. It probably wouldn't keep them inside for very long once things got going, but any time at all would be a help.

Now for the warehouse. The wide door opened easily, and once inside, I used my torch. I whistled softly between my teeth as I played the light over the stacked plastic-wrapped bales of opium. There were hundreds of kilos of the raw drug here, and once it had been transformed into heroin, it would be easily worth the annual budget of an average developing country.

Back behind the stacks of raw opium were worktables containing a complex array of laboratory equipment whose function I couldn't begin to comprehend, but whose overall purpose was very clear. Khan had set up a complete processing factory, and was turning out massive quantities of deadly heroin on a regular basis.

I clicked off my torch and sat quietly in the darkness, thinking. Khan must receive shipments several times a week. It was a near-perfect setup: raw opium would come into Sri Lanka daily, in any number of ways – Indian and Pakistani merchant traders, tourists, and blockade-runners. The Palk Strait between India and Sri Lanka was only a few miles wide, and poorly patrolled. It would be child's play to bring opium in and get it to Mahasona.

And once fifty or a hundred kilos had collected in Colombo, it would be equally easy to get it out again, to the Maldives. Any passing freighter could unload some, but the easiest way by far would be to use tour groups. The Maldivian customs inspectors never checked their baggage carefully, out of respect for all the hard currency they brought.

So the opium could easily be run out to Madirifushi from Malé in the cigarette boats, and refined heroin could be brought back the same way, given to the same tourist mules to take to Europe, or hidden in the deck plates of a passing freighter.

I could also see why Khan found the idea of establishing a secure base inside Sri Lanka itself an attractive one. It eliminated a risky and complicated step in the process, and would permit him to increase his production enormously. But surely the government of Sri Lanka would never tolerate such an operation. Either Khan wasn't as clever as Osbert thought he was, or else he had something up his sleeve.

I got to my feet. So much to do, so little time. Before I could get Shanti to safety, I needed to destroy the warehouse and lab. Otherwise, it would be like leaving a pile of radioactive waste around.

I looked around at the opium. There was plenty more where this came from, of course, but it would take Khan a while to build up his supply again. Since a drug dealer's stock is his capital, getting rid of the warehouse would be the equivalent of forcing Khan into bankruptcy.

Leaving the warehouse, I slipped quietly back around behind the radio room, to where the tiny Honda generator sat. Just as I'd hoped, there was a large two-hundred-gallon gasoline tank beside it, together with half a dozen five-gallon jerricans and five or six feet of plastic hose. Perfect.

The Midnight Auto Supply couldn't have done it better. I cut a short length of plastic tubing, and using it as a siphon, I quickly filled the jerricans. Then I carried two of them over to the warehouse. Once inside, I carefully poured gasoline all around the perimeter of the shed. The walls and roof were made of cadjan palm fronds, and they'd burn very nicely once the gasoline got going.

I went back for two more jerricans, dumping the last ten gallons of fuel on top of the piled plastic packets of opium. I had no idea how well opium burned, but I was going to find out in just a few minutes.

Then I unzipped the large pockets of my vest, took out the plastic-wrapped bundles of dynamite, and checked them for damage. The detonators were still firmly embedded in the end of the sticks, the fuses still attached.

I hefted one of the bundles in my hand. Easy to throw, and with enough weight to ensure accuracy. Four sticks of this stuff wasn't going to be enough to do any real damage, but it would certainly blow out one of the warehouse walls and start the gasoline blazing, and who could ask for a better deal than that?

I stuffed the dynamite back into my pockets and went out into the night. Time now to see what Mr. Khan was doing.

* * *

I've saved the best until last, I thought as I crouched on the stairs outside Khan's bungalow, peering in the open window. Khan had his back to me, and he was stuffing bundles of money into a cloth sack, making tiny marks with a pencil on a notebook open on the table in front of him. From time to time he would pause to take a drink from the whiskey bottle at his elbow.

Shanti sat at the table across from him, her wrists bound together with rope. Her hair was in disarray, and there were dark smudges on one of her cheeks, but she looked unharmed. Her dark eyes glared at Khan. I shifted position then, and she caught the movement. Her eyes widened in surprise and her mouth opened as she recognized me. I put a finger quickly to my lips. She gave me a barely perceptible nod, and went back to staring at Khan.

Khan looked to be in his mid-forties. He had a small potbelly and a big head of curly, prematurely grey hair that shone like pewter in the light of the gooseneck lamp at the end of the table. He turned then, and I got a glimpse of a strong handsome face, hawk nose and thick well-groomed moustache under bushy brows. As he counted the money, I caught the gleam of a gold Rolex on his wrist.

The air-conditioner's hum was loud, but I had no trouble catching his words. "Two more days, my dear," he was saying. "That's all the time I need. Just until the full moon Poya. After that, it really doesn't matter."

What doesn't matter? I asked myself. It was hot under the house, and I was sweating like a courtroom lawyer in my wetsuit.

"Give it up, Khan." Shanti's voice was firm and strong. "Uncle Bertie will never turn the manuscript over to you. And it does matter, even after Poya. Do you think for one moment that the rest of the world is going to stand by and actually let you get away with this?" She paused. "Max and Uncle Bertie are probably on their way to England right now. In a matter of days, you're going to be front-page news, and then your time's up. Why don't you admit it?"

Khan stood up and took a pistol from his belt. He laid it on the table, and then reached across and slapped

Shanti's face, hard. She stifled a cry and glared at him, her eyes blinking back the pain.

"Your time is up, too, my dear." His voice had taken on a purring quality. "This morning when Mahasona brought you here, you were sure that you were going to be saved by your wonderful uncle and Mr. Duncan."

"His name's Donovan. Max Donovan."

Khan shrugged. "His name could be Krishnakumar for all I care. He and your uncle will both be dead very soon, whether they are in London or still in Colombo. Mahasona will see to that, believe me."

He took a drink of whiskey and came around behind her. "You're all alone now, Miss Wickramanayake. You'd better get used to that." He paused, tracing her cheek with a thick finger. "We don't have to be enemies, you know. You're quite a pretty little thing, in fact. Did anyone ever tell you that?"

"No one as ugly as you."

He smiled. Then he reached down and ripped open her blouse. He cupped her breast, moving his fingers over its contours slowly. She shrank from his touch, but he only laughed, holding her securely. He moved his hand up the side of her neck, forcing her neck back.

Quick as lightning, she turned her head and sank her teeth into his hand. He gave a roar of pain and stumbled backward, spilling the rest of his whiskey.

He grabbed her long hair, jerking her head back, and slapped her again. Shanti cried out then, and I got ready to kick the door in when Khan began to speak again. "You stupid filthy cow. Do you think you're going to get out of here alive?" He put his face very close to hers. "Do you think I can't touch you if I want to? Do anything I want with you?"

She spat full in his face.

He drew back as if stung. "All right, bitch." His voice was low and dangerous. "I have six men here with me.

None of them have had a woman in weeks. If you don't want me to touch you, let's see how you like the others."

Khan was looking off to the right, an ugly smile on his face. "All of them would like to make your acquaintance, I'm sure. Suppose we start with Lal, eh? Would you like that, Lal?"

From off to the right, a muffled grunt, and then Lal walked into view. He was a huge, hairy man with a spade beard and tiny pig eyes. He wore a filthy T-shirt that was far too small for his bulging belly. He smiled drunkenly, his eyes fixed on Shanti's exposed breast.

"Take her, then." Khan's voice had turned ugly, and I realized he, too, must be drunk. "Bloody hell, man, you're welcome to her." He lapsed into Urdu then, the two of them talking back and forth.

Lal nodded and started forward, unbuckling his belt. Khan turned away from her, pouring more whiskey. Shanti looked once at me, her eyes filling with tears. I nodded. Hang on, kid, I thought. Shanti began to cry.

I jumped off the stairs and sprinted to the radio shack. Beside the transmitter was the autostart switch for the Honda generator, still grinding away outside. I turned the key to OFF, watched the lights flicker and die, and moved into position behind the door.

The next phase wasn't slow in starting. In the dark silence, I could hear cursing coming from Khan's house, and then, the slamming of the screen door. I braced myself, thumbing the change lever on the Kalashnikov to the automatic fire position.

As it turned out, I didn't have to shoot him. Lal stood outside the door and shouted something in a drunken, irritated voice. I kept quiet, trusting to his curiosity and arrogance to bring him closer. After a moment, he poked his head inside, and that was all I needed.

I grabbed him by his beard and pulled hard, running him into the cinder block of the far wall before he had time to do much more than squeak. He hit with a dull boom, tried to rise, and caught the full force of the Kalashnikov's stock in his solar plexus. Without a sound, he collapsed onto the dirt floor and lay there, unmoving.

Everything had to happen very fast now. I ran outside, scooped up the last jerrican of gasoline I'd left beside the generator, and headed back toward Khan's house. Leaving the gasoline on the porch, I raised the Kalashnikov and kicked in the door.

Khan whirled around. He had found a candle somewhere, and now he looked a little like a South Asian version of Vincent Price, his eyes widening as he saw the gun in my hand. Shanti was back against the wall, her hands loose, arms folded tightly across her breasts. Her blouse was in tatters, and her face was streaked with tears.

"Show's over, Khan," I growled. "Let's go."

I've got to admit, the man was quick. He scooped the pistol from the table and raised it, finger tightening on the trigger, just as Shanti's long leg came up like an Ivy League punter and booted the weapon across the room. Then she grabbed the half-empty whiskey bottle from the table and cold-cocked him with it, snapping his head back hard. She was drawing back to see if she could break something with another try when I grabbed her arm.

"Not now," I said. "We'll take him with us, though. You'll probably get another chance." I scooped up the money on the tabletop and stuffed it in my vest. It was Australian currency, I was pleased to see. "Any more of this around?"

Shanti gestured to the corner, where an ancient steel safe sat. "There's more in there. Lots more. Listen, there's—"

I turned to Khan. "Open it," I said.

He snarled at me. "Go to hell."

I jammed the Kalashnikov's barrel between his legs and pulled up, hard. "Pretty please," I said.

He wheezed and emitted a strangled croak.

I was just about to stop being polite when I heard shouts coming from one of the Quonset huts outside.

"Uh-oh," I said. "Time to be moving on. We'll have to leave the safe." I grabbed Khan's pistol and handed the Kalashnikov to Shanti. "Here," I said. "It's set to automatic. If he moves, if he even so much as farts, shoot him. Think you can do it?"

She looked at Khan, then at me. "He tried to rape me," she said. "It would be a pleasure to shoot him."

I held up my hand. "Not unless he moves, okay?" I grinned. "You have to play fair, after all."

The shouting from the Quonset huts was getting louder, and I could hear metal banging. I went outside, got the jerrican, and sloshed gasoline all around the room. Then I picked up Khan's pistol, and placed the barrel against the back of his head. "Move."

As we were going down the steps, Shanti grabbed my arm. "Listen, I've got something important to tell you."

I pulled the dynamite bundles from my vest and lit both fuses. "Can it wait?" I asked, chucking one bundle inside Khan's house and the other in the general direction of the warehouse.

Then I ran for the beach, pushing Khan and Shanti in front of me.

CHAPTER TWENTY-TWO

The blazing compound reminded me in some ways of places I'd been a long time ago, in Vietnam, but this wasn't the time for nostalgia or a trip down memory lane. Khan was hollering his head off, the whole damn forest seemed to be on fire, and from somewhere back there in the darkness, shooting had started.

The muzzle flashes strobed back and forth, but none of the bullets seemed to be coming in our direction, and I assumed that in the general confusion, Khan's men were firing at each other. That wouldn't last too long, if they were any good. Sooner or later, they'd figure out that the boss was gone, and then everybody would head for the same place at once.

Right where we were headed. The beach.

Shanti was in the lead, and I was right behind her, pulling Khan with one hand and sweeping the shadows with my pistol at the same time. I looked back. The warehouse was blazing merrily away, a super-big Yule log out here in the middle of the Indian Ocean, but I couldn't seem to get into the holiday spirit. The game had started and the odds still weren't in our favor. Khan's men were on their home territory and they had plenty of firepower, factors which gave them a pretty big point spread as far as I could see. We had to get off the island damned quick, and every second counted.

So I ran as fast as my legs could carry me, and nearly slammed into Shanti, standing in front of the open fence gate. "Keep going, woman," I growled. "What are you waiting for?"

"Wait, Max. There are dogs out there; I've seen them. Big, vicious dogs."

"Not anymore," I said, using my best Inspector Clouseau accent. Just then three men appeared around the side of the blazing warehouse. "Damn," I said under my breath. I snapped off three shots with the pistol, forcing them to hit the ground. Then I grabbed Khan by the collar, and we all took off at a dead run for the beach.

The cigarette boats were right where I had left them. I threw Khan into the third one, got Shanti settled in the cockpit, and kicked the chocks out from under the boat. We rolled down the inclined rails and hit the waters of the lagoon with a splash. I cranked the prop down and fired up the motor. It caught immediately, just as a group of men burst out of the undergrowth, armed with automatic rifles, and began taking shots at us.

I grabbed the wheel, straightened it, and slammed the throttle forward. We erupted into motion, planing almost instantly, careering across the smooth water of the lagoon. I turned my head to see the men jumping into the two other boats, and heard their cries of triumph as their motors roared.

Shanti grabbed me by the shoulder. "They're coming after us, Max! We'll never be able to outrun them! What are we going to do?"

"Keep your head down," I said. "They're going to be very busy with other things in just a few moments." As I spoke I heard one of the pursuing engines die, as the thirsty carbs gulped up the ounce or so of fuel in the float tank. The yells of triumph turned to screams of fear as someone noticed the open bilges. I hoped for their sake that the boats had buoyancy chambers.

I raised our prop to clear the reef, coasted across it, and then cranked down and opened the throttle, setting a course across the channel. Osbert ought to be out there somewhere with the *Bombay Duck*. I let out a rebel yell.

Shanti tapped me on the shoulder. "There's still one boat behind us," she said, pointing back at the lagoon. "And I think they're gaining."

I twisted around in the seat. Somehow, the second boat had cleared the lagoon and was right behind us. They must have an auxiliary fuel tank. As I looked back, I saw muzzle flashes, and felt bullets crunching into the wooden hull of our boat, inches away from me.

I spun the wheel, sending our boat on a zigzag course. "Shoot back!" I shouted at Shanti.

She raised the Kalashnikov awkwardly and pulled the trigger. It was still set to automatic, and in seconds, all thirty rounds in the magazine had been fired. She turned to me, her face stricken. "It's empty," she said. "And they're still coming. What now?"

"Pray," I muttered. We were almost across the channel, and I could see the outline of the *Bombay Duck* up ahead in the water, but at the rate we were going, we weren't going to make it.

Just then, the deck of the *Bombay Duck* was illuminated by bright flashes, and the harsh coughing noise of a machine gun came across the water, music to my ears.

"Osbert's firing back at them!" I shouted.

"Uncle Bertie's doing that? I can't believe it!"

I cut the wheel hard to starboard, giving Osbert a clear field of fire. He had our pursuers in range, and as I watched, he walked his shots straight across the water toward their oncoming boat, just like a professional. They managed to get off one short burst, and then the front half of their hull seemed to simply explode into splinters.

I yanked the throttle back and saw two figures splashing in the water a hundred yards behind us. "Help us!" one of them cried.

"Don't be silly," I shouted back. "Swim to the small island, you'll be fine." I waved and moved off.

We raced across the water toward the *Bombay Duck* and safety, leaving the blazing island behind. The moon was a giant Japanese lantern hanging in a dark blue velvet sky lit with millions of tiny candles. I put my arm around Shanti's shoulder and gave her a squeeze.

"Well, that's over," I said.

"Not yet," she replied. "Wait till you hear what I've got to tell you."

CHAPTER TWENTY-THREE

Osbert took Shanti in his arms as she came aboard the *Bombay Duck*. I boosted Khan up on deck with a not-so-gentle poke in the backside from the barrel of the pistol, and tied him securely to the wheelhouse. Shanti let go of her uncle and turned to me, her face grave.

"We've got problems," she said. "Are you both ready to listen now?"

I nodded.

Her eyes grew serious. "Something awful is about to happen. When– when Mahasona kidnapped me, he–"

Uncle Osbert leaned forward. "Who on earth is Mahasona?"

"Later," I said. "Let her continue."

"Mahasona took me to Colombo," she continued. "The next morning, we flew out to Khan's island in that seaplane you saw. There was Mahasona, me, and the pilot. They loaded a bunch of plastic-wrapped packages into the plane, too. Opium, probably." She paused. "Money, too. Mahasona brought Khan quite a bit of money. Some of it was on the table, Max, when you broke in."

"I took everything I could see," I said. "You think there's more?"

She nodded. "Much more. He keeps it in that old safe in the corner of the room. I saw him going through it earlier. There are ledgers in there, stacks of banknotes, all sorts of things."

I looked behind us. Madirifushi Atoll was still faintly visible on the horizon, the glow of the fire making it look as if a miniature sun were coming up over the water. The safe had looked sturdy enough to survive a fire, and I toyed briefly with the idea of turning the *Bombay Duck* around.

I shook my head to clear it. Silly boy, I thought. "Go on," I said to Shanti.

"Anyway," she continued, "Khan and Mahasona sat around talking and drinking all afternoon. I heard every word." She dropped her voice. "It was them who stole the tooth relic, Max. Mahasona and his men."

Uncle Osbert shook his head in disbelief. "They stole the Lord Buddha's tooth? Whatever for? What on earth would a bunch of drug dealers want with a religious relic?"

"That's the awful part," said Shanti. "Khan's going to use the tooth relic as bait for a trap."

"A trap? What are you talking about? A trap for what?"

"For the Maha Sangha," she said. "He's going to kill them all."

Osbert and I sat down on the gunwales and stared at her. Finally I said, "Begin at the beginning."

She glanced at Khan. He glowered back at her. "All right," she said. "Remember Khan's plan to set up a heroin laboratory somewhere in Sri Lanka? You wrote about it in the book."

Osbert nodded. "Yes, of course. He wanted to set up a network of drug-processing factories, on the Colombian model. But I still don't see—"

"Wait. What would have to happen in order for Khan to achieve his objective? Think about the Colombian situation: in order for a large-scale drug operation to run successfully inside a country, you need a weak government and a population that is either apathetic or powerless. Given those two conditions, Khan could operate freely, couldn't he?"

"I suppose so," Osbert said thoughtfully. "Yes, I can see your point. And we certainly do have a weak government right now." He looked up. "But an apathetic population? Oh, no. The Sinhalese would never allow large-scale drug operations on the island. The Buddha's precepts are very clear: no intoxicants. How on earth could our people accept heroin dealers in their midst?"

"They could if the Maha Sangha told them to," Shanti said softly.

Osbert stared at her as if she'd gone mad. "But the Maha Sangha would never do such a thing. Never. Good heavens, girl, do you realize what you're saying?"

He turned to me. "The Maha Sangha, Mr. Donovan, is the governing body of the Buddhist clergy – the senior order of monks. Rather like the College of Cardinals in Rome, those chaps who pick the new pope." He paused. "Only we don't have popes in Buddhism, so the Sangha is even more powerful, I suppose. The Maha Sangha deliberates all matters of Buddhist doctrine."

"Precisely," said Shanti. Her face was flushed. "You know as well as I do, Uncle: the Maha Sangha is even more powerful than the government itself. In fact, they run the government from behind the scenes. The government can't really do anything the Maha Sangha disapproves of, everyone knows that. And on the other hand, if the Maha Sangha wants something to happen, it almost always does. Am I right?"

Osbert nodded. "Yes, of course you are. Everyone knows that. But I still don't see—"

She grasped his hands in hers. "Listen to me. Suppose you could get rid of all the members of the Maha Sangha, all of them, all at once, and put other people in their place. Suppose those other people were willing to do business with Khan's gang. Just suppose that."

Osbert smiled. "But that's ridiculous, my dear. No one could simply replace all the members of the Maha Sangha at a single stroke – they're elected for life. Why, to do that, you'd have to—"

He stopped, confusion and horror clouding his face.

He looked over at Khan. "But– but that's monstrous. Absolutely monstrous." Osbert's voice was a whisper.

Khan snorted derisively.

I tapped him hard on the ankle with my gun barrel. "Shut up," I advised.

Shanti nodded solemnly. "Yes, Uncle. You'd have to kill the monks. You'd have to get them all together and kill them."

Osbert was shaking his head. "Kill the Maha Sangha? But how? They only come together once or twice a year, for ceremonial occasions. They don't normally meet for any other reason."

Shanti smiled grimly. "Suppose someone had stolen the most sacred religious relic in the land. Suppose that same person pretended, instead of having stolen it, to have found it. Suppose that it was to be given back to the clergy at a special ceremony. Wouldn't that be reason enough to bring them all together?"

Osbert drew back, his mouth open in shock. "Good God, is this true? Is that what Khan and this chap Mahasona were talking about?"

"I'm afraid so," she said.

"There's an easy way to find out," I said. I turned to Khan, grabbing him by his wrist-ropes, pulling him up on tiptoes so that it hurt. "What do you say, friend? Is what she says true?" I twisted the rope, increasing the pressure.

He hesitated.

I stuck my face close to his and spoke softly. "We're only a few miles from your island, shitbird. The sharks in the lagoon are probably still hungry. Couple of Dobermans and one or two of your men were only the first course." I put my hand on the wheel. "We can go back there right now if you want."

He seemed to sag then. "No," he mumbled. "No, don't go back. Please."

"Then answer the question. Are you planning to kill the Maha Sangha?"

"Yes." Khan's voice came out like a snake's hiss. His eyes glowed in the moonlight like dark jewels. "We will kill them, kill them all." His face was twisted in a mask of fear and anger. "They are old men, reactionaries, people with whom it is impossible to do business. Earlier, we had offered several of them a share of the profits. They turned us away."

He gave a bitter smile. "Some in the government were not so stupid. We have people – even at the highest levels – who turn a blind eye to our operations in return for their percentage every month." He paused. "Once we have eliminated the monks, the rest will be easy."

"How?"

Shanti put her hand on my arm. "After they talked, Mahasona showed Khan some kind of device. Something with a timer and a switch."

"A bomb," Osbert murmured.

I nodded; a bomb made sense. I remembered the package that Mahasona had handled carefully as he'd climbed back into the seaplane earlier in the evening. I jammed the barrel of the pistol against Khan's neck. "You're a real sweetheart, you know that? Okay, so the monks get blown up. Where, and when?"

He stared at me. I held his gaze steadily.

"Tell us," I said, "otherwise, there's no real reason for you to go on living, is there?"

"Tomorrow night," he said finally. "At the temple on top of Sri Pada – the Holy Mountain."

"Tomorrow night?"

He nodded. "You're too late, Donovan. Far too late. Mahasona's already there, with the bomb. There's nothing you can do to stop us now."

Khan laughed then, throwing his head back and spitting full into my face.

CHAPTER TWENTY-FOUR

We wound our way slowly out of Colombo through the backside of the Pettah, rumbling past wretched tenement flats covered with peeling paint and washing hanging from the narrow balconies. The train consisted of a steam locomotive and its tender, three boxcars, and three empty passenger coaches. We were crouched in the second boxcar, peering out the half-open door. Khan, now tied securely, lay on his side out of sight, not looking comfortable at all.

We passed the busy commercial district of Maradana, running parallel to Jayantha Weerasekera Mawatha, and moved through the yards of the railway workshops in Dematagoda, slowly picking up speed. With a blast of the whistle, we hit our stride as the train crossed the wide Kelani Ganga at Kotuwila. Three work elephants lay in the shallows of the river below us, and one of them raised his long ropy trunk in response to the engineer's long whistle.

The ancient American steam locomotive was cranking by that point, thundering out its power in a vast belch of vapor and coal dust, heading for the hills in the hazy green distance. I felt my heart begin to thud in rhythm with the locomotive's pulse. We were on our way, we were going to make it, we were going to win.

It was going to be close, however. Osbert had insisted on us taking the slower goods train instead of the Udarata Menike express mail, because, as he pointed out, rebels had attacked the Udarata Menike on its last three runs, and with a batting average like that, it was likely to happen again. The slower goods train would still get us into Hatton by mid-afternoon, which would give us plenty of time to find a taxi up to the foot of Sri Pada, the Holy Mountain.

We'd arrived back in Sri Lanka mid-morning after a bone-jarring ride of nearly ten hours in the *Bombay Duck*, bouncing across the water at forty knots. Fortunately, the seas had been calm and our fuel tanks were nearly full. We anchored the *Duck* just off Crow Island Beach a little north of the city and walked down Sea Beach Road until we found a three-wheeler to take us into town. Our boat had enough weaponry to start a small rebellion, but I left it all and took only the Webley. I was still vibrating from the ride, but the swaying motion of the ancient steam train was doing a lot to make me forget one form of motion sickness and concentrate on another.

We'd needed a way to get into the highlands quickly and without being spotted, and hopping a train had seemed like the best bet. If past experience was anything to go on, Khan's men were everywhere, and if anyone spotted us, our life expectancy would be measured in minutes. So we were riding the rails as non-paying passengers.

At the Colombo Fort Station, Osbert, disguised in a makeshift turban and dark glasses, had examined the schedule boards and selected a goods train. "This will get us upcountry fairly quickly," he had said. "Goes to Kandy first, then switches to the Badulla line there. We should arrive in Hatton in about five hours."

Hatton, high in the tea country, was the nearest railway station to Sri Pada. A tiny hill station surrounded by terraced tea plantations, the town consisted of little more than a couple of streets of shops. Its main claim to fame was that it served as the jumping-off place for pilgrimages of Muslims, Buddhists, and Christians to Sri Pada, also known as Adam's Peak, the second highest mountain in Sri Lanka, and one of the island's holiest religious shrines. Once we arrived, we would join thousands of others converging on the area.

The Colombo papers had been full of little else that morning. The holy relic had been recovered, the nation was rejoicing, and the Maha Sangha was preparing the ritual of purification. This would occur at dawn tomorrow, in the temple atop the mountain, at the spot where the Buddha himself was reputed to have placed his footprint. The tooth relic would be transported to the top of the mountain this evening, the papers reported. Throngs of pilgrims would carry it, climbing up thousands of steps cut into the rock.

The elder monks of the Maha Sangha would follow close behind. They would spend the hours until dawn in prayer, emerging as the sun rose to show the tooth relic to the assembled crowd.

That was the plan, at any rate, but we knew better. And unless we could get there in time, Mahasona and Khan would have the last laugh.

Uncle Osbert was murmuring something in my ear. I jerked to full attention. "What?" I raised my voice to make myself heard over the roar and the rattle of the train.

"What I said," he shouted in my ear, "was that we're approaching Polgahawela. This is where the main line divides. One line goes north to Kurunegala, but we turn east, straight toward Kandy. We'll also begin to climb now. After Kandy, we go through Gampola and Nawalapitiya, on up into the mountains. We'll get to Hatton by mid-afternoon if all goes well. "

"You've ridden this train a lot, I take it?" I said.

He shook his head. "No, never. But I have a replica of the Colombo–Badulla line at home."

I looked at him. "A replica? What the hell do you mean?"

Shanti leaned forward. "Uncle Bertie's a model train enthusiast – remember, I told you that? Well, he's duplicated entire sections of the line out in the servants' quarters of his house in Colombo."

"You're kidding."

Osbert blushed. "Not at all. Damned difficult, actually, to fit it all in, but I managed to do it. Oh, not all the tiny towns are there, but I looked at the maps quite carefully, and put in the ups and downs, the bridges and level crossings, that sort of thing."

He looked wistful. "The only thing I haven't managed to do is get just the right sort of locomotive. This one we're riding in is an American model, actually; a 2-8-2 Mikado. The locomotive weighs over two hundred tons, and burns about three tons of coal an hour when it's up to speed. They shipped rather a lot of them out to India and Ceylon in the old days. This is the last one left on the island, I believe."

"Thank God," I muttered, wiping soot out of my eyes.

"Oh, no," he said. "They're marvelous old trains, absolutely smashing. Develop enough horsepower to pull the pyramids."

I lay back on the hard boards and closed my eyes, trying to blank out the racket and roar of the train. "Just as long as it gets us to Hatton," I muttered. "Before tonight."

* * *

Osbert mopped sweat off his forehead with his handkerchief. "What on earth are they doing now?"

I slid the boxcar door open a crack and peered out. A solitary goat was picking his way carefully between the cars, sniffing suspiciously at cigarette butts and scraps of paper. Behind us, a gang of men in uniform was laboriously pushing a caboose-like structure up the tracks toward our train. Something was odd about the way it looked, and then I saw that there were sandbags on the roof. I looked again at the men, and realized that they were soldiers.

"Come over here," I said quietly to Osbert. "Tell me what you make of all this."

We had spent two hours whistling through tunnels and crossing ancient iron bridges built years ago by British engineers, climbing steadily into the mountains, but at Kandy we had been shunted into a siding, and there we had sat for the better part of an hour, baking in the heat. From time to time the ancient locomotive would jerk us forward a few feet, only to shudder to a stop once more. I had assumed that we were taking on coal or water, but this looked like something else altogether.

"Soldiers," whispered Osbert, his moustache tips quivering. "What the devil are soldiers doing on a freight train?"

"I don't know," I whispered back. "Look – what's that they're carrying?"

We craned our necks out the boxcar door. At the end of the train, the soldiers were loading half a dozen heavy metal cases. It took four men to carry each, and as they struggled along the tracks, they were watched with anxious eyes by other soldiers, their rifles at the ready.

"Oh, dear." Osbert pulled me back into the train and sat back against the wooden wall. Sweat beaded his face. Across from us, Shanti and Khan watched us carefully. Khan was bound hand and foot with rope, his mouth stuffed with a gag. We'd found him to be a much better traveling companion that way.

"I'm afraid we, ah, may have made a ghastly mistake," Osbert began.

"I can't wait to hear the rest of this," I muttered.

"This isn't an ordinary goods train, apparently," Osbert continued.

Just then there was the hoot of the locomotive's whistle, followed by a bang and a jerk. With a lurch and a shriek of protesting metal, the train began to move.

"It's a payroll train," he said.

"A what?"

"A payroll train," Osbert said. "For the tea plantations. The payroll train goes upcountry once a month. It carries the payrolls for all the tea plantations in the area, from Kandy to Badulla."

"How much money?" I said.

Osbert shook his head. "Heavens only knows. Millions of rupees, I suppose. That's why the soldiers are there."

I leaned back against the rough wooden wall of the swaying boxcar and took a deep breath. "Jesus, Osbert," I said. "Why did you pick a payroll train for us to ride on?"

"I didn't know it would be carrying the payroll," Osbert protested. "The Udarata Menike – the train we didn't take – normally carries the payroll. I suppose," he added thoughtfully, "that's why it's been attacked so often." He paused. "I'm dreadfully sorry, but how could I have known?"

True, I thought morosely; how could any of us have known? We'd chosen to go in the freight train because it seemed like the safest option, but looking back at the soldiers crouching behind their makeshift wall of sandbags atop the swaying caboose, I wasn't so sure. Nobody had told me that I'd be riding in a train full of money.

All that money would be like honey to the bears, and if I were an insurgent living up in the jungle and wondering where my next bullet was coming from, the sound of the train's whistle would be music to my ears.

I sighed. Not much we could do about it now. We were picking up speed again, and I stared dully out the boxcar door at the passing jungle scenery. The dense green mat unrolled itself endlessly, punctuated here and there by small clearings in which were set tiny storybook houses made of cement and corrugated-iron roofing, with neat flowerbeds around them and groups of smiling brown children who bounced with glee as the train steamed past. It was all very picturesque, but Spiro Agnew would probably have agreed with me – once you've seen one jungle, you've seen 'em all.

I sat and thought about what our next move was going to be. We could trust neither the police nor the army, and in any case, I couldn't see what they would do even if we could. The Maha Sangha was fully assembled, and whatever Mahasona was planning for them would happen tomorrow morning as the temple's trumpets announced the dawn. People said that if you stood on the top of Sri Pada and looked west, there would be a brief moment when the rising sun would create a gigantic triangular shadow across the entire western part of the island, all the way out to the Indian Ocean and the Gulf of Mannar, practically to the coast of India.

It sounded nice, but I probably wouldn't have time to enjoy it. I didn't know what Mahasona was planning, but whatever it was, it was likely to require my full attention. I patted the comforting bulk of the Webley through the cloth of my bag, closed my eyes, and settled back to see if I could enjoy the ride.

* * *

I woke up to the screech of brakes and tumbled forward as the train slowed. Crawling to the door, I peered outside. The jungle was going by slowly as the train ground to a halt. Then it shuddered to a complete stop and stood still, hot metal pinging in the sudden silence. Two loud explosions came from the locomotive area, sounding like grenades.

I craned my head up and looked up the track, seeing nothing but a curtain of greenery. "You got any idea where we are, Osbert?" I called back into the boxcar. "Is there a station or something up here? I can't see a damned thing but jungle."

Osbert looked up. "There's no station along here, Mr. Donovan. Not for many miles, in fact. Oh dear, I hope we haven't broken down. That would be quite serious, wouldn't it?"

Movement at the rear of the train caught my eye. Soldiers were jumping off the top of the fortified caboose as fast as they could, leaving their guns behind and heading for the bush. On the other side of the tracks, men were walking out of the jungle, carrying rifles. In the lead was someone who looked terribly familiar. He had a pistol in his hand and a large white bandage covering his nose. As he came closer I saw that it was Podi Putha.

"Is it a breakdown?" asked Osbert.

I turned. "Everybody, get your stuff," I said.

I moved to Khan, unclasped my knife, and cut his legs free. From somewhere up toward the front of the train there was the muted stutter of automatic weapons fire.

Osbert cocked his head. "What's that noise I hear?"

I picked up my shoulder bag and threw open the boxcar door. "That's chickens, Osbert," I said, "coming home to roost. Let's get moving."

CHAPTER TWENTY-FIVE

We crouched in the wet jungle and watched Podi Putha's men swarming over the now-deserted train. There was no sign at all of the soldiers, or of the train crew either, for that matter. They had, simply and without fuss, fled into the jungle at the sound of the first shots.

I didn't blame them. Dying in the middle of nowhere for the Brooke Bond tea plantation payroll wasn't my idea of a noble cause, and I doubted that the Sinhalese saw it any differently. Guard duty on a payroll train was a shortcut to trouble, and at the first sign of danger, the sensible thing to do was to head for the tall grass.

We lay in the thick underbrush, twenty yards away from the raised roadbed, and watched Podi Putha's gang whooping with delight as they snatched up the abandoned guns and ammunition belts. It was wet in the jungle, and uncomfortable, but a hell of a lot better than still being on the train. All we had was the Webley, and it was fully occupied, being dug into Khan's ribs in order to keep him from thrashing around.

Moisture was dripping off the end of my nose and I was muddy and uncomfortable in my filthy clothes, but that wasn't the main thing on my mind. I turned to Osbert. "You say you know this part of the train route?"

He nodded. "Yard by yard, practically. You really must come to the house sometime and see the whole thing. It takes up most of two rooms. Why, I've even–"

"Just tell me this," I said quietly, "how far are we from a road?"

"A road? Why? What do you mean?"

"See those guys out there? Any of them look familiar? If Podi Putha finds out we're here, he'll make the sack of Rome look like a game of tag. We've got to get the hell out of here."

"But the train – they're robbing the train!"

"What do you think I am, blind?" I hissed. "I can see that, for Christ's sake."

"But it's not right. Damn it, man, we've got to stop them – we've got to do something!" He started forward, but I grabbed him by the back of his neck and sat him down on the ground, hard.

"Where the hell do you think you are?" I whispered. "In one of your novels? Let them have the money, Osbert. Let them have the guns, too. We've got to get to Sri Pada and save the monks. I'll ask again. How far are we from a road – somewhere we can find transportation?"

Osbert shook his head sadly. "There's no road near here, Mr. Donovan."

He pointed to a white-painted mileage marker beside the track, down a hundred yards from where we lay. "We're, oh, perhaps ten miles beyond Nawalapitiya. Down the line in front of us is a little village called Watawala. And after Watawala, the line meets the road, and runs more or less parallel to it all the way into Hatton."

He frowned. "But from here, it's miles to the road, straight through the jungle."

I grimaced, glancing back into the shadowy forest behind me. I knew jungles, knew them well, and if ever there was a case of familiarity breeding contempt, this was it. I knew how to survive in the jungle, and how to use it for my purposes, but that didn't mean I had to like it.

The thought of trying to find my way through dense bush with Shanti, Osbert and Khan in tow wasn't at all appealing. We had to try something else.

Podi Putha's men had almost finished dismantling the makeshift bunker that the soldiers had set up on top of the caboose. As I'd suspected, the abandoned guns and ammunition were first priority – to a low-budget group of bandits, they would be worth as much as money.

There were at least a dozen bandits that I could see. While three or four kept a casual lookout along the track for any of the soldiers who might be foolish enough to show themselves, the others worked with crowbars and wrenches, ripping into the wooden walls of the caboose. We watched them, peering warily out of the undergrowth at the train.

"What I don't understand," I whispered, "is how they got the train to stop." I pointed up the tracks. "Look – the rails aren't torn up; there's not even a barricade."

"That's easy," Shanti replied. "There have been so many attacks on trains in the past few years that the procedure is pretty straightforward. The bandits send someone down on the track with a white flag. When the train comes in sight, they fire a few shots, let off a few grenades. And the train stops."

That explained the explosions I'd heard. "Just like that?"

"Well, the assumption is that the bandits have put more explosives on the tracks, and that if they go past the man with the flag, they'll be blown up."

I looked up the rails. "I don't see anything that looks like dynamite."

Shanti shrugged. "They mine the tracks about half the time. But the engineers almost always stop now, since they have no real way of knowing."

I nodded. "Clever." I looked back at the caboose. Podi Putha's men had discovered the payroll safe, and they were busy prying to drag it out onto the back of the caboose through the splintered door. It was massive and heavy, and they were having a tough time. As I watched, they shouted to their comrades on watch to come help them.

It would take most of them to get the thing out of the caboose, and then they'd have to blow it open unless they wanted to lug it through the jungle. So for the next few minutes they'd be concentrating on the safe. Time to make our move.

The train stood there like a large black dinosaur, steam leaking out from its underside as it grumbled and hissed to itself. "Osbert," I murmured, keeping my eyes on the locomotive, "tell me something."

He moved up close to me. "What is it?"

"That locomotive. You said you knew what kind it was?"

"A 2-8-2 Mikado, yes. Rather splendid, isn't it?"

"It certainly is," I agreed. "Do you know how it works?"

"Of course," he said. "Locomotives are quite simple machines, really. In fact—"

I rose to a crouch. "Good. Come on. We're going to steal it."

CHAPTER TWENTY-SIX

Holding the Webley in one hand and pushing Khan ahead of me with the other, we moved up beside the massive locomotive. I climbed the steel ladder to the walkway which ran along the side of the tender and pulled Khan up. Casting anxious glances toward the back of the train, I helped Shanti and Osbert up. A moment later we were all standing on the steel plate of the locomotive's cab.

A hundred and fifty yards away, Podi Putha and his men were jammed onto the back of the caboose, busy packing some kind of explosive around the door of the safe. "They'll blow the safe in a few minutes," I said. "What usually happens then? Do they just take the money and run back into the jungle?"

"Well, yes," Osbert said. "Eventually. But they usually set fire to the train before they do. That's become almost traditional, I believe."

"Jesus. Well, let's get this thing moving, okay?" I turned and surveyed the inside of the locomotive.

I've admired trains all my life. I couldn't begin to count the nights I've laid awake in bed, listening to a whistle in the night. When I was a kid, a rail line ran less than half a mile away from my house, going God knows where. Nights when I couldn't sleep, I'd lie in the dark and listen to the whistle, wondering about the beginnings of things, and the ends.

But for all my lifelong love of trains, I knew very little about how they worked, and the inside of a locomotive cab was a bewildering mess of gears, levers, handles, and gauges. Over everything lay the hot smell of oil, grease, and steam. It was about forty degrees hotter in the cab than outside, and already my shirt was soaked. I can drive most things, from airplanes to bulldozers, but I'd never tried a train before, and I wasn't very confident of my ability to learn on the job. We'd have very little time to figure things out once we uncoupled the locomotive, and I wasn't aware that trains had a lot of acceleration off the line.

I stared at the array of controls in front of me as if it were the dashboard of a UFO. "Go to work, Osbert," I said after a moment.

"With pleasure," he replied, his bright eyes moving over the controls. "First, however, we must uncouple the train's cars. Fortunately, that's relatively easy. And we're in luck, which makes things considerably better than they might be."

"In luck? How?"

Osbert gestured back down the track. "We're headed uphill. If we release the coupling, the rest of the train should just slide away from us."

I grinned. "You mean the bandits will just roll away downhill?"

He smiled back. "Precisely, Mr. Donovan. Let's give it a try, shall we?"

He reached over and moved a lever. There was a loud whoosh and a cloud of steam billowed out from somewhere under the locomotive.

I looked back anxiously. "Osbert, can't you do this more quietly?" I said. "If they figure out what's going on–"

"Can't be helped, I'm afraid," he said briskly, releasing another cloud of steam. He was peering at the dials and gauges, testing the levers, playing with the control wheels, looking for all the world like a South Asian version of the Wizard of Oz behind his concealing curtain.

After a moment, he straightened up. "Perfect," he muttered to himself as he tapped the glass face of the steam pressure gauge. "Two hundred forty pounds of steam – that'll do nicely. Now for the sand." He pulled another lever.

"Sand?"

He turned to me. "Of course. You have to have a lot of friction to get the train to move when it's at rest. Otherwise, the big wheels tend to simply spin on the spot. This dumps sand under the front wheels to improve their bite."

He turned. "Now," he said, grasping a handle, "we'll uncouple the locomotive and tender from the rest of the train, and be on our merry way."

He yanked hard, and I heard a dull clunk from behind the tender.

"There," he said. "That should do it."

We all turned to watch the train. Nothing happened.

After a moment Osbert frowned. "The rest of the train should be moving away from us, rolling back down the hill. It's not budging at all, is it?"

"You're certainly right about that," I said. "Any idea why?"

"Someone must have set the brakes on one of the cars," Osbert said after a moment. "They're supposed to do that, actually, but I'd rather assumed that in the excitement no one had got around to it."

"So the brakes are still on," I said. "What happens now?"

Osbert looked at me. "Well, someone's got to release them."

I looked at Osbert, and then at Shanti. Then I looked back at the train. I sighed, and took the Webley out of my bag.

"Be right back," I muttered, slipping off down the catwalk.

* * *

The cars were deserted, and I moved through them quickly, the Webley held high. Each car had a large metal wheel at one end, which served as a brake on the bogeys of that car. Osbert had instructed me to make sure that they were all turned as far to the left as possible. I did the three boxcars first, and then started on the three passenger coaches. I was just doing the second coach when I ran into trouble.

I was wrestling with the big metal wheel when Podi Putha appeared at the door at the end of the car. He stopped when he saw me, surprise and confusion clouding his face. The big bandage across the bridge of his nose made him look like a raccoon in reverse. His confusion changed to rage as he recognized me.

"You!"

"In the flesh," I said in a conversational tone of voice, showing him the Webley. "Come on inside and we'll discuss things."

He snarled and dived back out the door, shouting for his men, and a moment later, I heard the first shots. I finished turning the brake wheel, and felt something under me give. Then the train began to move, slipping inch by inch back along the tracks.

Time to leave, I thought. In a shootout, there are far worse places to be than inside the steel-plated cab of a locomotive, and I wanted to get there as fast as possible.

I jumped out of the coach and came face to face with one of the bandits, his rifle raised and pointing straight at me. I shoved my forearm into his face hard, grabbed the metal ladder, and pulled myself up to the top of the car.

The cars were definitely moving, rolling backwards down the line, carrying me further away from the locomotive. I began to run along the tops of the cars, leaping across the gaps between them, feeling like I'd just entered the nightmare hurdles. The bandits fanned out on either side of the train, taking potshots at me.

The string of cars was picking up speed with every passing second as gravity worked its magic on the tons of wood and steel under my feet. I came to the end of the last car and jumped, landing with a grunt in the cinders of the roadbed. I rolled once and then I was up and heading for the locomotive, fifty yards away, shots raising little puffs of dust all around me. Shanti hung off the back, her arm outstretched like someone out of an old Russian movie.

"Osbert, start the train!" I yelled, looking back to see Podi Putha right behind me. "Start the goddamned train!"

Shots clanged off the steel plates of the boiler as I ran for my life. Osbert opened the throttle. There was a huge cloud of steam and a screech of hot metal. A shudder passed through the giant locomotive, and then, miraculously, it began to move.

Steam gouting from under the wheels in explosive bursts, hot oil wafting back across me, the locomotive majestically gathered its skirts and began to pick up speed. I reached the ladder behind the tender and began to haul myself up.

I clambered aboard, puffing like a walrus, and crawled across the top of the tender. Climbing down into the cab of the locomotive, I pulled Shanti to me and hugged her. "All right!"

I expected her to hug me back. Instead, she screamed.

I whirled to see Podi Putha coming fast across the top of the coal tender. He had a Sterling submachine gun slung across his back, and with one smooth motion he dropped to a crouch and brought the gun around to bear on us. I heard the safety snick off.

Shanti bent, scooped up a lump of coal, took one precise step forward, and threw. It caught Podi Putha square on the forehead, knocking him backwards, off the tender and onto the tracks.

As we rounded a bend, we got a last glimpse of Podi Putha standing alone, his fist upraised, his bellows of rage being reduced by the Doppler effect to mere whispers.

"Nice shot," I said to Shanti.

She grinned and wiped sweat from her nose with a grimy hand. "Ladies' College Cricket Team. I was first bowler when I was in sixth form." Then she kissed me. A real one this time.

* * *

Osbert hummed and fussed under his breath as he adjusted the controls. The locomotive was blasting along, moving at nearly forty miles an hour through the jungle, roaring its metal defiance to the skies.

"Stoke the boiler!" Osbert shouted to me.

"What?" It was hard to even hear myself over the pistons' roar.

"The boiler! It needs coal!" He opened the door to the firebox. I got a quick glimpse of hell with the lid off and a blast of hot air that would peel paint.

"Warm in there," I said, drawing back and feeling to see if my eyebrows were still there.

"Over two thousand degrees," he shouted. "The hotter it is, the faster we go. Get busy."

I got the idea. I turned, found the shovel, and began to throw coal into the dragon's maw, as fast as I could.

If you stuck your head and shoulders out the side of the cab, the breeze made the roaring hell of the interior almost bearable. We were all hanging out the side, looking like dogs in a station wagon on a Sunday ride in the country, when Osbert pointed to a white-painted concrete post coming up ahead. There was a large black 'W' on it.

"Blow the whistle," he said. "That brass rod, there. Pull on it – hard."

I pulled it. An unearthly shriek arose from somewhere deep inside the bowels of the locomotive and forced its way out the top, nearly taking my ears with it.

"Again," said Osbert, and so I gave it another shot, grinning from ear to ear as I did so.

The cab was full of the smell of burning coal, smoke, steam and hot iron. I blew the whistle again, feeling the raw power of thousands of horsepower throbbing underneath my feet. This was a hell of a lot more fun than flying, I decided. Shit, this was living.

"There's a village coming up, you see," Osbert explained. "And a level crossing. One must sound the whistle at every crossing." He paused. "And if I recall correctly, there's a curve just after the village. Ah, yes." He pointed to another post as it flashed by. "That means 'reduce speed'."

He let go of the red throttle rod, reached down and turned the brake handle. Then he frowned and turned it some more. Then he turned it as far as it would go. The locomotive kept on plowing along. In fact, it actually seemed to be picking up speed slightly.

I waited a decent interval. Then I cleared my throat and said, "Takes a long time to slow one of these suckers down, doesn't it?" I waited a couple of beats. "Actually, it doesn't seem to be slowing down much at all."

Osbert turned to us. "I'm afraid I've got some bothersome news," he said at last. He pointed to a set of gauges above the brake controls. "We've lost steam pressure in the condenser."

"What does that mean exactly?"

"The condenser produces compressed air, which is used for braking. But we, ah, don't seem to have any compressed air. Or any steam pressure in the brake system."

I thought back to the explosions I'd heard earlier when Podi Putha's men had stopped the train. As if reading my thoughts, Osbert nodded. "Those grenades must have ruptured the compressor pipes and the brake rigging system," he said. "You're quite right, Mr. Donovan, the train isn't slowing down. And apparently we, ah, can't actually slow it down."

I looked out at the jungle rushing by outside, feeling the thunder of two hundred tons of uncontrolled machinery under my feet.

Suddenly, playing with trains didn't seem like so much fun anymore.

CHAPTER TWENTY-SEVEN

Osbert glanced outside at the foliage flashing past us, and back again at the big dial in front of him. "This isn't good," he said after what seemed like an awfully long time.

"I can understand that as a general statement," I said. "But is there anything more specific you'd like to tell us?"

He turned to me, his expression clearing, as if he had been lost in abstract thought. "But on the other hand, I think I know where we are," he said.

"That's always helpful," I agreed.

He pointed to the dial he'd been monitoring. "This reads the steam pressure from the boiler itself. See the needle? Our pressure's dropping. We've stopped stoking the firebox, and the boiler's cooling off. We're running out of steam."

I brightened. "No steam, no power. So the locomotive will just stop, right?"

Osbert gave me a small smile. "Well, in theory, yes. On a level track, that's more or less what would happen, although it would take many miles. But this isn't a level track."

We all looked back at the metal rails snaking off behind us through the jungle. "But, Uncle," Shanti said after a moment, "aren't we climbing? We were on an upgrade when you uncoupled the cars, and it seems as if we're still going up. We should slow down even faster, shouldn't we?"

Osbert sighed. "We won't be climbing for much longer, my dear. What goes up must come down. If I'm correct in my reckoning, we'll come to the crest of the ridge we're on in just a few miles. And then it starts down." He paused. "Fast."

I looked at him with alarm. "Can you, ah, give us a little more detail on that last remark?"

"Certainly," he said, wobbling his head in agreement. "We're climbing a sort of gentle ridge right now, and soon, we're going to come over the top. Then we start down, into a sort of steep valley."

"Steep valley?"

"Yes. And at the bottom of the valley, there's a tank — what I believe you call a reservoir. The railway crosses the tank on an old steel bridge. Then the track climbs back up the other side to the station at Hatton town."

We were all very quiet for a moment. Then Osbert said, "We'll be moving very fast by the time we get to the bridge. We're at forty-seven miles per hour now, for heaven's sake. Once we cross the crest and start down, we'll pick up even more speed." His eyes grew wide. "Do you know what that means? By the time we start across the bridge we'll be moving at nearly sixty miles an hour!"

"Bad, huh?"

"Impossible is more the word," he replied. "If I remember correctly, they have the trains stop at the crest above the valley and test their brakes for the ride down. They're not supposed to go more than fifteen miles an hour across the bridge. It's curved, you see – to enable the train to start up the steep switchback on the other side."

I nodded, thinking. "And what happens if we come across it at sixty miles an hour?"

Osbert spread his hands wide. "Good God, man, that's obvious," he said. "We fall off."

I kicked at a lump of coal, sending it out into the jungle rushing by outside. "What about this bridge?" I said after a moment. "You know anything about the bridge?"

"Of course I do," he said. "I had to build a scale replica of it for my model railroad. Let me see." He closed his eyes, thinking.

"Wide steel girders," he said after a moment. "Two hundred and fifty yards long. The track runs straight into it off the descent on one side, intersecting the river at an angle of approximately forty degrees. The bridge curves counterclockwise as it crosses the tank."

He opened his eyes. "Yes, that's it. The bridge has to curve, you see, in order to start the train up the other side at a proper angle to the slope." He paused. "And that's why the train can't be moving more than fifteen miles an hour as it goes across."

I nodded. I'd stopped thinking about the train by that point. I was concentrating on the bridge. "And this bridge – how far over the water is it?"

His eyes widened as he caught my intent. "Good heavens, you can't be thinking of jumping?"

"Thinking's free, Osbert," I said. "And anyway, have you got a better idea?"

* * *

"Everybody understand what they have to do?" I was shouting to make myself heard over the roar of the train, looking anxiously from Shanti to Osbert to Khan and back again.

They nodded, looking down at the ground flashing past. We were outside the cab, on the narrow catwalk along the side of the massive locomotive's boiler, hanging on to the rail which ran along the top at shoulder height. The catwalk had been designed for inspection purposes while the locomotive was at rest, and it was a hell of a place to be while it was moving at over forty miles an hour. I'd cut Khan's ropes, and as far as I was concerned, if he wanted to jump off, he was welcome to do so.

He hadn't seemed all that keen, however. So we were all out there together, hanging on for dear life, and running through the steps in our minds. The plan was dead simple: jump off the train before the train jumped off the bridge. But we had to be very careful how we did it, because if we timed it wrong, we'd find the train falling on top of us. But if we jumped too early, we might miss the reservoir altogether.

"The reservoir," I yelled. "How deep is it?"

"Very deep," Osbert replied. "Why, I remember once talking to one of the old British engineers who did the design. This was years ago, of course. They had the devil's own time–"

I looked up to see a large sign flashing by. It said 'STOP 300 YARDS – CHECK BRAKES.' I held up my hand. "Osbert."

He stopped, nodding sheepishly. "Yes, of course. Sorry. Well, the water is deep."

We were over the crest by then, starting down the incline. Through my feet, I could feel the locomotive picking up speed with every passing second.

"All right," I said, trying to keep my voice calm. "Remember – we've got to jump all together. And we've got to do it very soon after the train starts across the bridge, because we want to get clear before it goes over the side." They nodded, watching me with serious eyes.

"When we start across the bridge, we'll link elbows," I continued. "I'll count to three and then we'll jump. Just like in school, all right?"

They nodded again.

I took out my knife and sliced through Khan's gag. He glared at me, his Adam's apple bobbing furiously.

"You have a problem with any of this?" I asked him.

He shook his head.

"Good," I said. "Because otherwise, I'll just let you ride the locomotive down."

The locomotive was swaying, rocking back and forth across the tracks as it accelerated, rushing down the steep slope to the bottom of the valley. Through gaps in the trees I could see sunshine reflecting off the surface of the reservoir below.

I steadied myself. Just like a physics problem, I thought. If we jumped too soon, we might miss the water. If we hesitated, we might go down with the locomotive. I remembered that I'd nearly flunked physics in high school.

We thundered down into the bottom of the valley, the trees opening up before us, the jungle whipping by in a dark green blur as we shot out of the woods and onto the bridge.

There was a sudden shock as the jungle opened up to reveal a wide, brilliant sky full of light. I caught a glimpse of open water, three elephants in the shallows near shore, and a nearly-naked mahout bathing them. The mahout stared at us, his mouth a perfect O, as we shot out over the bridge.

I knew instantly that we had to jump, because we were moving far too fast, and the locomotive was going to fly right off the rails at any moment.

I grabbed Shanti's hand on one side, and Osbert's on the other. "Ready? One, two–"

"One thing," Osbert said, in a voice barely above a whisper.

I stared at him. "What is it now?"

"I can't swim," he said.

"Hell of a time to bring that up," I muttered as I pulled us all off into space.

We seemed to fall forever. It reminded me of times when I'd parachuted – plenty of time to look around and think things over as you dropped toward earth at an ever-accelerating rate. I turned on the way down and caught a glimpse of the train roaring blindly on, smoke pouring from the stack like a blast furnace.

A shock as I hit the water, and then we were down, going under. My nose and mouth filled up as I sank, and the pressure mounted in my ears. A pause, and then I started to rise, moving through the blood-warm water toward the light and the air, following my bubbles up. I grabbed Osbert's collar as I rose, pulling him with me.

We all broke the surface together, spraying a rainbow of drops into the bright sunshine, just in time to see the locomotive plunging off the side of the bridge about a hundred yards away from us.

It happened slowly and majestically, in a style worthy of Cecil B DeMille. The train plowed through a six-inch steel guardrail as if it had been a piece of string, and hung miraculously in mid-air for a fraction of a second. Then it dropped straight down into the water, pulling the tender after it.

Water and steam exploded as the red-hot boiler went under, sending a geyser of warm spray washing over us. Then there was an awful silence.

I held on to Osbert, treading water. Shanti and Khan were beside us. Everyone was looking at the spot where the locomotive had gone in, as if waiting for the second act to follow. Nothing happened. The turbid water roiled, bubbles rising to the surface. When the waves had subsided, the reservoir was as before. The locomotive and tender had disappeared without a trace.

Khan shot me a glance. Keeping hold of Osbert, I pulled out the Webley and raised it up where he could see it.

"Don't get any ideas about swimming off somewhere," I reminded him. "If you do, I'll have to see if this thing will fire when it's wet." I smiled. "I'm betting that it will. What do you think?"

He stared at me, saying nothing, treading water.

I looked at Shanti. "Guess we'd better get out of the water, don't you think?"

"I think that would be an awfully good idea," sputtered Osbert, hanging on to my arm as if there were no tomorrow.

I nodded and began to pull him over toward the bank, near where the elephants lay in the shallows. They seemed unconcerned, but their mahout was standing as if mesmerized, staring at us as we drew slowly closer.

I dragged Osbert up out of the water and extended my hand to Shanti, pulling her up beside me. Khan staggered up on the bank a moment later.

The mahout approached and stood a respectful distance away, watching us carefully, trying to make sure we weren't going to suddenly burst into flame.

I turned to Osbert. "Ask him how far it is to Hatton."

There was a rapid exchange of Sinhala. Osbert turned to me. "About five miles, he says, through the forest. It's a trail, not a road." He paused. "He wanted to know if I was the train driver." His eyes twinkled. "I told him you were."

"Well, yes," I said. "I guess I am. I mean, it was my idea to steal the train in the first place."

I reached down into my bag, pushing aside the Webley to find a roll of soggy banknotes. I pulled out a handful of rupees and showed them to the mahout. "We'd like a ride into town on your elephants," I said, brushing my wet hair back.

The mahout looked at me for a moment. Then he grinned and said something to Osbert.

"What did he say?" I asked.

Osbert was smiling, too. "He says he'll be happy to give you a ride. And that elephants appear to be much safer to ride than steam locomotives. But he also says he'd like to drive this time, if you don't mind."

CHAPTER TWENTY-EIGHT

Elephant rides might be exciting when you're a little kid at the circus, but when you're older, it's a different story. It isn't nearly as much fun as it looks, and it feels like being on a very small sailboat in a choppy sea.

And another thing: if you're going to ride in an elephant convoy, get up front. In the past hour, I'd discovered that elephants are flatulent creatures, and the blow-back for people riding on the animals behind can be pretty overpowering.

Khan and I were on the third elephant, Shanti and Uncle Osbert were in the middle, and the mahout was on the lead elephant, all alone, singing softly to himself through his nose. We were making about five miles an hour through the jungle, and as we swayed along, I checked my watch anxiously. Five o'clock now, little more than an hour until dark.

I sat close behind Khan. I had the Webley out, just to keep his attention focused while I spoke softly in his ear. It was time to talk turkey, time to get the next steps down clearly in our minds. Because the clock was ticking, and if we didn't get this right, a lot of people were going to die.

"I want you to believe that what I'm going to say to you is true," I began, speaking quietly and pressing the Webley's barrel hard into his right kidney. "I'm going to ask you a couple of questions, and if you lie to me, I absolutely promise you that I'll kill you. Do you understand that?"

Khan turned his head and smiled thinly. "You're too late, Donovan. There's nothing you can do now. You can't stop this anymore."

"Shut up," I said mildly, "and listen to me. I haven't finished."

"Why should I? What the hell can you do to me now, Donovan? It's too late – you ought to know that."

"It might be too late to stop things," I said, "but it's not too late to deal with you."

"Deal with me? What the hell do you mean?"

I pointed down at the elephant. "Read much history, Khan? Do you know how the Sinhalese kings dealt with thieves and traitors?"

"Hah?"

I patted the elephant affectionately. "This is how they did it, Khan; with elephants. They dug a hole and buried someone in it, up to his neck. Left just the head sticking out. Then they led the elephant over the top." I grinned. "Squashed his head like a watermelon."

"You wouldn't do that." His voice lacked conviction.

"Maybe not," I agreed. "There are so many other attractive possibilities, after all."

"Other possibilities?"

"Sure. Put a rope around your neck, throw it over a tree branch, tie the other end to the elephant, and stick him in the ass with the goad. Kind of like the cowboys used to do." I thought for a moment. "Or maybe I could tie one leg to one elephant, one leg to another. Get them going in different directions."

He twisted around, glaring at me. "You're crazy, Donovan."

I smiled. "Not crazy," I said. "Just pissed off. Want to know why? Think about it. You make heroin for the kids in my neighborhood. You kidnapped my girlfriend and tried to rape her. You wanted to kill her uncle. You've got a plan to blow up all the monks. You're an annoying person, Mr. Khan; the kind of guy who'd piss almost anybody off." I pulled back the hammer on the Webley. "Would I let an elephant step on your head? You bet I would. I'm just trying to decide whether it would be more fun to shoot you myself and leave you dead in the jungle here."

"I don't believe you." Sweat beaded his forehead.

"I wish you would," I said, "because it's true. Consider this, Khan. You've already lost, no matter what happens. There's only one choice now for you: living or dying." I grabbed his chin and pulled his head around, staring him in the eyes. "And let me tell you, friend," I breathed, "it doesn't matter a damn bit to me."

He stared back at me, and I could feel him trembling. "What do you want to know?" he said at last.

I let go of him. "I want to know how it's going to happen." I prodded him with the Webley. "Tell me all about it."

"It's a bomb," he said at last.

I poked him harder. "I know that already," I said. "Tell me something I don't know."

"All right, all right. Mahasona's going to do it. The bomb is ten pounds of Semtex, wired to explode on a radio pulse from a dual-function timer. Mahasona put it together himself." His voice was a whisper, barely audible.

"How, Khan? How's he going to do it?"

"The casket. The small golden casket that holds the tooth relic. They've built an ornamental platform, a kind of pandal, on which to carry the relic up to the top of Sri Pada. He– he's going to put the bomb in the pandal."

He looked straight at me, defiance flickering in his dark eyes. "And when all the monks are assembled, it will blow them all to Kingdom Come, or Nirvana, or wherever they all think they're going. And you'll never be able to stop him."

I smiled. "We'll see about that."

* * *

It was just after dark. We walked slowly through the crowds of pilgrims in Hatton, and headed toward the bus station. We still had to get to the base of the holy mountain, and time was running out.

I walked close behind Khan, my finger on the trigger of the Webley, which was concealed under my loose shirt. I smiled and nodded to all the happy pilgrims that passed us, keeping a firm grip on Khan's elbow.

"Don't even think about trying to get away," I hissed to him through smiling, clenched teeth. "I'll drop you before you've gone five feet."

"We need food," Osbert declared, pointing to a row of tea shops beside the market. "The climb up the mountain takes hours, and we'll need energy. At least some tea and rolls."

I nodded. It had been hours since we'd last eaten. I stopped, surveying the line of tiny cafés.

"Which one?" I said to Osbert.

Just then, a voice came from behind us. "Wikkie? Wikkie, is that you? Where on earth have you been?"

We all turned to see Wimalananda Thero, the monk, standing a few feet away, a broad grin on his face.

* * *

"That is a truly amazing story, Wikkie." The monk's face was grave in the dim light. We sat in the smoky café, wolfing down sticky buns and drinking sweet white tea. The bhikku had declined food, reminding us that monks did not eat after noon. Instead, he had listened with wide eyes to our account of our adventures since we had all parted company at the monastery at Kurundugama.

"This is the event of the century," he said quietly, his hands folded in front of him. "The relic was found yesterday morning. Someone – presumably this man Mahasona – sent an anonymous note to the Hatton police station, directing them to look in the baggage storage room at the train station. The casket was in a large trunk, just as the note had said it would be. Now, Buddhists from as far away as Europe are arriving here, to see the tooth restored to its rightful place." He looked up at me. "And now you tell me that this man Mahasona intends to kill all the members of the Maha Sangha?"

I swallowed the rest of my bun and nodded. "No doubt about it." I pointed at Khan, sitting silent beside me. "Ask this guy, if you don't believe me. We've got to get to it before the monks assemble." I leaned forward. "Maybe you'd better tell me what's going to happen up on the mountain tonight."

The monk nodded. "The Maha Sangha are assembling now, at the foot of the mountain. They must perform a special purification ceremony this evening, in the temple at the summit. Tonight is Purim Poya, you see – the night of the full moon. The astrologers say that this is an auspicious time for new beginnings, and therefore, an excellent time for the ceremony. And Sri Pada is the logical place; it is one of the spots on the earth's surface where multiple lines of spiritual force intersect, you see. The mountain is holy not only for followers of the Buddha, but also for Christians, Muslims, and Hindus. It is known and respected across South Asia; the place where Adam's footprint first appeared on earth. Each morning at dawn, the monks from the temple hold a ceremony to greet the new day. It is a ritual centuries old."

"And they're going to perform the purification on the top of the mountain tomorrow morning?" I asked.

"Yes. The tooth relic, in its golden casket, will be carried up the mountain tonight, on the pandal." He checked his watch. "They should be starting up soon, in fact."

"And then?"

"The Maha Sangha will follow the pandal. They will climb the sacred stairs slowly, chanting prayers until they reach the summit."

I looked outside. It was fully dark. "You say they're starting up soon?"

"Any time now, really. The pandal is a kind of painted wooden platform. It is large and heavy, and it will take the crowd four or five hours to carry it up the trail to the peak. By midnight, everything should be ready for the Maha Sangha. They are old men; they walk more slowly. When they reach the top, they will shut themselves in the temple." He opened his hands. "And at dawn, they will bring the casket out into the light of the new sun, and show its glory to the people."

I stood up and grabbed my shoulder bag. "Not if they're dead," I said. "Let's go. We've got to get to the mountain as fast as possible."

* * *

An hour later, we climbed out of an ancient taxi that I had managed to rent with the last of my rupees. We emerged into a dense crowd of pilgrims, some carrying burning torches, all headed in the same direction: up the mountain.

I peered up into the darkness, seeing a line of lights ascending the side of the ridge. "Is that the trail to the summit?" I asked Thero.

"Yes. There are stone steps leading to the temple." He pointed to the lights high above us. "Look, the pandal is already on its way up."

Heart sinking, I looked up at the crowd, hearing their shouts of excitement as they followed the ungainly wooden platform. There were thousands upon thousands of pilgrims in the crowd. It would be impossible to even attempt to force our way through them. "Then we're too late," I said at last.

The monk shook his head. "Not necessarily," he said. "There's another trail, about a quarter of a mile from here. It's much steeper and more difficult, and not often used." He looked at me. "Do you want to try it?"

"It seems to be our only chance."

The monk turned and began walking down the path, away from the surging crowd. "Follow me, then. And mind where you put your feet once we get on the trail. There are quite a few snakes around here, I'm told."

CHAPTER TWENTY-NINE

It was dark on the trail, and we stumbled often as we climbed, our breath rasping in the humid night air. Off to our left we could hear the shouts and chants of the faithful, a mile or so away, as they followed the brightly lit pandal up the side of the holy mountain.

Thero had shown us the track leading to a smaller, lesser-known trail. It was little more than a narrow footpath through the dense jungle, climbing steeply along the side of one of the main ridges. The main route up to the temple had stone steps, and was lit with electric light bulbs for much of the way. We were enjoying no such comforts.

I went first, pushing Khan in front of me. Shanti, Thero and Uncle Osbert followed. It was hard going in the dark, with only the moonlight to help us pick our way, but we had little choice. The main stairway was choked with pilgrims, all of them moving by slow degrees into a trance-like state as they followed the pandal up on its long journey to the temple, and in its present frame of mind, the crowd would tear to bits whoever was foolish enough to try and meddle with things.

As I climbed, I tried to piece it together in my head. Mahasona's specialty was explosives, and if Khan had been telling me the truth, he'd somehow managed to turn either the pandal or the tooth casket itself into a time bomb. Once the Maha Sangha were assembled on the summit, he'd blow them, the tooth, and the temple to bloody bits. We had until dawn to stop him.

We pressed on in the darkness, our breathing harsh and ragged. Shanti and Thero were doing all right, but Osbert was starting to fade. Khan, who had shown little enthusiasm for the climb in the first place, was slowing everyone up.

It was difficult to track our progress in the dark, but I could feel the air growing cooler, a degree at a time, as we climbed. Sri Pada was over six thousand feet high, one of the tallest peaks on the island, and it would be bitterly cold on the summit in the hours just before dawn. I kept putting one foot in front of the other, staring up into the darkness ahead, to where the Holy Peak waited.

* * *

An hour later, we were perched on a rock outcropping, high above the valley. All of us were soaked with sweat and breathing hard, shivering in the chilly air. Through an opening in the trees we had a clear view of the opposite ridge, and the stairway trail. Light bulbs were strung above it as if for a gigantic garden party, and in their illumination we could clearly see the hordes of pilgrims carrying the pandal up the steps toward the temple. They were at least a mile away from us, but we could distinctly hear their cries of "saadhu, saadhu!" as they inched up the mountain.

As I watched, my heart sank. They were going to get there first. Although we weren't that far from the summit ourselves, they were well ahead of us. They would be entering the temple soon, and depositing the pandal and its casket within it.

Thero pointed down the ridge. "The senior monks," he said. "They're on their way."

It was true. Below us, the stairway lights clearly illuminated the orange robes of the Maha Sangha as they slowly climbed the ridge, half a mile or so behind the pandal.

I turned to the monk. "We've still got a chance," I said. "We won't get to the temple before the pandal does, but if we hurry, we can probably beat the monks. What do you say?"

He shook his head, pointing to where Osbert sat, exhausted, on a boulder, his arms around Shanti. "Wikkie is tired, Mr. Donovan," he said quietly. "He simply can't go any faster. And as for him" – he indicated Khan, sitting off to the side – "he won't be any help to us."

I glanced back and forth between Osbert and Khan. "Then we have to go ahead on our own," I said.

I got up and walked over to Osbert. Reaching into my bag, I pulled out the Webley and gave it to him. "Thero and I are going on ahead, Osbert," I said. "You and Shanti guard Khan. With any luck, we should be on top within the hour, and if I can get into the temple, there's a chance we can find the bomb and defuse it before the monks get there." I motioned to Khan. "He's exhausted; he won't give you any trouble." We'll be back to pick you up when it's all over."

Shanti looked up at me and nodded. "Be careful, Max," she said. "Remember that Mahasona's still out there somewhere."

I nodded. "I know." Then I turned and, together with Thero, began to climb the trail again, moving as fast as I could.

* * *

Four o'clock now, the hour before dawn, and very cold. The bhikku and I lay sheltered from the wind, hidden in the rocks just below the wall of the temple. We looked across at the masses of pilgrims crowding the narrow trail leading up to the entrance. They had already placed the wooden pandal inside the temple and closed the massive door. Now everyone awaited the arrival of the Maha Sangha.

The summit of Sri Pada lay less than a hundred feet above us. The rocks looked like grey ice in the moonlight, which had none of the warm friendliness I remembered from lower altitudes. Here, over a mile high, it shone upon the landscape with a cruel, cold light that I found far from reassuring.

I turned my attention to the temple. Its huge stone doors were set into the rock and flanked by two statues of the Buddha, his hand upraised in blessing. No windows pierced the rock. Outside, the pilgrims made a solid human wall extending down the mountainside.

I looked again at the surging throng. "How do we get in? Knock at the door?"

"There's no one in the temple, Mr. Donovan. Everyone is outside, waiting for the senior monks. And the doors can only be opened by one of them. Or a guardian of the temple."

"Guardian of the temple?"

"Yes. There are a dozen of them. They live here on the mountain and tend to the temple room during times between the full moon. They are old men, soon to die. This is merit – karma – for them, you understand?"

I nodded. "Is there no other entrance?"

The monk pointed to the side of the temple, into the shadows. "Only one other. A narrow tunnel which comes out there."

"A tunnel?"

He nodded. "Hardly more than an airshaft. It leads to the inner temple hall, where the pandal now sits. The tunnel was built hundreds of years ago, during the time of the Portuguese. To enable the monks to escape if ever they were attacked here." He peered into the darkness. "Only the monks know about it. Come; I'll show you."

We began to creep along the side of the cliff. The path was very narrow here, with a virtually straight drop several hundred feet down to the forest below. I shivered, and not entirely from the cold.

"Careful," whispered the monk as we moved along the ledge.

"I'm being careful," I replied testily. "How much further? This is making me nervous."

"It is just here." He pointed to a cleft in the rocks. "There is the entrance."

I peered at the tiny hole in the rock. It looked barely wide enough for a man to crawl through. "Okay," I said finally. "Who goes first?"

Thero drew back. "You must go alone, Mr. Donovan. I am forbidden to enter the temple."

First a secret passage, I thought to myself, and now I have to crawl through it alone. Of course – why did I even ask? I turned to the monk. "Go back and join the others, then," I said. "I'll be back as soon as I can."

Thero nodded. Turning, he pointed down the mountain at the long line of orange robes. They were much closer now, and I could clearly hear the sound of their voices as they chanted prayers.

"The Maha Sangha," he whispered. "Hurry, Mr. Donovan. And good luck."

I nodded, took a deep breath of air, bent over, and entered the narrow tunnel.

* * *

The tunnel was no more than two feet wide, roughly square in cross-section, and damp with condensation. The rock was rough to the touch, and my knees and palms were sore and scraped before I'd gone more than a hundred yards. It was hard to crawl in such a tight space, and it reminded me, vividly and unpleasantly, of a time in college when I'd accepted an invitation from one of my crazier friends to accompany him on a spelunking expedition. I hunched along like an inchworm, trying very hard not to think about the fact that what was waiting for me at the end of the tunnel wasn't the proverbial light, but a powerful bomb.

The blackness was total. Not a single ray of light penetrated into the tunnel. I turned sideways and extracted my battered Zippo, spinning the wheel until it caught. Holding the light out in front of me, I tried to get some sense of where I was. The walls of the tunnel dripped with age-old slime and mold, and ahead of me I could see a small army of insects scurrying to get out of my way. The air was damp and stale, with a smell of boiled cabbage and deep decay.

I heard movement behind me and turned my head, banging my elbow on the rock in the process. The Zippo fell to the ground, but not before I caught a glimpse of two small eyes, a flattened hood, and a very long, narrow body, sliding along the edge of the tunnel wall. Then the light guttered out, and the blackness closed in again.

Snake. I lay rigid as a stone, unbreathing, straining my ears to catch even the faintest sound. There it was again – a slow rustling slither. Using all my willpower, I forced my hand to reach out and pick up the Zippo and light it.

As the light flared, there was a hiss. I cringed in the narrow space, terrified at what I saw. Not ten feet behind me, a huge cobra stared intently at the flame of my lighter, its hood flared and at full alert, its tongue probing the air for signs of danger. Its tiny eyes glittered as it weaved its head from side to side, mesmerized by the flame.

Keeping the flame lit, I moved back a foot or two. The snake stayed in place, watching me. I moved again. Still no response. Jesus Christ, I thought. Is the damned thing just going to sit there?

My overriding desire at that moment was to get out of the tunnel, and had the snake been on my other side, no amount of glory, money or the love of fine women would have induced me to do anything other than flee the tunnel and never return.

But the snake was between me and the open air, so I crawled on, further inside the mountain, into the darkness. Toward the bomb.

And sooner or later, I knew, the Zippo would use up its fuel.

The next hundred yards were agony. I did most of it on my backside, lighter in one hand, as I glanced back and forth between the snake behind me and the tunnel wall in front. I refused to think about what I would do if the snake came for me.

At last, I reached the end of the tunnel, and the large flat stone which served as a hatch. I could feel fresher, colder air blowing in from behind it. I put my shoulder to the stone and pushed, feeling it move a few inches. I pushed again, harder, moving it a foot this time. One more time, and then finally the opening was wide enough to crawl through.

I emerged, gasping, into the central temple room. Holding the Zippo high, I saw that the stone chamber was about twenty feet square, ringed with carvings and murals. There were scenes from the Jataka stories, and between them, carved columns with inset moonstones.

In the center of the room stood the pandal, and on it, the tiny golden casket which held the tooth relic. In the dim light of my Zippo, the gleaming casket seemed almost to pulse with life.

It was beautiful, but I didn't have time to admire it. From behind me I heard a low hiss, like air escaping from a bicycle tire in a slow leak. I turned quickly, pushing at the heavy rock which closed the end of the tunnel, but it was already too late. The cobra was already inside the temple, its tail disappearing silently into the darkness beyond the range of my lighter.

I looked around, finally spotting a candle set into a niche in the stone wall. Lighting it, I saw the snake in the far corner, behind the pandal. It had curled into a tight coil, its upper body raised, the hood flared in alertness. It stayed still, showing no signs of agitation or aggressiveness. As I moved carefully around the room I could feel its eyes on me, watching. Waiting.

Not good, I thought. Not good at all. I'm trapped here in the temple room, inside a mountain, together with a cobra and a time bomb, while outside, a screaming horde of religious fanatics waited. And coming up the trail, I knew, was a bunch of monks who would have my balls for beads if they caught me in here. What more, I wondered, could possibly go wrong?

I heard a creaking noise straight out of an early Karloff film, and turned to see a panel in the top of the pandal coming off. I was about to find out, I realized.

Mahasona stood up from inside the pandal, smiling as he stepped out onto the stone floor of the temple. In his hand was a long shiny cutlass.

Behind me, I heard the cobra stir, and then stay still.

CHAPTER THIRTY

"Donovan." Mahasona's voice was soft, almost a caress. From somewhere, a faint breeze ruffled the candle flames, casting eerie shadows along the walls. The cutlass in his hand flashed briefly in the flickering light.

I moved back and then stopped short, remembering the coiled snake behind me in the darkness.

Mahasona stretched his muscles. "Sore," he grunted. "I was carried all the way by those silly buggers." He patted the sides of the brightly painted pandal. "Very pretty, no?"

"Wonderful," I said. "Is that where you hid the bomb?"

He nodded vigorously. "Oh, yes, indeed. The bomb is there. Ten pounds of Semtex." He flashed a wide smile. "Enough to kill them all."

"If you set that off in here," I said quietly, "you'll kill yourself as well. Did you think of that?"

He gave me a scornful look. "I will be gone," he said. He squatted down, placing the cutlass across his knees, and leaned forward. "The bhikkus are coming now. They will come inside, pray, and wait for dawn. Then they'll pick up the pandal, put the tooth box on top, and march outside." He laughed. "Then the sun comes up like thunder, eh? Like the poem."

"How?" I whispered.

His eyes brightened in the candle flame. "Radio timer. Very simple. I like these bombs best of all." He reached under his shirt and pulled out something the size of a calculator. "Very accurate, very fine quality. Made in Japan." He held up the black plastic box, showing me its tiny switches and lights. He moved something, and I saw a red light come on and start to blink.

"I know about the tunnel also," he said, pointing to the entrance. "But the tunnel is for getting out, not getting in." He turned, smiling, and clicked the timer off. "It's not time yet. I need to kill you first, then wait for the bhikkus to come. When the temple doors begin to open, I'll set the timer, run quickly into the tunnel, and escape." He lifted his shoulders and spread his hands, palms out. "The bhikkus will all die. Very sad."

I took in a deep breath, trying to keep my heartbeat under control. "There are hundreds of people outside," I said. "You can't really think that—"

"Nobody will be near the tunnel entrance. If they are" – he shrugged – "they die, too. No one outside can hear us. The walls are stone, very thick." He smiled. "Go ahead, shout. Loud as you can. Shout, Donovan. Nobody will hear."

He laughed, loud and long. Behind me, I heard the snake stir.

Mahasona stiffened as he caught sight of it, and his breath hissed in fear and surprise. "Naja," he murmured, drawing back two paces. "A temple snake. Sometimes good luck." He turned back to me, his expression serious. "But not for you, Donovan." He started toward me, the knife held in front of him. "You should die now, I think," he said quietly.

I took off my shirt and wrapped it around my left hand. "Maybe," I said, circling around to my left. "Maybe not. Let's give it a try, shall we?"

"Wait."

Both of us started at the sound of the new voice. I turned to see Khan emerging from the narrow tunnel on his hands and knees. He had the Webley in his hand.

Mahasona's mouth opened in surprise. "You?"

Khan stood up. "Me," he said. "Donovan brought me." He laughed. "And left me guarded by an old man."

"The island–"

"He burned the warehouse, destroyed the lab. I think most of the men are gone."

Mahasona's single eye blinked in the dim light. "And the money?"

"Still there," said Khan. "Still in the safe." He raised the Webley. "Pity you won't ever get your share, old man." He fired three times, punching Mahasona back against the stone wall.

Even before the shots had died away, I was moving. I leaped up across the temple floor, and snuffed out the candle with one quick swipe of my hand.

Total darkness enveloped us.

* * *

203

I lay flat on my stomach, trying not to breathe, thinking about the bomb's timer blinking silently in the darkness, counting down the seconds, and wondering whether I'd really been all that smart.

Here I was inside a stone temple that might as well be a tomb, sharing the available space with a man with gun, another man with a knife – who might or might not still be alive – and a cobra. And ten pounds of high explosive, set to go off in a few minutes' time. Maybe I shouldn't have put out the candle.

Still, it was one way of evening the odds a little. I'd made my move; now it was up to Khan. I certainly wasn't going to budge until I'd figured where he was. And where the damned snake was.

The timer was what had me really worried. I could see the blinking red light in the darkness, about fifteen feet away from where I crouched. Mahasona had been holding it when Khan shot him; his fingers must have tightened on the switch. The bomb was armed, the countdown started. How long, I thought, was the countdown?

Now we had a classic no-win situation; practically a textbook case. If nobody turned off the timer, the bomb would go off, blowing Khan, myself, the snake and the Buddha's tooth into the local equivalent of Kingdom Come.

But to stop the timer, one of us had to actually go over, pick it up and turn it off. And the minute one of us did that, the other one would know where he was.

So it was a kind of Mexican standoff. If we waited it out, we'd both be blown up. If one of us made a move, the other one would move in immediately. How long did we have left?

I felt in my pockets very carefully, looking for useful items, but all I found was the Zippo and a few rupee coins. I drew out one of the coins and scaled it across the room. It hit the wall on the far side with a satisfying ping and skittered to rest somewhere in the darkness.

Almost immediately there was an orange flash and a thunderclap, and I heard the Webley's heavy bullet singing around the inside of the stone chamber as it bounced from wall to wall. I kept very still and hoped very hard.

One shot to get his approximate location, I thought. One more to get his exact position. Unless the ricochet killed me. I took out another coin and hefted it, watching the timer's light blinking in the darkness. Just do it, I told myself; time's running out. I tossed the coin into the opposite corner, and was rewarded an instant later with another blast from the Webley.

And this time I was looking in the right direction. Like a flash frame in negative, I glimpsed Khan's outline as he crouched against the wall, the gun up and questing, the other hand back on the rock, steadying him. It lasted a mere fraction of a second, but I had him.

Gritting my teeth in the darkness, I started crawling toward him. I had gone perhaps five feet along the damp wall when my hand fell on something cool and smooth. When it moved and slid out from under my touch, I almost screamed.

I froze, rooted to the spot, listening to the blood thudding through my veins. *Can snakes see in the dark?*

This is no time to find out, I decided. After a long moment, I backed slowly off and began to work myself around in the opposite direction.

By then, I was completely disoriented. I had formed a pretty accurate idea of where Khan was with respect to where I'd been at the time of his second shot, but now, as I crawled around the wall in the opposite direction, I realized that the relative positions were all wrong, and I had only the vaguest idea of where Khan would be by the time I got to the other side. I stopped every few feet, straining my ears in the darkness. To hell with Khan, my nerves screamed at me. Where's the snake? Where the hell is the snake now?

And then it didn't matter, because with a grunt, I bumped up against Khan's back. I took one wild swing which ended with a flash of blinding pain as my fist hit the stone wall, and then I was down, feeling his feet thudding hard into my ribs and kidneys.

I drew myself into a tight ball and rolled away, trying to escape, but I hit the wall and bounced back. Then the heavy butt of the Webley connected with the side of my head. A hot tropic sun exploded silently inside my brain, and when its light died, there was nothing but the pain and darkness of eternal night.

* * *

The candle's light flickered unsteadily in the stone room as I levered myself up on my elbows, blinked, and brought the scene into focus. The back of my head felt like it had been worked over with a jackhammer, but that wasn't important right now. My full attention was focused on the timer that Khan held in his hand. I had no idea how long I'd been out, but however long it had been, the situation hadn't improved any.

Khan looked over, bringing the Webley up. His face was bathed in sweat, and the gun barrel trembled.

"The bomb–" I began.

He held up the timer. "Not to worry, Mr. Donovan. I've turned it off."

"You'll never–"

"–get away with this?" He smiled, his teeth very white in the dim light. "Of course I will, Mr. Donovan. And here's how. I'll tell you exactly how it is going to work." He held up the detonator. "Mahasona is – or was – a very clever chap. This will explode the Semtex hidden in the base of the pandal. It can be set as a timer, but it can also be used another way: as a vibration detonator."

He held up the plastic box. "It's very simple. Such mechanisms are used, for example, to blow up cars, sometimes even aircraft. This one has a mercury switch.

As long as the box lies flat, the circuit remains open. Movement, however, will jiggle the mercury inside, bridging the switch contacts."

"And detonating the bomb."

"Exactly. Mahasona and I had worked this out on the island, some time ago. We were not entirely sure what the situation would be here on the mountain, so it was decided to cover all eventualities. If a simple timing device were needed, then he would simply start the clock and draw back. If, however, the time of the explosion could not be predicted, we decided to use a vibration sensor."

He set the box down on top of the pandal. "I think that this will pose no problems. Once the detonator is placed inside the pandal and armed, all it will take is a slight movement to set it off."

He glanced at his watch. "The monks will enter the chamber in just a few minutes. Here they will perform their mumbo jumbo, and when they are done, what do you think they will do?"

I shook my head, staring at him.

"They will pick up the pandal, Mr. Donovan. They will pick it up to carry it outside." His eyes gleamed. "Ten pounds of high explosive in a stone-walled room should make quite a blast, don't you think? I would be surprised if anyone survived, wouldn't you?"

I watched him, saying nothing. If I could stall him long enough, perhaps the monks would arrive.

He was obviously thinking the same thing. "Time to conclude our business, Mr. Donovan. You, of course, will have to die." He hefted the Webley. "How ironic that it should be with your own weapon." He shrugged. He turned toward the pandal, and the ornate golden casket that sat on top of it. "But before I shoot you, there is one other thing that remains."

"What?" My voice was barely more than a whisper.

He pointed to the casket. "Have you forgotten the Buddha's tooth? It is quite literally priceless, as we both know. It would be a terrible tragedy if it were to be destroyed in what is about to happen." He looked at me, his eyes glowing. "I need the Maha Sangha dead, of course. But the tooth relic itself need not disappear."

His expression grew thoughtful. "There are those in the world, you know, who would pay a great deal of money for the relic. Enough to permit me to rebuild my business again." He took a step back toward the pandal. "Obviously, then, the tooth is far too valuable to leave here."

"You're forgetting something," I said.

"What am I forgetting, Mr. Donovan?"

"There's no tooth."

"I beg your pardon?"

"There's no tooth," I repeated. "Didn't you know that? The tooth relic is a myth, a religious fairy story. When the Portuguese sacked Kandy in the eighteenth century, they not only burned the temple, but they took the tooth relic and destroyed it."

I was babbling, the words spilling out, trying desperately to gain time. Any moment now, the monks would arrive, and although they were a far cry from the US Cavalry with The Duke in the lead, they'd have to do.

"The Portuguese were Catholics," I continued. "In a way, they had the same idea as you. Take away the religious symbol of the Sinhalese, and they could bend them to their will. They found the tooth, carried it away from Kandy, and destroyed it." I paused. "I don't think it did them much good in the end, however."

Khan's eyes flashed. "This is rubbish," he spat. "I have heard that silly story, too, Mr. Donovan. There is another version, however, which you neglected to mention. And that is that the monks cleverly substituted a replica of the tooth in place of the real object, and that the Portuguese destroyed that. The Buddha's tooth exists, Mr. Donovan. And it is here, in this casket."

I shook my head. "The casket is empty, Khan."

He smiled. "Well, there is one way to find out, isn't there?"

Keeping the Webley trained on me, he stepped up on the pandal. He put his hand on the top of the tooth casket and paused. "Before I kill you, Mr. Donovan, I'm going to do you a favor. I'm going to open this box, and show you one of the most extraordinary religious relics of all time."

Behind Khan, I saw movement in the shadows, and my heart stopped. Slowly and silently, the huge cobra was rising up, out of its hiding place behind the pandal. It stood straight up, its hood flared wide, trembling slightly. Its eyes were fixed on Khan's hand, resting lightly on the top of the casket box. I swallowed hard and stayed quiet, not daring to move, speak, or even think.

"You're a lucky man, Mr. Donovan," Khan continued. "You will have a moment to gaze upon an object as extraordinary in its way as the Shroud of Turin or the Holy Grail." He pursed his mouth. "And then I will shoot you, take the relic, and leave by way of the tunnel."

"The box is empty," I whispered. "There's no relic."

"Of course there is," he said, and opened the top of the box. "And I'll show it to you, right now."

His gaze dropped to the inside of the box, and even in the dim light, I saw his eyes widen with surprise. A split second later, he saw the cobra. His mouth opened, but before he could make a sound, the snake struck, hitting him at the base of the neck.

He screamed then, a long, horrifying sound, and fell back from the pandal, striking his head with a crack on the stone floor. The revolver dropped from his numb fingers as blood began to pool under his head where he had struck it. His eyes were open, but as I came near, I could see the life leaking out of them as he lay motionless on the cold stone floor of the temple under the flickering light of the candle.

I got slowly to my feet, walked over to Kahn's body, bent over and picked up the Webley. The cobra remained fully erect, hovering over the casket. I looked over at the snake. It gazed back at me, its tiny eyes pinpoints in the dim light, revealing nothing. "Nice work," I murmured.

Carefully, I approached the pandal. The snake watched me, swaying gently from side to side.

"Don't get excited now," I whispered. "But there's one more thing I've got to do."

Moving very slowly, I slid my hand up and under the pandal, found the detonator, and carefully drew it out. I had no idea how sensitive the mercury switch was, but a jolt or sudden movement at this point would almost certainly set it off.

I drew the detonator across the top of the pandal, felt with my fingers for the switch, and turned it off. The tiny red light winked off, and I let my breath out with a long, slow whoosh. The snake stirred.

I glanced at the casket. What had Khan seen inside the box, in the split second before the snake had struck? Was one of Lord Buddha's teeth really in there, or was it – as I'd tried to make him believe – empty?

I leaned forward. The snake moved then, drawing closer to the casket, keeping its tiny eyes on me.

"Hey, sorry," I whispered, backing away. "It was just an idea." I shrugged. "Guess I ought to be cleaning up around here before the monks arrive, right?"

* * *

Shanti and I stood on the rocky summit, our arms around each other, and watched the sun edging slowly over the eastern horizon. The island was wrapped in dawn cloud, and we seemed to hover on our rocky pinnacle, far above it.

Just below us the elder monks of the Maha Sangha were pushing open the temple doors, and murmurs were rising from the assembled crowd like the throbbing of a huge engine.

"I wish Uncle Bertie were here to see this," she murmured, her cheek pressed against my chest.

"He's better off where he is," I replied. "He and his bhikku friend ought to be arriving at the hospital right about now. Couple of stitches and he'll be fine. He seems to have a very hard head."

There was a long blast from the horns, and then a double line of monks appeared. Between them, they bore the ornate pandal on top of which sat the golden *karanduwa* holding the tooth relic. A triumphant shout of joy burst from the crowd.

At that very moment, the sun emerged from the cloud bank, flooding the scene below us with golden light. An immense triangular shadow sprang forth from the Holy Mountain, clearly outlined against the clouds, shooting westward toward India. The crowd began chanting "saadhu, saadhu!" in unison, the strength of their voices seeming to make the mountain itself vibrate.

We clung together, overcome by the noise and the emotion, our eyes locked on the massive shadow stretching across the island. As we stood transfixed, the huge triangle raced backwards toward us, until in a matter of a few seconds, it was swallowed up again by the mountain.

CHAPTER THIRTY-ONE

I sat on the terrace of the Galle Face Hotel, looking out at the boundless blue of the ocean, admiring the way the waves crashed against the breakwater just in front of the hotel. A hundred yards offshore, the *Bombay Duck* lay at anchor, its tanks freshly topped up with fuel and water, its galley filled with provisions. Behind us, the workmen were almost finished repairing the damage to the room I'd occupied on the day that Mahasona had tried to blow me up.

The day I'd met Shanti. The day that everything had started.

She came down the steps to the terrace, a tall drink in one hand, a sheet of paper in the other. She moved with the liquid grace of a doe, her brown skin a startling contrast to her white shorts and halter top. Here in the relative privacy of the hotel she had discarded the more traditional sari in favor of something a little more casual, and I followed her with my eyes as she approached, thinking again about how good it was to be alive.

"It's a cable from Uncle Bertie," she said, waving the paper at me. "The publisher's upped his offer to seventy-five thousand, and he wants our advice." She plopped down beside me. "What do you think?"

"Pounds, not dollars, right?"

"Pounds. He says half is for you, whatever they agree on."

I grinned. "Tell him to take it, then. I'll pick up my share on the way home."

She frowned. "You're not leaving, are you? I mean, we've not yet– well, we haven't had..." She stopped, embarrassed.

I smiled and put my hand over hers. "I wasn't thinking of leaving just yet, no," I said. "And you're right – we haven't. But with Osbert away in England..." I let the end of the sentence drift off.

"–the mice can play," she said, her eyes dancing with mischief. She squeezed my hand, and settled back on the beach chair, gazing out across the water.

"Did you read *The Island* today?" she asked after a moment. "They've arrested that policeman, Abeyratne. The one who came to the nursing home that night, remember?"

"I remember, all right," I said, with a shiver.

"And there was a story about finding the bodies of Khan and Mahasona up on the side of Sri Pada. They've opened an enquiry."

"Good luck to them," I said. "Any mention of the explosives? I tried to scatter the stuff fairly widely among the rocks."

"No, nothing. Oh, yes. Podi Putha's gang released what they call a 'communiqué'. They deny responsibility for destroying the payroll train. They're claiming that it was the work of foreign agents."

I nodded. "Well, they're right about that, in a sense. Anything else?"

She shook her head. "Most of the rest of the paper was about the return of the tooth relic, of course. Interviews with members of the clergy, all that sort of thing. The government is going to declare a week's holiday as a gesture of national thanksgiving."

I grunted. Fine with me, I thought. I slid down in my chair, took another sip of my drink, and ran the past week quickly through my mind, looking for loose ends. We'd covered our tracks pretty well; there was nothing that would connect us to either Khan or Mahasona, or to the wreck of the train for that matter, unless the cops were willing to believe a slightly bemused elephant-driver.

And as far as I could see, the only other people who had anything to say about the events of the past week were Thero and Gaffar Abdeen, the merchant. And for different reasons, neither of them was likely to start talking.

So it was over, more or less. Uncle Osbert and the manuscript were safe in London, and there was an exciting final chapter to be written from an eye-witness viewpoint that would undoubtedly boost sales. Khan and Mahasona were dead, and with them, the plot to turn Sri Lanka into a vast heroin factory.

And the Buddha's tooth was finally back where it belonged, in the temple by the lakeside in Kandy.

All that was left, it seemed, was to enjoy ourselves. Uncle Osbert would return from London at the end of the month but, until then, time stretched out in front of Shanti and me like an endless summer vacation in paradise.

I half-closed my eyes, letting my thoughts drift lazily away on random currents, far out across the water. The Maldives were out there, I thought sleepily, sitting like green jewels in the brilliant blue ocean. And to the north of the chain lay Madirifushi Atoll, nestled inside its deceptively quiet lagoon.

The hammerheads in the lagoon were probably dead by now, I thought, if no one had been taking care of feeding them. They'd had one last banquet, though, which couldn't be beat. Already, creepers would be starting to poke through the burnt-out ruins of the drug warehouse, and rust would be forming on the barrels of the automatic weapons abandoned in the Quonset huts where Khan's men had been sleeping.

Shanti took off her shorts and blouse, revealing a tiny iridescent bikini. I watched her as she walked to the diving board and stood poised at the end. She dove in almost without a splash.

My thoughts slowly returned to Madirifushi, and to the large safe that I'd seen in Khan's house. The safe might still be there, I thought. And in the safe was the money.

It was all waiting out there in the middle of the tropical seas, drifting through the hot days and balmy nights. Hidden treasure.

Somebody else had to know about it, I reasoned. And they'd already have visited the island, cleaned out the treasure trove, and departed. Maybe some of Khan's men were still alive.

Or maybe not.

Maybe nobody else knew about it. Nobody but us.

I raised myself up on my elbow and looked out at the *Bombay Duck*, admiring its sleek, fast lines. I checked my watch; over an hour until lunchtime.

I lay back in my chair, thinking.

It might be dangerous. There might not be anything in the safe. The contents might have perished in the fire. The sharks might still be there.

Shanti emerged from the water, droplets forming a diamond web in her jet-black hair. She bent and gave me a long kiss, and I could feel the heat passing from her to me.

"I have an idea," she murmured, her hand creeping up my thigh. "It's getting warm out here. What do you say we go back to our room for an hour or so, turn the air-conditioning up, and see what develops?"

I took a last look at the *Bombay Duck*. "Well, sure," I said at last. "And then I've got a suggestion for you. How would you like to go for a little boat trip afterwards? See some interesting things in interesting places."

She smiled then, a brilliant smile that lit up her whole face. "Upstairs first, Mr. Donovan," she said. "And if I'm satisfied, then I'll come with you on the boat. Anywhere you want." Her eyes were sparkling with mischief and excitement. "Anywhere in the world."

I got up out of my chair. "You've got a deal," I said.

THE END

If you enjoyed this book, please let others know by leaving a quick review on Amazon. Also, if you spot anything untoward in the paperback, get in touch. We strive for the best quality and appreciate reader feedback.

editor@thebookfolks.com

www.thebookfolks.com

Also in this series

ONE BEATS THE BUSH (Book 1)

Vietnam vet Max Donovan discovers his war-time buddy
has been accused of murder. Suspecting his friend has
been framed and unable to come up with the bail money,
he must solve the case himself. The feathers of a rare bird
were found near the crime scene, and Donovan heads into
the dangerous jungles of Papua New Guinea and the
shark-infested waters of the Coral Sea to discover the truth.

WITH TOOTH AND NAIL (Book 2)

When a hitman kills a policeman and makes his getaway by
stealing Max Donovan's car, the army veteran makes chase.
His quarry is a cunning and violent man heading for another
kill and won't welcome Donovan's efforts to stop him. A
thrilling game of cat and mouse in the jungle and savannah
of Senegal ensues. Only one man will come out on top.

All FREE with Kindle Unlimited and available in paperback!

More fiction by the author

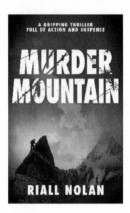

MURDER MOUNTAIN

A standalone action thriller

Wanted by the FBI and hiding out on a remote island in the Pacific, Peter Blake has an unwelcome visit. He's been rumbled by a man who "trades in information" and the price for not being handed over to the authorities is to use his mountaineering experience to lead a team on a dangerous mission to recover a fallen satellite. If he fails, it will cost him his life.

FREE with Kindle Unlimited and available in paperback!

Other titles of interest

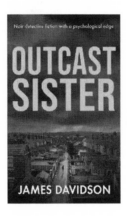

OUTCAST SISTER
by James Davidson

London detective Eleanor Rose is lured back to her home city of Liverpool by Daniel, an ex-boyfriend and colleague who's in danger. But when she retraces his steps to a grim housing estate, he's nowhere to be found. Has she walked into some kind of trap? Is Rose ready to confront the demons she finds there?

FREE with Kindle Unlimited and available in paperback!

A KILLER AMONGST US
by Mark West

When her husband invites Jo on a couples' hiking weekend, despite disliking camping she accepts, hoping they'll rekindle their former closeness. But her hopes are shattered when the group starts to argue amongst themselves, and then the unthinkable happens… a happy holiday quickly turns into a desperate fight for survival.

FREE with Kindle Unlimited and available in paperback!

Sign up to our mailing list to find out about new releases and special offers!

www.thebookfolks.com

Made in the USA
Middletown, DE
01 December 2023

44347855R00135